40

The Times
Bedside Book 2

The Times
Bedside Book 2

Edited by
Philip Howard

with a Foreword by
Sir Bernard Ingham

HarperCollins*Publishers*

HarperCollins*Publishers*
77–85 Fulham Palace Road,
Hammersmith, London W6 8JB

Published by HarperCollins*Publishers* 1992
9 8 7 6 5 4 3 2 1

A catalogue record for this book is
available from the British Library

ISBN 0 00 255159 4

Set in Linotron Times by
Rowland Phototypesetting Ltd
Bury St Edmunds, Suffolk

Printed and bound in Great Britain by
Hartnolls Limited, Bodmin, Cornwall.

Foreword

James Reston, the American journalist, once said: 'A news-paper column, like a fish, should be consumed when fresh. Otherwise it is not only indigestible but unspeakable.'

A succession of chief reporters and news editors kept me in my place as a junior reporter by describing various Yorkshire newspapers as: 'Today's news and tomorrow's fish and chip paper.'

These assorted sages were, in their different ways, trying to underline the ephemeral nature of the newspaper business. None of them got it quite right. Properly served, fish and chips can make a most informative meal. As for Mr Reston, he was talking bunkum and balderdash – as Philip Howard's selection in this book so enjoyably confirms.

Mr Reston is part of that eternal journalistic conspiracy to make you buy tomorrow's edition and forget about yesterday's. They have their reasons, as Simon Jenkins, the editor of *The Times*, has explained: '. . . the task of a newspaper is simple: to make the best possible stab at the truth in the time available.'

Consequently, journalists publish their mistakes while doctors bury theirs, as we told uppity medics in the Halifax Coroner's Court in the 1950s. They have no desire to be reminded of them. Nor do they wish to have recalled how better they might have expressed this or that; how juvenile their prose used to be; how hopeless their predictions; or how inadequate their response to the challenge of time. Journalists can blush, you know.

This is not, however, a book of blushes. Instead, it is an accolade – a testimony to the better products of a craft which hourly meets the imperative of filling the space informatively, entertainingly and provocatively. It also shows that, unlike Mr Reston's fish, good journalism can still come up fresh the second time around.

Bernard Ingham, 1992

Contents

Introduction

The Times has many attributes, but infallibility is not one of them, though we do our best. We are no longer the only notice board for the ruling classes, though hundreds of readers write to the editor each week hoping to get their opinions and names on the letters page. *The Times* is not the ultimate arbiter of English grammar and usage, or even of sloppy pronunciation by BBC presenters, though I get dozens of letters from readers each week seeking advice (or more usually confirmation of their prejudices) on these matters, and try to give them helpful replies, bashed out with one finger on a portable, in haste and swearing, the Agony Uncle of the split infinitive. The antidote to imagining that *The Times* was ever the guardian of correct usage is to read back numbers, and to note that it was from *The Times* that the Fowler brothers took examples of solecism in their lively books on usage.

Richard Cobden believed that one copy of *The Times* contained more useful information than all the historical works of Thucydides; Walter Bagehot said that it had made many ministries; and Ralph Deakin, a former foreign news editor of the paper, declared with endearing arrogance: 'Nothing is news until it has appeared in *The Times*.' Less controversially, *The Times*, produced in haste, is the first rough draft of history, a daily companion and a source of entertainment.

The scene of the paper's production would be a sad disappointment to romantic readers. It is not like an Oxbridge college or barristers' chambers, filled with grave men and women going calmly about their daily business of putting the world to rights, thinking great thoughts, and composing deathless prose in book-lined studies. This is the picture that Trollope gave of the *Jupiter*, his *nom de plume* for *The Times*:

> Who has not heard of Mount Olympus – that high abode of all the powers of type, that favoured seat of the great goddess Pica, that wondrous habitation of gods and devils, from whence, with ceaseless hum of steam and never-ending flow of Castalian ink, issue forth eighty thousand nightly edicts for the governance of a subject nation?

Trollope was being sarcastic about the rising power of *The Times* in calling for overdue reform of the political process.

Today, Mount Olympus has become the Valley of Wapping. We publish nearly 500,000 copies a night, each of them ten times bigger and with a much wider range of topics and treatments than in Trollope's time. What has not changed is the appropriate attitude for *The Times*: one implying that the world would be a better place if it were run by *The Times*. This is not always true, but it is a good working principle.

It all happens in a converted rum warehouse for the Port of London, in News International's plant at London Dock, a long, narrow shed with barred windows down one side, air conditioning that suggests that every breath has passed through fifty previous bodies, and a congestion of tables with men and women, shoulder to shoulder, staring into Atex terminal screens, and pecking at keyboards. Like all newspaper offices, it is systematic untidiness. Trollope is still right about one thing – that it never closes.

It is a daily wonder of the modern world, to arrive at the word laboratory in the morning, with fifty blank pages to fill for tomorrow – as many words as are in four novels of average length, and none of them written. Journalists have a daily phobia that their paper will come out with blank pages. It seldom does. But it is a daily panic, creating the adrenaline on which hacks run. Concentrated writing does not start until after lunch, and we all know what journalists' lunches are like, in popular myth if not in sad reality these days.

It would please Trollope to say that lunch was at the Garrick with a minister or senior civil servant. Sometimes it is. But more usually it is spent dropping bits of sandwich into the keyboard, while scrolling through a Niagara of old journalism on the database looking for bricks to build something fresh. Since Fleet Street is no longer the centre of things, and because of the vast improvements in instant information by screen and telephone, journalism has become less gregarious. You can find out what you want to know more quickly than by going in person and talking to people, a fact that has not necessarily improved the quality of journalism.

Whether the vast increase in news production and reporting during the last generation has made the world a better place is a topic for philosophers, or leader-writers, at a pinch. But it has certainly made newspapers more professional.

A life in the day of *The Times* is a remarkable experience, so much effort and hurly-burly to get the paper on breakfast tables from Exeter to Aberystwyth to Inverness. And twenty-four hours later it is all dead, wrapping for shoes and lining for budgerigar cages, and the machine has started up again.

This is not a matter for sadness. Most journalism is by definition ephemeral. That is what journalism means. It is the best job that can be done of producing the first draft of history in the terrifyingly short time available. Old newspapers are evocative guides to the spirit of the time, and pointers to how great events seemed to contemporaries. But they are fallible, breathless, full of errors and misconceptions, not so much published as carried screaming into the street. Better and more accurate versions of history will be provided by more deliberate historians, who have time to weigh the witnesses and think. Journalists get there first, with the best available version on the night.

Every day in the papers there are pieces that deserve more

than a mayfly's existence of twenty-four hours, that are worth preserving, and reading at leisure. The trick is to find them.

The Times has not made such a selection easier this year by introducing a third section, called 'Life & Times', which includes all the arts and features except the 'Oped', the main features page 'opposite the editorials'. Never in two centuries of daily newspapers have so many articles on such assorted topics been available in so many forms and so attractively presented every day of the year.

This has been a year of heavy and inscrutable politics: the continuing turmoil and confusion in the old Soviet empire, bloody war in Yugoslavia, doubtful elections from the United Kingdom to the United States, uncertainty in Europe as the Danish voted down the Maastricht treaty by a tiny majority in a referendum. It was a harder year than usual for the futurologists of the daily press to read.

This is the second *Times Bedside Book* to attempt to capture the feel of a year between hard covers. Like all human endeavours, especially in daily journalism, it is subjective, and produced in the constant stir of daily business. We cannot tell today which matters are going to interest readers a year from now, much less a hundred and a thousand years ahead. *The Times* employs dozens of writers on every topic under the sun, some of them the experts and master wits of their time. We have room to include only a tiny fraction of their daily party pieces, but they give a flavour of the year to be read at leisure, and a sample of some of our best writers. Meanwhile, back at the word laboratory, we are busy with tomorrow's edition.

Philip Howard, June 1992

Agony and ivory

Nigel Hawkes

The elephants browsing in Zimbabwe's Hwange National Park move slowly, with an air of mournful wisdom. They seem to know that for all their size and strength, their future lies in the hands of others, who are smaller, cleverer and more resourceful.

Wildlife campaigners believe that Zimbabwe's department of national parks and wildlife management will soon launch a new cull, slaughtering up to 4,000 elephants in the country's parks. This week, members of the Convention on Trade in Endangered Species (CITES) have been meeting to decide what response to make to a proposal from South Africa that the trade in ivory should be allowed to resume.

A fearful battle is brewing out over the heads of the elephants. At issue is the question of what to do when a species that has suffered a calamitous decline begins to make a recovery. Can the killing start again? The prospect sickens those who did so much to alert the world to the elephant's plight, but there are others, equally devoted to the elephant, who say that game management really means doing your best for the species, not preserving every single member of it.

Ironically, it is the nations that have done best in looking after their elephants – Zimbabwe and South Africa – against whom the fury of the conservationists will be directed if the ivory ban is overturned. The growth of elephant populations in the national parks of both countries has put heavy pressure on the environment. The worst effect is the loss of mature trees, destroyed by browsing elephants who push them down simply to nibble a few leaves.

1

The destruction of trees impoverishes the habitat for other wildlife, depriving them of shade and nesting sites, and increases the rate of soil erosion. A park with only scrub vegetation and no full-sized trees is also far less attractive to visitors.

The answer, the southern African states have always believed, lies in regular culls of elephants to keep numbers within bounds. Culling has gone on for thirty years at Kruger National Park in South Africa, where elephant numbers are maintained at 7,000. Culling has also been used, more discreetly, in Zimbabwe, whose national parks department produced a scientific report in 1989 justifying the policy.

The need for culling to preserve the parks, itself controversial, has now coincided with another argument, forcefully put by some conservationists. The preservation of wildlife, principally to provide something for tourists to look at, has often been at the expense of local people. Chased from the land and offered no share of the income brought in by tourists, the people of Africa have little to thank the conservationists for. In this view, wild animals are a luxury enjoyed by the rich in the West at the expense of the poor in Africa – just another form of colonialism. From poverty to poaching is a short step.

The answer, according to a growing number of environmental economists, is to change the basis of wildlife management and give the animals an economic value to local people. At last year's general assembly of the International Union for the Conservation of Nature, this view was put forward strongly by Graham Child, who works for the IUCN in Saudi Arabia, and Brian Child, from Zimbabwe's department of national parks and wildlife management.

The Childs believe the failure to protect wildlife results from 'centrally regulated management of game, relying on protectionist devices and policing', which provide no incentives for local people to cooperate. The answer is to decentralize the system, and give ordinary people a reason for protecting the animals rather than poaching them.

The same argument was taken up by Professor David Pearce, of University College London, and three of his colleagues in their book *Elephants, Economics and Ivory*, published in early 1991 by Earthscan. Pearce has served as an adviser to the environment department, so his views carry weight. They were heard with horror by the elephants' self-appointed friends.

He concluded that the crucial factor in the decline of the elephant was not the ivory trade *per se*, but the failure of some states to use it constructively. 'The ivory trade ban must be considered an interim measure, not a solution,' he wrote.

What is needed, in Pearce's view, is to generate a flow of revenues from a diverse range of wildlife uses – including tourism, hide, meat and ivory – in order to create a safe niche for elephants. To do so, his calculations showed, depends on the maximization of aggregate value, which in turn depends on exploiting the value of the ivory. In short, the best chance of preserving the elephant is to use the ivory trade, not try to suppress it.

This view is music to the ears of Zimbabwe, South Africa and Botswana, the three states that are leading the fight to resume controlled sales of ivory at next year's CITES conference, but it infuriates others. Dr Richard Leakey, director of Kenya's wildlife service, has been touring the world to warn of the consequences, and British conservation groups have held secret planning meetings to ensure they can create a united front.

'Once there is a change in the rules, then Hong Kong and Japan will be back in the business of buying ivory,' Leakey says. 'That will definitely force up the price, because the southern African states alone cannot produce enough. The minute that happens it will be funnelled by more poaching. Then we're right back where we were.'

In Kenya, at least, the elephant was in a spiralling decline. 'We had gone from a population of 65,000 elephants twenty years before, to 16,000,' Leakey says. 'You can't sustain that sort of loss to the breeding community – it's the big elephants with the big tusks that are going, the matriarchs and the bulls, and you can't do that and keep the herds viable. That is my concern.'

Bill Travers, chairman of Elefriends, is equally alarmed. 'The ivory ban has been in place only two years and when it came in we said that it would take fifteen years for elephant populations to recover. To talk of resuming the ivory trade now is premature, based on the figures we have.'

The figures, of course, are another source of controversy. Travers admits that statistics of elephant numbers in Zimbabwe and South Africa are sufficiently reliable at least to make a case, but he is sceptical about Botswana, and says: 'Lord knows what's happening in Zaire, Cameroon, and the Congo, the forests that used to be thought of as the last safe refuge of the elephant.'

Counting elephants, despite their size, remains an inexact science. Zimbabwe estimated that in 1989 it had 51,700, with 21,600 of them in the Hwange National Park alone, at a greater density than at any time this century. Populations are continuing to grow. Elephants are efficient breeders, they have no effective predators but man, and they no longer die in large numbers during droughts. Water holes in the national parks are topped up artificially, and the control of fires makes enough food available to sustain the elephants through dry periods.

By last year, some estimates put the number of elephants in Hwange at 27,000, almost double what the park authorities reckon to be its elephant 'carrying capacity' of 15,000. The last cull at Hwange was five years ago; since then the damage to the trees has become more obvious. In many places, the only tall leadwood and mopane trees are those that date from before the growth in elephant numbers. More recent trees are broken off, to form a dense and shapeless scrub.

*

A beautiful animal but not a very efficient one, the African elephant spends sixteen hours a day feeding. This is hard on the teeth, so elephants grow six sets, one after another. When the last set wears out, at the age of sixty to sixty-five, the animal can no longer feed and will die a natural death. Apart from those that die as calves, and the few that are killed in fights, there seems no reason why most elephants in the national parks should not survive for their full life span.

Until, that is, the culling parties move in. One of the terrible things about culling is the way it must be done. Picking off the old and infirm, or allowing wealthy European hunters to take pot shots at elephants close to the end of their last set of teeth, does almost nothing to control numbers. The only way to counter the natural growth rate is to take out whole herds, eliminating extended families in a single lethal fusillade.

While adult male elephants may function as loners or link up with others to form bachelor groups, younger males and females of all ages travel together in breeding herds under the guidance of a senior female, the matriarch. Research has shown that they communicate using sounds too low to be heard by the human ear, which can carry for six miles or more, to warn of danger or to signal distress.

Populations cannot be reduced by killing only males, because there will always be enough left to continue breeding. In parks where visitors expect to see a natural population, shooting only the older elephants is ruled out because it would disturb the social balance and alter the age structure of the population. Shooting part of a herd, leaving the rest to scatter and spread distress throughout the whole park, is equally unacceptable. The only effective method is the elimination of entire breeding herds.

The hunters gather with their guns and start by shooting the matriarch. Deprived of her leadership, the group panics and is quickly picked off with a series of fast, accurate shots.

Any escaping or wounded animals must be followed and killed. In about three minutes, an entire herd of sixty to one hundred elephants lies dead.

Nobody pretends that this is a pleasant business, and the national parks department in Zimbabwe suggests, redundantly perhaps, that: 'Culling should not be done near tourist areas or roads.' With the lovers of the elephant ever ready to spring to its defence, the chances of keeping a cull quiet are negligible. The fear in Zimbabwe is that tourists will shun a country that is known to kill its elephants, even if the need to do so has only arisen because they are well protected.

Travers takes the view that the need for the culls has not been proven. He believes that, left to their own devices, the elephants will find their own level, expanding in numbers until the habitat is so changed that it can no longer support them. Then the population will crash as thousands die, before the cycle starts again. Even if true, this pattern of events seems hardly kinder to the elephants, and allowing them to starve to death in national parks would attract even worse publicity than culling them.

Other alternatives are to try birth control, shooting or injecting contraceptive pills into the elephants. The Zimbabweans say that contraception has not been tried, and doubt whether it is practical for wild elephants.

Leakey, although not opposed to culling in principle, believes that selling the ivory from the elephants that are killed will be a disaster. Once the trade begins again, the poaching of elephants will follow. 'If the value of the ivory is really so important to Zimbabwe, and if they are going to lose, say, £15 million of revenue from a sustained take-off of ivory, then we should get the international community to buy the ivory off them for the next five years to keep it off the market,' he says. 'They'll get their money, but the ivory trade mustn't resume. To buy it and destroy it would be cheaper than fighting a poaching war across Africa. It's very costly and very difficult to fight a guerrilla war, and a guerrilla war that is aimed at animals in national parks is almost impossible to win.'

Leakey believes the ivory ban has been a huge success, reducing the incentive for poaching and enabling the game wardens in Kenya to get a grip on the problem again. 'It's not because we've got the bigger guns, it's because the poachers aren't in the parks, because where are they going to sell the ivory? They can't sell it. Who wants to walk for five days without food and water to make $2 a kilo? For the moment, the poachers have turned to banditry.' If so, then once again it is the local people who will suffer: the elephants' gain will be their loss.

The Worldwide Fund for Nature has yet to make up its mind where it stands on the issue, but Simon Lyster, a senior conservation officer of the organization, has no doubt of his own opinion. While he agrees that culling may be 'a horrible necessity', he says that it is far too soon to resume the trade in ivory. 'The last thing we want is to risk the resumption of poaching in countries such as Zaire,' he says.

A possible compromise, in his view, is to resume trading in products other than ivory, principally elephant skin, which can be sold to the United States to be made into cowboy boots. Skins could raise only half as much as ivory, but would provide some revenue. 'Nobody poaches elephants for skin,' Lyster says. 'It takes too long to remove and prepare to be worth the poachers' while.'

Like the whale, the elephant is proving an interesting test case of what we really mean by conservation. The old game wardens had no doubt; they culled old animals to sustain a healthy population that could then be shot by hunters or, later, simply gazed at in awe and admiration. If individuals had to die to maintain the health of the species, that was a cruel fact of nature.

The modern animal-lover has a much more sentimental approach. Mass-marketed concern about animals has detached them from their context, by suggesting that everything in the jungle is lovely and only man is vile. Left alone, we are encouraged to believe, wildlife would flourish in an atmosphere of cooperation and mutual respect. In fact, most wild creatures have always died unpleasantly from hunger, disease or predation.

The difficulty is that, for many people, it is impossible to love a species while acknowledging that individual members of it are dispensable. By turning animals into people, with individual rights, we risk closing off the very options that may be needed to maintain the same animal as a species. In addressing this problem, the conservationists have some difficult choices to make.

3 August 1991

Moscow's road to ruin

Mary Dejevsky

Images of 19 August 1991 flash through the mind on fast-forward: the early morning call from Australia trying to verify an improbable coup story. 'The source is what? The official Tass news agency? Are you sure?' The first modest military vehicles sped along the special central traffic lane (in Gorbachev's time, they travelled with the rest of the traffic). Solemn newsreaders intoned Gennadi Yanayev's takeover statement. The coup committee made a rambling appeal to the nation.

Then came the first armoured personnel carriers crossing the Kutuzovsky bridge beneath our block of flats; the tanks drawn up in formation outside the Russian Parliament; Boris Yeltsin, tanned and resolute, calling for a general strike from the top of a tank – like Lenin in 1917, said one breathless admirer.

The mixture of confusion and insecurity brought Muscovites at first hesitantly and then in anger to the barricades. The state bread lorries were diverted from their route to hand out free loaves to those preparing the resistance. This brings to mind not only Petrograd in 1917, but Paris in 1789.

Only with the loss of Gorbachev, it seemed, did Russians appreciate what had been theirs: a respected, reforming leader of world repute who was striving against seventy-three years of Soviet history to make his country normal. Any who were uncertain about Gorbachev's political stance had their answer yesterday when his real opponents came out of the shadows.

He was less than thirty-six hours away from bringing off a political coup of his own: the wholesale restructuring of a union that could no longer be held together by either exhortation or coercion. It still cannot be held together by those means, whatever Gennadi Yanayev and his emergency committee believe. The barricades that appeared in Moscow streets towards evening testified to that.

Yesterday's military coup, for it can be called nothing else, was accomplished in the midst of unaccustomed and uncanny political calm, when Gorbachev's victory appeared to be not only within grasp, but virtually complete. He had, it seemed, squared his fiercest opponents in the Communist party last month, persuading them to accept a programme that was only secondarily Marxist, lest a worse evil befall them, then looking on as party committees meekly left the factories. Last month, he seemed to have circumvented his grasping ministers by bringing all state property under the personal control of the President.

Yet while these institutions squealed their protests, representatives of the three related structures upon which the Soviet state is built had been strangely silent: the military command, the chiefs of the KGB and the heads of the giant military industries had not spoken.

Last autumn, when Gorbachev was on the verge of accepting the rapid route to a market economy, these giants blocked his path. Their ultimatum, it was said, put the reform programme on hold, brought the law and order lobby to the fore and earned the military a brief hour of 'glory' in Lithuania before they were outmanoeuvred in April.

The eight men who yesterday emerged at the head of the 'emergency committee', it must now be assumed, are those formerly nameless members of the self-styled National Salvation Committee who let the tanks loose on the Lithuanian capital, Vilnius, last January.

Between the time of the Baltic crackdown and his renewal in April of his alliance with the Democrats over the new Union structures, Gorbachev's policy can be interpreted in only one way. He did not embrace the hardliners, nor did they constrain him. Gorbachev the reformer waged a constant battle to keep to his chosen course. He was a limited reformer perhaps; he was an ideologically hidebound reformer, but none the less he was a reformer. There was a limit beyond which he would not go. Yesterday, that limit became clear, as did his real opponents. Gorbachev would not use military force to bring people into line. The hardliners kept calling for a state of emergency, but he continually placated them with half-promises and half-measures. He would not cross that line.

When he took on additional powers, as he did twice in that period, it was to prevent them being taken – and used – by others. The new powers he assumed, each time with the assent of Parliament, were not used. A threat to reintroduce censorship was never enacted; joint army and police patrols never marched the streets under Gorbachev's rule, except on the very first day, for show. He restructured his government; he shuffled his cabinet. He brought reputed hardliners to the fore and shaded his liberal advisers from the limelight.

Many of his moves were shadow-play. He had to show the hardliners that he was capable of maintaining control and that the country would not descend into chaos. He had to confront statistics that said economic chaos was on the horizon, even though local successes were just starting to show. He had to confront casualties, especially in ethnic violence in the trans-Caucasus, which were his fault only to the extent that age-old enmities had surfaced as repression was loosened.

The last overt challenge to Gorbachev came in June from his Prime Minister, Valentin Pavlov, who mounted a clumsy attempt in Parliament to draw some of the presidential powers to himself. So clumsy was this attempt at a constitutional coup that it was generally ignored. Yet a closed session of Parliament heard doom-laden statements from military, interior ministry and KGB leaders, which read just

11

like the appeal issued by yesterday's coup committee. If Gorbachev will not use his special powers, Pavlov told Parliament firmly, then I will. Now he has.

Gorbachev has nerves of steel. One liberal Soviet commentator remarked that the best prospect for the Soviet Union was to leave the economy alone and allow it to rebuild itself along natural market lines. In a way, Gorbachev was doing just that, and perhaps he had no realistic alternative. But he had always tried to follow the public consensus and the historical reality rather than mould them.

Over the past year, the centralized Soviet economy has been breaking down, and the Soviet leader, apparently deliberately, took precious little action to stop it. The supremacy of the party has been collapsing too, and Gorbachev took little action to stop that either. He was trying to 'manage' a transition, staying half a move ahead of his opponents and moving with the public opinion.

In the past two months, Gorbachev could be seen fighting and manoeuvring, apparently with brilliant success, for his political life and his version of a new Soviet Union, to be governed by the new Union Treaty. Every tiny concession, it seemed, inched him closer to his goal. But he had to act fast. He had to agree a Union Treaty which offered different concessions to different republics. He had to rush through a piecemeal signing of the Union Treaty, and he had to bring it forward to the summer holiday season while his institutional opponents were unable to organize their forces.

Those leaders whom he had taken into his confidence – Yeltsin from Russia and Nursultan Nazarbayev from Kazakhstan – understood the urgency: they took their concessions and agreed to sign.

On 23 April, at a mysterious meeting outside Moscow, they were apparently given a choice between a depleted, looser union bound by a treaty and no union at all. Yesterday, as Boris Yeltsin addressed the crowd from his tank, a Russian democrat and constitutional expert said with regret: 'Our mistake was to delay the establishment of firm statutory guarantees for our democracy. We should have signed the Union Treaty earlier.'

On 19 August, one day before his new union was to have come into being, Gorbachev's time ran out. His opponents, quietly this time and with more guile, had beaten him to the line. But the stark choice remains. Either the Soviet Union becomes a smaller, looser union bound by voluntary treaty, or there will be no union at all. Yanayev's militarized unitary state is no model for the future happiness or prosperity that Gorbachev, however diffidently, still held in his sights.

Without Gorbachev, or someone of his stature, the union will fall apart. The centre can no longer hold.

20 August 1991

Prints in homage to his subjects

Quentin Crisp

In the autumn of 1939, when London was plunged into darkness, I met Angus McBean by braille in Buckingham Palace Road. A tall, thin shadow passed me and stopped a few yards further on. Hearing his footsteps fall silent, I also paused. He retraced his steps and, within two minutes, had uttered the words: 'I will photograph you.' I was frightened by his proposal and hastily explained that I would never pay for a picture of myself. I need not have been alarmed: he expected no fee. He was the duck-billed platypus of the camera; he felt that if he did not consume his own weight in celluloid every day he might die.

He asked me how old I was and, when I admitted that I was thirty, he told me he was thirty-four. I tried to keep my face absolutely expressionless, because I had assumed that he was about fifty. He was as thin as an excuse, as tall as a fisherman's story, bald, and his features clung desperately to his skull, but this unfortunate appearance, of which he was acutely conscious, turned out by and by to have its advantages. As middle age overtook him, he became slightly fatter and, as the years went by, he looked younger than he had in youth.

Several days after our first encounter, I went to his studio, which was then in Pimlico. As far as I can recall, this was a large, but by no means vast, basement room with grey walls and a stone floor containing nothing that did not refer to the owner's craft. From it, doors led into the dark room under the street, where in happier times somebody had kept coal, and to a small office and an even smaller bedroom.

Some months later, I was escorted on a pitch-black journey to McBean's country cottage in a Hertfordshire village, the name of which I have forgotten. There I met his mother – a tiny lady with a strong Welsh accent, who was a Scrabble demon. McBean cultivated my friendship, but was in a perpetual panic about the consequences of being seen with me. What would the world think – particularly the famous actresses on whose patronage he depended?

This consideration inevitably caused a long hiatus in our relationship, until he had become rich beyond the reach of censure. By that time, he had lived in a series of houses in such rarified localities as Gibson Square and, finally, an Elizabethan manor in Suffolk. The moment I caught sight of this edifice, I began to laugh. It was too grand to be taken seriously: it was even surrounded by a moat.

Although I once heard McBean reprove a young friend with the words, 'You can't go around with self-confessed interior decorators', he himself became deeply immersed in this pernicious craft, and on a huge scale. Wherever he lived he tore down walls, put up ceilings and uprooted vines. Everything that was made of wood he painted to look like marble, and everything that was made of stone he painted to look like wood. To this astonishing showplace came innumerable celebrities, including the novelist E. M. Forster and the choreographer Frederick Ashton. Ultimately, all this frantic rebuilding caused McBean's back to give out, and he was compelled to sit down for long periods of time, a posture that, until then, he had hardly ever assumed.

It was his assistant, a certain Mr Ball, who changed McBean's life style so noticeably. As he was later heard frequently to say, 'I never made much money from photography; my affluence has come from buying, refurbishing and selling houses', and that was a way of life instigated by his young friend.

This continual interior decorating was a three-dimensional form of the meticulous retouching that characterized all his photography. To put it mildly, McBean was not a realist. I once asked him to explain the fundamental principle on which he worked. His reply was that his sitters wanted to be beautiful because they thought they would then be loved. This delusion suited his temperament perfectly, and he could maintain his rosy view of the universe because he had the good fortune to live at a time when everyone could be good-looking, because all photographic negatives were glass. Every surface on everybody's face that was at half-moon – passing from white to black – was treated so that it abandoned the texture of an orange and took on the smoothness of an apple.

The genius who effected this transformation was a Miss Towler. One evening when I was sitting in the Belgrave Road studio, she entered the room, carrying with great care the negative of some great lady's portrait. 'What shall I do about that?' she asked her employer, pointing to some detail that I could not see. After a few moments devoted to technical discussion, he replied: 'I should remove everything except her title.' He played that life was happy; he played that all women were lovely – even Edith Evans; he played that love was everywhere. This philosophy made him delightful to be with, impossible to talk to and infinitely sad.

He worked hard for his success and, when it arrived, he enjoyed it chiefly because it brought him into close contact with so many illustrious people. Unlike most of the men who work among the rich and famous, he was genuinely starstruck. I never heard him speak badly of anybody well-known. In his eyes, celebrity made anyone adorable. In spite of his success, he remained mysteriously modest. Wherever we went he always insisted on paying for everything, as though he might otherwise not be so readily acceptable. In the days before I started to behave as though it was a privilege to know me, I once remarked on his unfailing generosity. 'You don't have to pay all the time,' I said. 'We are pleased to be with you.' To this he replied: 'What does it matter, when I would gladly pay so much more?'

28 September 1991

ITV auction fiasco

Nobody – neither minister nor television company, programme-maker nor viewer – believes that the way the commercial television oligopoly was reordered yesterday was anything other than a fiasco. The prime beneficiaries are a mere handful of private shareholders and the Treasury. That the new structure has at least some of the better features of the old one is largely due to the Independent Television Commission. Making the best of a terrible job, it has led the bull of market forces out of the china shop of British television licensing without too many breakages. The government should never ask such a task of it again.

Just four of the sixteen incumbent television franchise-holders were sacrificed to shake up the industry, let in new blood, and warn the others against complacency. In no case does a franchise appear to have been lost simply because more money was bid by a competitor. This negated the central, and silly, principle on which the 'auction system' was supposed to work: that the more money a company gave the Treasury, and thus the less money it had left for programme-making, the greater was its entitlement to a franchise. The ITC determined to let what are termed 'quality' considerations override financial ones. The discretionary judgment of a panel of the great and good – the very mechanism the government wanted to replace with simple market forces – has thus saved the bacon of the old industry moguls.

Some of the resulting justice is rough. That LWT and Sunrise should have riches showered on them while Thames and TV-am are cast into utter darkness seems cruel. None of the existing franchise-holders was a public-service

17

broadcasting angel. The ITC's susceptibility to 'loss leader' programming and lobbying shows how little has changed from the old system. But whether the losers can cry all the way to the courts is doubtful. The Broadcasting Act 1990 was carefully drafted to avoid any such unedifying review.

Nor is the outlook all gloom. Some of the losers may move into satellite and cable, expanding consumer choice there. The existing franchise-holders have made great strides in slimming down their bloated establishments and in encouraging independent producers. Both the BBC and the commercial companies must now move further in the direction of shared production and programmes 'bought in' from independent producers. Two of the four newcomers, Carlton (replacing Thames in the weekday London slot) and Meridian, TVS's successor in the south of England, propose to rely heavily on outside production for entertainment and drama while concentrating their in-house output on news and current affairs.

These 'publisher/contractor' companies operate by commissioning programmes from other producers, in the manner pioneered by Channel 4. This should expand finance available to the independent production sector, the most creative area in British television. Carlton has been an independent producer, involved in such well-acclaimed programmes as *Inspector Morse*. In a reversal of roles, Carlton could make room for Thames to become an independent programme-maker itself. Thames is potentially the largest independent in Europe.

So much, so good. But auctioning terrestrial commercial television was always intended to benefit the Treasury not the television viewer. The result must be fewer resources available for programme-making and thus for competing with the cheap products on offer from the American television industry.

Certainly the ITC has encouraged a trend away from the corporate uniformity of television in the 1970s and 1980s, towards a richer mixture of franchise-holders and independents. With luck it has also paved the way for a greater diversity of non-terrestrial programmes on the nation's screens. But as this year's equally chaotic award of commercial radio franchises showed, Britain is no nearer a coherent broadcasting policy. With the BBC's franchise next in line for renewal, that lacuna must soon be filled.

17 October 1991

Samoans relish their role as rugby's warriors

Andrew Longmore

The winds which buffeted the north for most of the week may prove an unwelcome omen for the Scots this afternoon at Murrayfield. As the Welsh, Australians and Argentinians will testify, the Western Samoans do not need the fourth anniversary of the October hurricane as an excuse to uproot trees.

A glimpse of the Samoan team room might not lift the locals' morale either. So many messages have spluttered through the fax machine at the team's hotel, the walls are papered with good will. Many of them reflect the religious conviction which has imbued the Samoans' Rugby World Cup journey with more than a touch of the crusading spirit. 'To Fats and the Boys,' says one from the Western Samoan Visitors' Bureau, 'Read aloud Philippians, Chapter 4, Verse 13. I can do all things through Christ which strengthen me.' From the Boys' Brigade of Western Samoa: 'We are still behind the curtains in prayers for the team.'

Intercepting the latest batch of messages is one of the most pleasant tasks of the day for Tate Simi, the team manager, who would otherwise be contemplating another day at the Labour Commission offices in Apia, the capital of Samoa.

Simi rises early, partly because he cannot sleep, partly because he does not want to miss one second of the adventure. 'I lie awake thinking about what we have done. It was a pipe dream before, but now we are competing with the top nations and with our success, rugby is not just a pastime for Samoans anymore, it's becoming part of the culture.' So much so that at 1 a.m. tomorrow, Western Samoan time, 20,000 people will flock to the main stadium in Apia to watch the quarter-final against Scotland. No rugby is played on a Sunday in the islands, but strict observance of the day has been set aside for observance of a different kind.

Courtesy of Television New Zealand, who installed a satellite dish in Apia, the Samoans have watched their team live on screen for the first time. So many have done so, two extra screens have had to be added to the five already in the stadium. 'They are travelling miles by bus from the villages to be there,' Simi said. 'And the good thing is that a lot of the old people are watching us too. It's not just the new rugby generation.'

'Fats' (Peter Fatialofa, the captain) and 'the Boys', of course, are loving every minute of the exposure. For a race which has repelled, absorbed and survived generations of foreign influence – from the United States, Germany, France and New Zealand – this is a heaven-sent opportunity to even the score, and the Samoans have no intention of letting it go just yet.

After their final full training session on Thursday, the team sang a special 'thank-you' anthem for the benefit of an Australian television crew. The distinctive harmonies were swiftly borne away on a numbing wind, but, just for a moment, a bleak Scottish day was warmed by an image of Pacific island sunshine.

Anyone transferring such romantic notions to the rugby field, however, had best take a look at limbs which have felt the full weight of the Samoans' worship of the physical. They might learn their rugby with sticks or sandals instead of footballs, might learn their close-handling skills because space is so tight six matches have to be played simultaneously on one small piece of ground, but the main influences on their game come from Australian rugby league and American football.

At least a dozen Samoans already feature prominently in American football and Timo Tagaloa has a letter from the Los Angeles Raiders to prove how close he came to joining them. Samoans, as their technical director, Bryan Williams, so aptly puts it, just love banging into people. 'Samoans are combative, warrior-like. That's why they like rugby. Soccer is regarded as a namby-pamby game.'

Williams has harnessed this enthusiasm to the limit. A little beyond, some of the Argentinians might say. 'Tackling can be taught, but really aggressive tackling is instinctive. If you have fifteen guys committed to the idea of knocking people over, that gets the opposition in two minds. The difference, I think, between us and some of the home teams is that we regard tackling as an offensive, not a defensive, weapon.' Asked if he has been surprised at the reaction to the team's tackling, Williams barely conceals a smile. 'A little.'

Manu Samoa, the legendary warrior whose spirit the team embodies, would share the smile and doubtless see eye to eye too with Fatialofa, the most famous piano-shifter in rugby and the outsize symbol of the Samoans' success.

Fatialofa has seven sisters and eight brothers, which is a fair tonnage for the planet to shoulder, and his seven-year-old son has inherited his father's instincts. 'He has already been told to cool it by his teachers because he tackles too hard,' he says. Fatialofa can hardly believe he will be leading his team into a World Cup quarter-final this afternoon. 'The whole thing has built up a momentum of its own.' Like the man himself that might take some stopping.

19 October 1991

No treasures in an empty box

Anthony Burgess

Despite the controversy over Margaret Thatcher's intervention in the great Channel 3 debate, the fact remains that we all spend too much time watching the box, which, since we've all become idiotic, is no longer known as the idiot's lantern. So the time has come to ask ourselves what precisely we get out of it.

I plead as guilty as the next man to excessive gawping. The adenoidal ocular gulp was, in the late Fifties, my response to the rediscovery of civilization after some years in Malaysian kampongs. I was often asked what kind of television we had 'out there' and was met by incredulity when I replied that there was, as yet, none. Even in the old black-and-white two-channel days, there was an assumption in the West that the amenity was essential to the full life. Indeed, the need had long antedated its satisfaction. Is there not a television system in Robert Green's play *Friar Bacon and Friar Bungay*, first produced in the 1590s?

For more than two years, as television critic for the now defunct *Listener*, I was glad to allay the guilt of excessive gaping by reminding myself that I was being paid for it. Leaving Britain for good in 1968, I was freeing myself from the seduction of three colour channels. I did not think I would be any longer seducible, for I would be an outcast at the feast of alien cultures. But I was soon addicted to high-kicking *Canzonissima* on Radiotelevisione Italiana. Language was no real barrier. It soon seemed natural to hear Gary Cooper entering a salon with, '*Ciao, ragazzi*'.

In Monaco, the televisual feast was multinational, with all of France and Italy pounding in over the notional frontiers.

Lengthy stays in the United States revealed that vast regions were ascetically provided with only a single channel, although New York's provisions were so rich as to provoke genuine illness: the old movies that one had to see came on in the early hours of the morning and the rhythms of regular sleep were dangerously disrupted.

At present I spend much of my time in southern Switzerland, where there are uncountable channels in four languages, to say nothing of dialects. It is all too much. I also spend odd months in my native country searching out an honourable grave. Viewing goes on, but there is little of the relief of a return to my own language: I hear far too much unintelligible yobspeak. But I have to concede that Britain's is the best television you are likely to get, though praising it reminds me of the damned in Ezra Pound's *Cantos* who praise one kind of human excrement at the expense of another.

The truth is that what we call television is not television at all. There was once talk of the Art of Television, meaning the exploitation of accepted limitations. The parallel was the Art of Radio, which genuinely flourished in the 1930s: an ambitious expressionism, which owed much to the Weimar Republic, functioned before blattner-phone recording came in, when gramophones were hand-wound and fade-outs were accomplished by gently shutting doors. Early television was live, and there was the faint thrill of knowing that lines could be muffed and things could go wrong. Characters could not change their clothes. A door could be opened to disclose a staring camera. There was the sense of limitation without which no art can properly be said to exist.

Nowadays, television is a poor sister of film. With the advent of the video cassette recorder, it has become possible to regard one's television set as the disgorger of the materials of one's personal film museum. The television play no longer exists: the television film, an impoverished relation of hypertrophic cinema, follows cinematic rules. But the experience of watching film on television is mean and lacks a sense of occasion. It is too easy: one lolls in one's slippers and shirtsleeves instead of sitting with others in a wet raincoat. This domestication of the cinema diminishes a great medium. We see one film, yawn, and at once demand another. We zap, and we do not sufficiently zap off.

I do not deny that I have learnt things from television – chiefly about animals – but I have not, when I consider the hours I have given to it, learnt nearly enough. There has not been one single television revelation to compare with, say, the first hearing of *L'après-midi d'un faune* or the first reading of *A Handful of Dust*. The cramming of each minute of the day and night with viewable material ensures that no transmission shall be particularly important. Everything is levelled down to easy eye-fodder; we are not encouraged to discriminate.

In its first days – I am not referring to such events as that transmission on the Baird system of Pirandello's *The Man with the Flower in his Mouth*, which I saw in 1932; I am going back merely to the 1950s – one was addressed directly by the medium. Orwell's *Nineteen Eighty-Four* reproduced the condition of 1948, when old ladies were shy of undressing before that seeing eye. At least there was a sense of rapport. To have lugged the victim of IRA bullets into the studio and shown him, as it were, dead live, would have been shocking and violently condemned by Parliament, but at least it would have been a televisual act. These days we see coloured film of the victims of every conceivable atrocity, and its epistemological impact is that of an aftershave commercial. Death is entertainment because it is processed as entertainment: film is manipulable and hence fictional.

A few years ago, I met a Hollywood producer who was convinced that BBC television transmitted a Shakespeare or Chekhov play once a week, showed the odd documentary of a potter's wheel, dealt briefly with the news, and then lapsed into blankness. It was a false memory of the 1950s and a response to the blaring, glaring TV diet of Los

Angeles. But some of us can recollect a time when television sets had doors which were ritually opened on an occasional evening and closed at the hour of the sleep-inducing malted drink.

Commercialization has disposed of the genteel era of limited viewing. The filling of the day and night with material so mediocre that it imparts artistic value to commercials is imposed on the BBC because the BBC has been taught to believe it has entered the competitive market. It is up to the viewer to learn discrimination, but this is difficult when homogeneity of value – and, it increasingly seems, of content – animates the programmers.

The answer is to keep the thing switched off until a re-run of *The Birth of a Nation* or *Metropolis* is announced. Even then, of course, television will be behaving, not as itself, but as a mere servant of a greater medium. Or perhaps *Parade's End* by Ford Madox Ford (made in 1964) will emerge from the BBC2 archives: that was television serving literature, a wholly laudable action. I think we have to liquidate the notion of the TV evening. We seem to have forgotten that there are other things to do. We can listen to a concert on Radio 3, read, make love, play the piano or the guitar. The trouble is that we have become afraid of *missing something* on the box.

In fact, we are missing nothing. We get more news from newspapers and more entertainment from library books. Television has to exist, but it does not have to enslave us. But then, the franchise winners are the real slaves.

19 October 1991

An author in search of
humility

Kate Muir

For a man obsessed in his books with metamorphoses, Ben Okri is in great fear of changing himself. Ever since he came to England from Nigeria, aged nineteen, he has danced an uneasy path between assimilating and observing this second culture, avoiding being crushed and remoulded to fit his new home. If he slots nicely into the space provided by the establishment, he fears he will become a cardboard, two-dimensional writer.

Keeping that slight distance and unease will be harder now he is branded with the mark of British literary acceptability. At this very moment, in bookshops around the country, Mr Okri is being made into enticing window displays, and each book is being rewarded in the corner with a bright sticker 'Booker Prize Winner, 1991'. Sales are even now quad-rupling.

Mr Okri's euphoria, coupled with physical suffering due to recent excesses of champagne, cigarettes and conver-sation, has temporarily precluded him from taking up his Biro and his black Ryman's notebooks. 'The problem with winning something like this,' he says hoarsely, 'is that it takes away your uncertainty. When I am certain about what I am doing, I tend to write rubbish.' Sensibly, he is taking a break until his humility returns, and in the meantime doing the penance which accompanies such an award, the endless interviews, photo-sessions and drinks in the Groucho Club.

Fortunately for his humility, the Ben Okri who wrote *The Famished Road* is dead. 'It seems to be very harsh, but you have to die with each work or otherwise you end up endlessly recycling the same narrow spaces in your consciousness.'

27

He fears the same-plot-new-clothes syndrome which plagues many other writers.

Already it should be clear that Mr Okri takes his writing seriously; himself less so. For instance, he can keep a straight face when he says he divides readers into two sorts, Homerians and Virgilians, and admits: 'I have never disguised my love of Homer', and adds that he loves Flaubert, 'of course.' If another author were to talk the way he does about his craft, he would be slammed for his pretentiousness. But in his wise-innocent way, Mr Okri gets away with it. Mostly.

'When I get to the table to work, half the time I don't know what will turn up. But if you are truthful in an idea, everything is incarnate. You can take almost any single aspect, any sentence of the book, and it will have the whole thing contained in it.' He believes in 'deep listening', waiting until he hears something clearly in his head, and then putting it down. This is coupled with 'mood writing', more rhythmic and musical than logical.

He needed to get away from Nigeria to see it clearly. He believes if you stay in a place long enough, you become part of that environment.

Poking further into whether he rewrites or streams consciousness meets with a refusal, as though one has asked to look in his underwear drawer. 'When other writers talk about their methods, I want to run away. I don't want to know their methods. It's like someone telling you how to make love.'

He moves the conversation on swiftly from the physical to the spiritual, although his books slide happily between the two. He believes people are composed of more than three dimensions and the problem with modern England is that it prefers to keep any fourth dimension, any spirituality, hushed up, or safely pocketed in churches. Mr Okri's books are filled with ghosts, animism and magic. His protagonist in *The Famished Road* is a spirit child, who straddles the two worlds, in order to make sense of one. Life in Nigeria is so chaotic that it can only be understood by going beyond the reality.

'We have not explained everything yet, although people here behave as if we have. The world is full of mysteries. One can still tremble in the face of all-knowing, inscrutable forces, but at the same time realize that that might mean we have forces within us, and we can acknowledge that power.' This is easier to say coming from another culture. For a British author, admitting spirituality is – well, a little *embarrassing*.

Back in Nigeria, Mr Okri thinks it is perhaps easier for people to be religious in the wider sense, because they are closer to suffering. In the first world, it is possible for a large number of people to cut themselves off from that. 'Those living with suffering are in the prerequisite position for the religious state. Their egos are stripped bare, and they become aware of their own mortality. But anyone who is in that state must wonder: how can this just be it?'

Mr Okri has been down there too, less so in Nigeria, where he was the child of middle-class parents, his father a lawyer. But when he arrived in London, after a stint of comparative literature at Essex University, he tasted the life of the starving artist, becoming homeless at one point, and sleeping in tube stations. Although he now has a flat in Maida Vale, north London, the Booker £20,000 means more to him than the other big names on the list.

He wrote two short stories in a burst of anger when he came to this country. 'Why was I angry? It's so obvious, I don't need to tell you – the racism, the homelessness, the problems of getting accommodation . . .' Now, at thirty-two, looking sleek in a blue blazer and paisley scarf, he is pleased he recorded what he felt at the time. He has lost those rough edges, and finds he becomes more subtle as he understands more. After all, he has, this week, gone from being perceived as a slightly-known, black Nigerian writer, to a big name in English literature, who happens to come from

Nigeria. 'I am aware of all the ironies, of what people have said. Not a single nuance of tone has escaped me.'

The baggage of cultural assumption can be seen in many of the reviews of his two novels and short story collections. He says the biggest mistake is that most critics do not simply open the book and read it. He puts on a flat, stuffy voice. 'They say: "Ooh dear, I'm reading an *African* novel. Ooh dear, it's bound to be a bit strange. Ooh dear, there are bound to be rituals and things." '

His books, he says, become three books – the one he wrote; the one that comes out of the collision between the reader and the book; and 'the worst one, when they put a set of their own assumptions on top of what they're reading, and then attribute it all to me.'

He loathes being categorized at all and particularly as a magic realist. His latest book is told in the first person and from the realist point of view of Azaro, your ordinary, average spirit-child. 'For Azaro, seeing a room of spirits, or two-headed people is normal. He would find this space here,' he says gesturing round his publisher's genteel office, 'full of other beings', presumably the ghosts of starved authors waving rejection slips.

Mr Okri is beyond this now, although he denies any intentions of becoming part of the literati. In fact he is secretly rather disappointed in all that. He chose to come to Britain rather than America, because of Dickens and Shakespeare. Surely a land which produced such greatness would have people to match? 'I expected it to be a land filled with giants. It wasn't.'

25 October 1991

Should auld acquaintance
be forgot?

Gavin Stamp

On the top of Calton Hill – Edinburgh's Acropolis – stands a fragment of a Greek Doric temple, an apparently ruined Parthenon. It is the unfinished national monument, and the fact that it remains incomplete so long after the Napoleonic struggle it was intended to commemorate might make it seem a monument to the legendary meanness, no, careful-ness, of the Scots, if that was not belied by the sheer mag-nificence of the great city below. For Edinburgh, as it used to be, seems to me to be the nearest thing to perfection achieved by man in the building of cities. It is the visible monument to the Scottish Enlightenment, when the intellec-tual capital of Great Britain was some 500 miles north of London: a thought uncomfortable to the English.

The English never really took to the Greek revival. In contrast, the Scots, like the Prussians, made the pure aus-terity of Greek architecture a symbol of nationhood and so, in the early nineteenth century, Edinburgh was recreated as the 'modern Athens'. One of its finest monuments is the old High School nestling on the side of Calton Hill. This severe Doric temple of learning, designed by Thomas Hamilton, seems much too grand to be a mere school. Indeed, it may soon perform a more important function, for behind its cen-tral portico in the former assembly hall is a debating chamber, complete with microphones, electronic voting systems and a speaker's chair – all the over-optimistic work of the Property Services Agency, in preparation for a posi-tive result in the 1978 referendum on a Scottish Assembly.

Now, it seems, this assembly hall may soon be in use, and Hamilton's High School would make a magnificent home for

31

a Scottish Assembly – a suitably imposing building in a fine capital city. But the thought of an independent Scotland cannot but make me ever so slightly uneasy. For, although I am now a citizen of Glasgow and my parents gave me a Scottish Christian name, I am in origin a Londoner, and do not have a drop of Scottish blood. Will I, and others like me, be sent away, like the Sudeten Germans, the Hungarians in Transylvania or, for that matter, the English in Ireland? For that is what can happen when empires collapse.

Edinburgh provokes interesting reflections on nationalism and the nation states of Europe, so many of which seem to be products of the political turmoil of the past two centuries. We English, along with the French, from our uniquely privileged backgrounds of ancient nationhood, tend to regard the struggles of the Estonians, or the Croats, with patronizing complacency. Do the Scots come in the same category? The train from King's Cross tunnels through the edge of Calton Hill to emerge at Waverley Station – that huge greenhouse which is the world's best sited railway station. Why Waverley? The answer lies with Sir Walter Scott, who sits under a colossal Gothic canopy next door to the station in Princes Street, for this great national author called his early books The Waverley Novels. But it may come as a surprise to find that the name Waverley is not Scottish at all, but comes from a ruined abbey in Surrey.

In fact, so much that the tourist industry sells as Scottish is an invention of the nineteenth century. Glasgow tends to be dismissive of kilts, bagpipes, haggis and the other principal manifestations of the Scottish heritage industry, and it is true that much of it derives from George IV's visit to Edinburgh in 1822. This partly farcical event was largely orchestrated by Scott, but Prinny was an intelligent Romantic, and his donning of the kilt made traditional Highland dress respectable again after its proscription at the time of Culloden (actually repealed in 1782). But so what? Scotland can claim precedence in the crucial nineteenth-century story of nations reinventing themselves, when Czechs disassociated themselves from Germans, and Finns from Swedes, through art, literature and language.

And why should we English be so smug? What are our symbols of nationhood? Much of our culture is imported from the Continent, and all many people can come up with as symbols of Englishness are twee country cottages and villages. The cult of the vernacular and the pastoral is also a modern, Romantic phenomenon, and the taste for the half-timbered cottage has much to do with the Shakespeare industry, essentially a product of the 1840s and '50s. After all, that ludicrous over-restored cottage in Stratford-upon-Avon compares unfavourably with Hamilton's Grecian monument, next to the High School on Calton Hill, which commemorates the Scots' national poet, Robert Burns.

As an Englishman in Scotland, I am increasingly conscious of the monstrous arrogance and ignorance of the English towards a great part of the United Kingdom. The problem, of course, is the way we are brought up. I still find it a great struggle not to say English when I mean British, and I am amazed at the number of educated, middle-class English who are prepared to confess, without apparent shame, that they have *never* been north of the Border; if they admitted they had not been across the English Channel they would be thought to be culturally deprived. It is this English ignorance about Scotland, translated into legislation, which makes an increasing number of Scots happy to contemplate some form of devolution.

For the fact is that Scotland *is* an ancient and different nation, with a separate history from that of England, and it preserves its own laws and customs – the local banknotes, issued by Scottish banks, are proof of that. The general merits of the distinct Scottish legal system are being demonstrated by the increasing unease about judicial processes in England, and anybody who has had to try to sell a house in England and buy one in Scotland will have no difficulty in appreciating the difference in, and the superiority of, the Scottish conveyancing system.

Although we speak, broadly, the same English language, many Scottish words are quite different – even basic ones (you ask for heavy, not bitter). With my English cloth-ears, I have often found myself as uncomprehending and as lost as if I were in a really foreign country.

Religion makes Scotland feel very different from England, with huge numbers of churches – so many now redundant – reflecting its terrible religious history. Scotland is a sectarian country, although that dark secret is kept well hidden. The established church, the Church of Scotland, is Presbyterian, although it is but one of many confusingly named churches owing to the fissiparous nature of Scottish Presbyterianism, while on the other side there is a strong, monolithic Catholic presence. In consequence, the exiled Anglican tends to feel alienated, for the small Episcopal Church of Scotland, in communion with the Church of England, can seem but a Victorian Anglo-Catholic invention.

Then there is education, in which the Scots still believe. Perhaps the English never did; certainly, schools in Scotland have not declined as far as they have in the south, for in Scotland education has always been highly regarded as a way of getting on, and out.

Whatever English schools do teach, they do not teach much about Scotland. I am now very aware of my ignorance of Scottish history, and have more sympathy for the historical complaints of, say, the Czechs about the former suppression of cultural identity through an imposed education. Who in England has ever heard of the Declaration of Arbroath, and knows anything of its significance? All we seem to know about is Bonnie Prince Charlie and the '45, and Robert the Bruce and that wretched spider.

Scottish history is complicated, and the religious convulsions of the sixteenth and seventeenth centuries are as confusing as they are depressing – but that is no excuse for not teaching something about Scotland in English schools.

Yet all I remember being taught about Scottish history concerned events that impinged on England, like James VI becoming James I, and the Act of Union. The rest was largely ignored, or taken for granted.

When I have mentioned this to Scottish friends, they have complained that they were not taught Scottish history either. Perhaps that is true: certainly many Scots need to be better informed about the Act of Union. Recently, members of the Scottish National Party (SNP) have compared Scotland's situation to that of the Baltic states. This is wickedly misleading. Latvia, Lithuania and Estonia were incorporated by force into the Russian empire. Scotland was never conquered by England. In contrast, the Act of Union, which resulted in the present representative arrangements in Westminster, was a union entered into voluntarily by both sides. That is the source of the stability, and greatness, of the United Kingdom.

The advantages to Scotland of the Union were immense. Some say that the extraordinary intellectual life of Edinburgh in the eighteenth century, which was the admiration of Europe, was a consequence of all the aristocrats and bureaucrats decamping south to London. (Indeed, Sir Nicholas Fairbairn, member of parliament for Perth and Kinross, argues that even today: 'The great benefit of the Scots is that they are the only identifiable, civilized European race who do not have the misfortune to have a government.')

In Glasgow it was different. At first the Union was violently opposed, but it became the source of the city's wealth and industry. After 1707, Glasgow could trade, for the first time, with America and other, now British, colonies, and it prospered mightily. In the nineteenth century, Glasgow became the 'second city' – not of Scotland, or of Britain, but of the empire. And the Scots ran that empire. If you look at the soldiers, the administrators and the engineers who built up the British empire, an astonishing number were Scots.

But now the empire has gone. Where does that leave

Scotland? Allan Massie, among others, has argued that the advantage to Scotland of the Union was the outlet in the empire, and that the disappearance of that opportunity for fame and fortune has brought the Union itself into question. I find that convincing. Why should able, industrious Scots want to run mere England?

Perhaps Scotland's destiny now must be in Europe, as the nationalists are arguing. There are historical reasons for this: the 'auld alliance' resulted in strange corruptions of French words in everyday use, such as ashet pies (from *assiette*), while the buildings of the Scottish Renaissance must be compared, not with English architecture, but with French. Scotland now likes to think of itself as a European nation, and Glasgow flatters itself it is a European city. It really was, and is, a city of culture, and its wealth of museums, art galleries and parks – all the product of a municipal paternalism that was Tory and Liberal before it was Labour – puts *all* other British cities to shame. But is Glasgow really a *European* city? Physically it looks, if anything, American, and many of its attitudes are American, not European. No civilized European city is still planning urban motorways: Glasgow is. This is one of the most depressing aspects of modern Scotland.

Scotland is even more in thrall to the motor car than England. I am appalled by my colleagues who drive to work when they could walk, cycle or travel by public transport. Unfortunately, whereas real European cities are fighting the car by improving public transport, Glasgow's once excellent bus system is not what it was, and it is filthy. Nor can all this be blamed on the English, and Mrs Thatcher. The only independent body seriously fighting the still active motorway plans in the city, Glasgow for People, is being crushed through legal costs by an alliance between the Secretary of State for Scotland and Labour-controlled Strathclyde regional council.

Nor is this backwardness peculiar to Glasgow. It has recently been found that atmospheric pollution caused by motor traffic in Edinburgh is well over European safety limits – the Scottish capital is evidently the Athens of the North in more ways than one. All over Scotland the railway system has been far too drastically pruned and is still being run down, while the interests of the car predominate. Roads get money when railways do not, and the typical Scottish environment is becoming one of hypermarkets and fast-food emporia surrounded by acres of car park. Is that what an independent Scottish nation wants to be like?

Much of what is wrong with transport policies in Scotland can be blamed on the Conservative government – Malcolm Rifkind is doing no more for Scottish public transport as transport minister than he did as Secretary of State. The Scots have a justified grievance against Westminster over many other things, including being made the guinea-pigs for a new local government tax. England was also a victim of Conservative reforms, of course, but at least the names of most of the ancient counties survived; in Scotland they did not, and there is a grotesque upper tier of local government that puts the glorious ancient town of Stirling into something called Central. I, certainly, would rather pay my poll tax to a Scottish Assembly than to that great bureaucratic monster, Strathclyde regional council.

In recent years, Conservative policies have consistently gone against the grain in Scotland. Perhaps the demise of the Conservative party in Scotland may allow the rise of a truly Scottish conservatism. It is sorely needed, for a devolved, or independent, Scotland is likely to be dominated by the Labour party which, at present, controls both Edinburgh and Glasgow. Perhaps that is no bad thing, if the result is Scandinavian-style social democracy. But although both these district councils behave with a welcome pragmatism towards business, and the politicians of Glasgow deserve applause for showing the prejudiced English that the city is much more than gang warfare and the Gorbals, there is a distressing tendency to promote proletarian culture as the Scottish norm. The decision of the SNP to be both nationalist *and* socialist is a symptom of this, as if the two were inseparable.

Of course there has been a vital working-class tradition in Scottish life, but the immense contribution of the middle class, of capitalists, to the power and prestige of Glasgow should also be acknowledged. Unfortunately, Scotland, like the United States, deludes itself that it is a classless society, when it certainly is not. It is true that there is much freer social contact and far less snobbery than in England (although professional life in Edinburgh could scarcely be more closed and elitist) and that the respect for education means that Scottish society is potentially mobile and fluid, but to claim that working-class culture is typical and authentically Scottish is absurd – and destructive.

I hate to criticize the great city that has treated me with such friendliness and tolerance, but some things I must publicly deplore. The average diet is appalling. Junk food flourishes, producing an all-pervasive litter, while the heavy consumption of sugar and fat is alarming. When this diet is combined with heavy smoking – the climate on the top of a Glasgow bus has to be breathed to be believed – it scarcely seems surprising that the average person in the street looks so unhealthy, and that the Scots have one of the highest death rates in western Europe. What Scotland needs is a healthy dose of English middle-class health-conscious environmentalism.

I do not include drinking in my strictures, partly because I can never find fault with the consumption of alcohol, but also because Scottish drinking, although still heavy, shows that habits can change. When I first visited Scotland, in 1968, I was amazed by the Dickensian scenes of distraught wives dragging paralytic husbands home at closing-time, and of the police putting drunks into coolers at lunchtime. No longer: the Scots were uncivilized because the licensing hours were barbaric – a product of the Calvinist tradition which I, as a foreigner, find hard to cope with. But these restrictions have been reformed and life is more civilized than in England. Now it is possible to get a drink (and go to the bank) any time in the afternoon. The only remaining inconvenience that prevents Glasgow being supremely agreeable is that off-licences are closed on Sundays.

Guilty as I feel about leaving London, I would not now choose to live anywhere else than Glasgow. It is a big city, a great city, rich in interest and culture, while the most magnificent countryside lies nearby and is easily accessible. Architecture makes a nation, and here, as with painting, the Scots have every reason to feel proud. Scotland has, for several centuries, produced distinguished *British* architects in numbers out of all proportion to its population, while Glasgow can claim as its own two original geniuses of European stature. One, of course, was Charles Rennie Mackintosh, who reinterpreted the traditional architecture of seventeenth-century Scotland and made it new. But my hero is Alexander 'Greek' Thomson, who, out of elements from Greece and Egypt, made a modern classical urban architecture which is at once European and quintessentially Scottish. Yet he hardly ever left his native land and never crossed the English Channel.

A nation that has given us Campbell, Adam, Playfair, Hamilton, Burn, Thomson, Shaw, Burnet, Salmon, Mackintosh, Lorimer, Tait and Spence, to name but architects, surely deserves respect. Yet something is wrong. Almost all Scottish cities have been grievously damaged, by the Scots themselves, while the worst new buildings in Glasgow – including the shaming and depressing new concert hall – have been designed by Englishmen. Even worse is the fact that Glasgow did its best to destroy its Victorian (and Georgian, and medieval) past, wiping out huge areas of stone tenement housing in an orgy of Utopian slum clearance, while driving through motorways to create urban wastelands without parallel in Britain. This was done partly out of class hatred – wiping out the black legacy of nineteenth-century industrialism and social injustice. But it was also done out of self-hatred.

Here is the thing that worries me most about modern Scotland. The damage to Glasgow has not only been the result of the usual factors – greed, ignorance, philistinism, indifference – but also of a disturbing lack of self-confidence. This can show itself in an extreme sensitivity to perceived criticism. For instance, there is that tiresome business of the Scots objecting to being called Scotch. This has long puzzled me, for, as anyone familiar with books published any time before this century will know, the Scots used to refer to themselves as the Scotch. I do not mind having a surname which is also that of a sticky label on letters; why should the Scottish think the generic name of one of the greatest boons that this land has given to civilization should be somehow pejorative when applied to themselves?

All too often, the Scots seem diffident about defending what is uniquely valuable and their own, and will only take notice when outsiders take an interest. This certainly has been true in Glasgow, with the precious work of both Thomson and Mackintosh; it is most depressing. Behind all this seems to lie a deep-seated, national inferiority complex – perhaps the worst legacy of the Union, the tying together of a small nation with a populous one. Why else should so many English be running the cultural establishments in Scotland? (On the other hand, why should there be so many Scots in Westminster running Britain?)

There is no reason for any feelings of inferiority, or any fear of lack of identity. Scotland's population is about the size of that of Finland, which has a much more severe climate and hostile landscape. Yet Finland is a proud, independent nation, with a distinct culture which has made an important contribution to twentieth-century Europe. Perhaps only separation from England can produce that vitality.

But divorce would surely be too painful and destructive for both England and Scotland, as our two nations' destinies have been for so long intertwined. In the cold and driving rain, I watched the Remembrance Sunday ceremony in George Square. The Union Jack flew on the City Chambers – that supremely opulent municipal pile – while the Cross of St Andrew flew on Glasgow's cenotaph. The two minutes' silence were preceded by the last post and followed by the plaintive, haunting music of a single piper. Then the sodden soldiers marched away, some in trousers, some in kilts, and the pipes played. Having fought two world wars together, having intermarried and interlocked, it seems inconceivable that the English and the Scots could separate completely. So for the moment, I feel safe, and can contemplate the old High School – one of the two finest buildings in Britain, according to 'Greek' Thomson – performing a new function with equanimity, if not with enthusiasm.

23 November 1991

Sleeping with the enemy

Anne McElvoy

Jana jerks open the door, peers cautiously into the gloomy corridor of her high-rise apartment block and whispers a welcome. Inside, in the light of the hall, dark roots are visible in the hair which until recently was perfectly preserved blonde. She catches my tactless glance and pats it self-consciously. 'I don't get out to the hairdresser now. The way things are, you understand. Why take risks?'

In the living room sits Milan, her husband, flicking disconsolately between the evening news of Belgrade television and the Croatian version. 'Two propagandas are better than one,' he says. 'Sometimes, you can even work out the truth using this method.' He proffers a half-tumbler of *slivovitz*, precursor to any heart-to-heart in Yugoslavia, and one of the few traditions which still unites a country in the midst of violent disintegration.

Jana and Milan are a kind, unremarkable couple in their late forties, devoted to their modest home, their daughter and each other. Their lives are now dominated by a factor they had long ceased to consider worthy even of comment: Jana is a Serb, Milan is a Croat.

At the beginning of September, as the attacks by the federal army and Serb irregular forces increased throughout Croatia, Jana greeted a neighbour and received no reply: 'I thought she hadn't heard me. But the next day it happened again, and the day after with someone else. When I climbed the stairs of the block, the doors would clang shut around me. When I closed the door of my own flat behind me, I suddenly realized what had happened. I was no longer their neighbour, Jana, I was a Serb. I was the enemy.'

She called a close Croatian friend to talk about her experience. 'By the way,' the friend said before she could start, 'I was just wondering, where did you say you were born?' Jana told her. 'Not that it matters,' her friend said, 'but is it true that you're a Serb?'

Twelve per cent of Croatia's population is Serbian. In Zagreb, a city of a million people, the figure was 100,000. Many, like Jana, have lived there for decades, arriving in the great movement of peoples in the early years of the new Yugoslavia after the war. Since the fighting started, an estimated half of this figure have left the city.

Jana blames the 'small terror' – the proliferation of insults, silences and denunciations which are now a part of everyday life for Serbs in Zagreb. We talk on the basis of no surnames, no photographs.

The National Guard had come round twice that week, claiming that someone had called *Zivjela Srbia* (Long live Serbia) from the balcony. The couple tries to joke about the ludicrous accusation, but the laughter peters out into an uneasy silence.

Contrary to the picture of ingrained ethnic bitterness invoked by the two sides to imply that this war is an inevitable consequence of a long feud, many Serbs and Croats lived side by side for years. And it is not the failure of integration of the two ethnic groups, but rather its success, which is the cause of much present anguish. Serbs and Croats cannot simply be prised apart, however much their leaders aspire to revive the homogenous societies of the nineteenth-century nation state. A new identity forged in the post-war period has been shattered by the collapse of Yugoslavia and there is only war-fuelled nationalism to take its place.

Milan was an officer in the federal army until a recent, and welcome, early retirement after an accident. His preference for watching both the Croatian and Serbian news at once bespeaks more than the mistrust of propaganda he claims. It is a symptom of his confusion about his own views and the fate of his country.

'I feel like a schizophrenic,' he says. 'I know how scared the army is: scared of the death of Yugoslavia, because that means the end of everything it stands for. But I shudder when I see those weapons raining down on villages. Rockets, for God's sake, air bombardment. Things I used to tell my recruits were there for the enemy outside, if ever we were attacked. Tito built up an army big enough to scare off the Russians. Now it has turned on its own people.'

As if to confirm his words, the air-raid sirens begin to wail outside. This is the third alarm this week, a regular chorus of threat, loud enough, it seems, to tear the night sky apart. There are distant thuds of shelling and mortar from the out-skirts of the city, like a background drumbeat. After a while, the *slivovitz* dispels the sound from our consciousness. Alcohol not as indulgence, but as an anaesthetic.

Zagreb is governed by fear of an all-out attack as the enemy forces edge nearer by the day. With grim humour, Croats refer to what is left of their unoccupied territory as Greater Zagreb. Little wonder that the mood towards Serbs is hostile. 'We are associated with destruction and aggression, no matter what our own views are,' Jana says.

Later, she admits that the war has affected the couple's relationship for the worse. 'I never thought of my marriage as a Serb-Croat affair. How many people think of their relationship as something political? Milan was just my husband and I loved him. But the longer this goes on, the more Serb I feel and the more there is a pull to identify with my own people.'

They had their first big row recently, when Jana wanted to go to a clandestine meeting of Serbs who have formed a support network in Zagreb. Milan said he did not want her to slide into a ghetto mentality and forbade her to go. 'Something snapped inside me,' she says. 'I shouted at him that I was forced into the ghetto by this damn country of his. I regretted the words, but I could not in all honesty take them back.'

She did not go, but the resentment lingers. Milan, clearly

anxious to stay in the mainstream of society, still speaks to Croatian acquaintances who have stopped talking to his wife. Jana explains her confusion: 'If you had asked me three months ago where my first loyalty lay, I would have said, "With my husband", without hesitating. But in this situation I think more and more about my people and my heritage, and I could see a day coming when my place would be with them.'

Jana and Milan live increasingly separate lives, no longer able to socialize together. Jana is uneasy in public places. 'We went out for a meal but the whole night I was watching the door to see if anyone who recognized me would come in. The whole conversation at the tables was about how murderous Serbs were and what should be done to them. I couldn't eat a thing.' Since then, Jana stays in the house most of the time and has given her husband an ultimatum. If it comes to physical attacks on Serbs in the city, she wants to leave.

Milan is uncomfortable with this topic, casts her a furious glance and says: 'The more Serb you become, the more Croatian you make me feel.' It is as if the ethnic enmity around them has begun to seep into their relationship, poisoning its candour and threatening its intimacy. 'Sometimes I feel that Milosevic and Tudjman [the respective Serb and Croatian leaders] are sitting in the living room with us,' Milan says. 'We begin to speak with their words instead of our own, and then we look at each other and wonder what is becoming of us.'

Attempts to avoid the subject of the war inevitably end in failure or in recollections of better times. Both know that their personal happiness will be restored only if the fighting stops and they fear that this is a long way off. Yet they are almost as afraid of the outcome of the conflict as of the war itself. Instead of living with violence, they will then live with the resentment of its aftermath. They agree that, win or lose, their national identity will be even more important than it is now.

Money is tight. Milan's pension comes from Belgrade, but all banking links with Croatia have been cut. Jana says: 'I came here because I wanted to be a part of the West, and this was a much more liberal place than Belgrade. Now it has become a prison for me.' Her elderly parents are in Belgrade.

Milan could not bring himself to move to Belgrade as long as Slobodan Milosevic is in power. 'If I went there and told people, "Here I am, I'm a Croat", I'd have the same problems my wife has here. If I went and said, "I'm a retired officer of the Yugoslav army", they might accept me, but I could not keep my mouth shut about the politics.'

The couple feels that there is nowhere inside Yugoslavia where they could live comfortably together. Under this kind of stress, many mixed marriages have fallen apart, with one partner often returning to Serbia, leaving the other in Croatia. Travel between the two republics is already extremely difficult, involving a lengthy detour via Hungary or the single open route through Bosnia.

The couple's daughter, Natasha, wanders in towards midnight to a voluble scolding about not telephoning to say where she was during the air-raid warning. She is twenty-one, fashionably dressed in the Italian casuals favoured by Croatian youth, intent on looking as western as possible. Sipping espresso in tiny bars to deafening acid-house music, they sport sunglasses, mock-gold jewellery and sharply cut jackets. Yet there is a compulsive edge to their glamour, as if the fantasy of fashion could obscure grim reality as husbands, brothers and boyfriends disappear to the front line, sometimes for ever.

Natasha looks vaguely annoyed to find that, having sought respite for the evening, on arriving home conversation is about the war. Her mixed parentage has given her a rare equanimity about the conflict. 'It's madness,' she says.

'Communism was nothing compared with this. I didn't lose friends in a war under the communists. I could travel where I wanted. Everyone talked about the freedom we would gain, but no one could call this liberty.' She is not a closet communist, she adds, it is just that she is tired of the modern convention which dictates that whatever comes after communism is automatically an improvement.

As is customary in the Balkans, Natasha took her religious and cultural lead from her father, and was brought up as a Catholic. This is the first time that she has thought about her Serbian roots. 'I have grown up in Croatia, gone to school and college here. It hurts to see the destruction of my country. Then I think of my mother hiding in the house because she is a Serb, and I feel angry that we are combating the old dominance with our own autocracy and narrowness.'

Under Tito, ethnic differences were subdued to the dogma of a united socialist nation. Many folk songs and poems were forbidden, points of differences between the republics hushed up. The post-war Yugoslav state acted as a heavy extinguishing blanket, cast over the fiery nationalist sentiments which had culminated in the mass killings of the Second World War. The arrangement kept Serbia, the restless giant, pegged down within the federation, but at the price of allowing it dominance over the country's institutions and the army.

This explains much of the bitterness towards Serbs in Croatia. Many of the top jobs were filled by Serbs, who also ran both the secret and the ordinary police. Now, old injustice is being exorcised by new, with many ordinary Serbs dismissed from their jobs in the past year without recourse to appeal.

Inside the Serbian Orthodox church in the centre of town, the breath of the worshippers hangs in the freezing air. There is no longer enough money from collections to heat the building. Milan Popovic, the priest, shivers visibly, even in his black robes, edged with silver. With his long beard and dark eyes, he looks like a benign sorcerer, an unapologetic eastern stranger in a city so intent on joining the West that the strain is palpable. The incantations of the Mass are a soft, mesmerizing drone, the candles flicker across the icons behind the altar. The congregation consists of eight elderly women.

There has been, Popovic says grimly, a silent exodus of Serbs from Croatia. Most of those who have remained prefer not to identify themselves by coming to the church. The list of services outside is routinely torn down. 'I can understand why they don't come,' he says. 'Anyone who enters the church is declaring themselves openly. In the present climate, our people are trying to lie low.'

He is now the only Orthodox priest left in Zagreb – his three colleagues packed their bags in October to return to Serbia – and he also ministers to what he calls his 'flock in exile', Serbs who have gone to Graz, in Austria, to escape the difficulties in Croatia. He no longer walks out in his robes after being attacked and spat at.

'Soon we will leave altogether,' he says. His wife, Slavica, a doctor, says nonsense, one must stay and resist. 'No,' he says. 'Soon we will have to leave. We will know when the moment comes and there will be no more fighting it.'

He ushers the way into an imposing stone building opposite the church. Another Serb stands guard as he tears down a giant tourist poster in the hall. Behind it, engraved in Cyrillic lettering, is a commemoration of the Borojevic family of Serb merchants who donated the house to the church in 1878.

Since the war, the house has belonged to the state. 'But anything Serbian offends people here these days. Even something more than 100 years old.' The next morning, a fresh Croatian poster is back in place. Popovic counsels families affected by the fighting. Outside his office sits a pale woman, chewing her nails and oblivious of her surroundings. She is a Serb, her husband Croatian. Their son has volunteered for the National Guard and has been dispatched to Virovitica, near the Hungarian border, in a counter-offensive to reclaim villages occupied by Serb forces. The outcome is precarious. A Croatian counter-assault is rare in these days of rapidly shrinking territory. The only certainty is that it will be bloody. 'I don't know which way to pray, for my son or my people,' she says, and begins to cry.

The priest has officiated at more mixed marriages than he can remember in his ten years at the church. 'I always enjoyed them. Each one seemed to me like a small atonement for the terrible things that happened between Serbs and Croats in the [Second World] War.'

The scar tissue over that particular wound has been forced open by the conflict, as both sides exhume the ghosts of a past war to justify a present one. Since the fighting began, there have been no more cross-cultural weddings. But this is a bad time for marriages of any description. At the nearby Catholic church of St Blaz, fifty of the eighty planned to take place in the past five months have been cancelled as the war kills hopes for the future.

The only friends who now visit Jana in her home are fellow Serbs. Milan meets his outside. The lines of segregation emerge more clearly by the week.

Two days after leaving the couple, in the town of Nasice near the front line with Serbia, the hotel receptionist tells me that her boyfriend has been killed in a battle with guerrillas. A National Guardsman who overhears shouts, 'Long live Croatia', and the entire lobby applauds. 'No,' says the woman, quietly, 'Long live everyone.' It was a rare and uplifting triumph of compassion over enmity. A moment of hope in a hopeless war.

30 November 1991

Madrid diary

Valentí Puig

Variously compared with Babel or Utopia, Madrid is a noisy place populated by sleepless chain-smokers who think midday means 2.30 and lunch is at 3.30. Certainly, dinner before 10 p.m. is a disgrace, and lunches are a long, premeditated joy. In such an expensive city, a whole generation of fixers lunch splendidly every day, later becoming showy with their portable phones. And this season's ties are as frightful as those in London.

Socialist Madrid has known the rewards and pleasures of making money. Everybody has learnt quickly how to sell something. Executives keep squash rackets at hand in their offices, but a few survivors from the old order still complain about a new society obsessed by takeover activities.

These are boom times for clairvoyants, and everyone seems eager to consult them. Rappel, for instance, provides the best advice for the spiritual migraine of the *Hello!* society through tarot. And mirroring new anxieties like a crystal ball, South American television soap operas *Rubí*, *Manuela* and *Leonela* have become a lachrymose must in television. Spain has quickly learnt zapping with the new private channels, and soap operas and Berlusconi's girl-shows have viewers agog.

Madrid taxi fares have gone up, but taxi drivers are in their usual bad temper, offering to throttle the mayor if it will help to cure the traffic jams. Radio stations blare the opinions of luminaries constantly from taxi speakers, as if words were more effective when unwritten. At night, journalists in trench coats flirt at the Cock bar with racy tales (mostly invented), and the trendy young set goes to Alaska's, the new night venue run by the singer Alaska, who has the looks of Cruella deVille, but with plenty of common sense. Away from late-night Madrid, in the suburbs, spontaneous anti-drugs vigilantes watch the streets, looking for heroin dealers. In most cinemas, people applaud the transvestism in *High Heels*, Almodóvar's new film: truly a sign of the end of Spanish isolationism.

Prime Minister Felipe González likes to take care of the bonsais in the gardens of the Moncloa Palace. There he meditates on the wonders of market economics and the counter-balancing of his party's left wing. Parliament was a good habitat when he was in opposition but now the opposition would like to see him there more often. How they would like to see him grilled like John Major at Question Time. Alas, they never will.

Far away from the rumour of lunches in the city of rumours, González thinks again about the next general elections. To get a majority, he may need the votes of Catalan and Basque nationalists, but they still seem inspired by the success of the Baltic states, when in fact they should see themselves more as a portion of a state split by language and culture, like Belgium. The prime minister's fellow citizens now like to think they are good Europeans but there was fury throughout the country when a rumour said that Brussels might abolish the tilde symbol from written Spanish, for example ñ. The Spanish will never allow bureaucrats to take away the identity of their language, which is as much a part of their history as financial scandals or plebeian duchesses. Even though bankers may be the heroes of the new Spain, the threat to the tilde was a bigger issue than the peseta going into the exchange-rate mechanism.

If any EC directive forbade the siesta, disobedience would be even more unanimous. Shrinks never invented anything so good – better than yoga. The only dilemma is whether to take to the bed or the sofa. Siesta may disrupt the day, but it stabilizes the nervous system. To keep siesta as a form of civilization deserves an opt-out clause.

When Gorbachev was in Madrid, people shouted at him: '*Torero!*'. It was the real end of a cold war that Spain had not always acknowledged. González was elected in 1982 to change everything, but only the socialists themselves did change. Out went beards; in came cashmere. Che Guevara's admirers became stockbrokers. They never had it so good.

Carmen Romero, González's wife, recently took part in a homage to Augusto Monterroso, a fine writer from Guatemala. The main contribution was Monterroso's dog barking to the audience. Now, call me old-fashioned but I think that in these circumstances, books should have the last word. It happens in Madrid that you get some of the fiercest literary arguments in Europe, although books are not sold quite so much. Nonetheless, everybody seems to expect some new golden age in which literature will be a top priority.

At the moment, talk is of Spain's bestselling book, *Scarlett*, as if the literary feuds of Café Bigón were just talk in a vacuum. Watching steamy videos when not writing a masterpiece, Spanish authors are frequently fêted by the state, but quickly forgotten. Barking must, then, be the lost link between the written word and the television image.

Among the wreckage of the Eighties *movida*, the trendiest young people have now gone back to the 1950s, a decade they never knew. Happily, *boleros* – those warm songs of absence and love – are again in fashion. Old hands, such as the singer Lucho Gatica, have come back and the group Los Panchos never went away. As the old *mañana* merges into today's high-tech bureaucracy, it may be one of the burdens of the age that designers and the neo-expressionist painters dominate Madrid's landscape. But then, bonsais are not quite the real thing either.

4 January 1992

The Decade of Evangelism was never going to work

Clifford Longley

Has there been a big mistake in strategy in the churches of Britain in the 1990s? Have they put too much stress on the possibilities of converting the unconverted, too much hope into the prospects of church unity? Would they have done better, before reaching outside, to have put their own houses in order first? The next few months may show a growing feeling among church members that the word whose time has come should not be 'evangelism' nor 'ecumenism' but 'renewal' – that deepening the pool of faith should come before widening it.

The churches' Decade of Evangelism is a year old. The 1992 Week of Prayer for Christian Unity starts tomorrow. But it is clear now that neither of these endeavours is going to set the world alight. The Decade has so far achieved little bar irritating the Jewish and Muslim communities. The Week will be not much more than a reminder of lost hopes. Yet depressing though these disappointments ought to be, none of the churches will spend next week in mourning. This is because neither the Decade of Evangelism (known to Roman Catholics as the 'Decade of Evangelization') nor the Week of Prayer for Unity has penetrated very far into the collective consciousness of church-goers – or even the consciousness of their pastors. Evangelism, unless it means rallies of the Billy Graham kind, is hardly understood as a concept. The thought of knocking on house doors looking for converts has little appeal. As for ecumenism, it has reached a stage at which it is normal for Christians of different denominations to be polite and warm to each other, but the stage beyond that is as unclear as ever.

*

All this is attributable to muddled leadership and uncertainties of purpose in every church, and an extreme evangelistic or ecumenical optimism that is near to dishonesty. The purpose of the Decade of Evangelism should have been defined before it began. Instead the idea was seized on with a kind of ecclesiastical 'me-tooism' when the Pope mooted some such thing in the mid-1980s. What he meant is still not clear, but it may have had something to do with offering Polish Catholicism to Europe as a role model. When the Lambeth Conference took on the idea for the Anglican Communion in 1988, the motive was different – a patronizing attempt to make Anglican Evangelicals feel they mattered, for instance – but not much more realistic.

As a result the Decade is wholly unfocused. To describe it as all things to all men is the polite way of saying it means nothing to anybody. But because it has become ecumenical property, nobody can say so. So the churches have agreed to play 'Let's pretend we are all doing something to convert the nation', just as next week they will play 'Let's pretend we all want to be united'. It is not that nobody believes in converting the nation or being united. In church terms, these are platitudes equivalent to motherhood. But they have no agreed meaning.

Leaving aside sophisticated theologies of evangelism and ecumenism understood only by the élite few, ecumenism still to most Anglicans means persuading people in the other churches to become Anglicans, and to most Roman Catholics persuading people in other churches to become Catholics. This hardly makes for unity. Equally, evangelism to Anglicans means persuading those not in any church to become Anglicans, and so on. The Free Churches are not so different. So the churches are still essentially working with the pre-twentieth-century competitive model of inter-church relations, though they are not allowed to face the consequences.

Renewal – deepening before widening – has two great merits as an alternative strategy: it can be done honestly, and the aim can be seen in sharp focus. Individually, renewal means nothing other than the Imitation of Christ, the pursuit of personal holiness through repentance, prayer and grace. Collectively, renewal means creating and nourishing a Christ-centred community of worship and service. Neither of these models of renewal requires any glances over shoulders to check on how good or popular is the 'image' being projected. Each means concentrating on raw religion rather than on the politics of religion. That is what people want.

By analogy with business, this change of strategy equals getting the product right before giving thought to its marketing. If the product were good enough, marketing and merging – the commercial equivalents to evangelism and ecumenism – might well take care of themselves.

18 January 1992

An enemy of the people

Janet Daley

I am always stunned with admiration by the ingenuity with which royal apologists defend the indefensible. Indeed, during my first years in Britain, I was almost convinced. It is the more subtle justifications that are so seductive: *of course* (the sophisticated engagingly admit) the idea of inheriting privilege, enormous wealth and political influence is, by modern political standards, repugnant. But go beyond such simplistic judgments, they urge, and think what the alternatives are.

The Queen 'embodies' the law and that, they argue mystically, raises civil order above the fray of party politics. The monarch's ceremonial function protects us from the invidious foreign tendency to idolize political leaders. Most persuasively for an ex-American repelled by materialism, they claim that hereditary nobility ensures that wealth is not the only measure of status.

That perennial sixth form debating topic 'Does monarchy serve any purpose in a democracy?' is generally dusted off by the media at every royal anniversary. But the current round, marking the Queen's fortieth year on the throne, is notably less anodyne than usual. Never have the critics' arguments seemed more confident. Doubts are being expressed in important quarters not about whether the throne *should* survive into another generation, but whether it *can*.

The fashionable theory is that the younger royals are dragging the whole thing into disrepute. The Queen looks more and more like a venerable headmistress who has lost control of the lower fourth; the press are turning the whole thing into a shaming circus, and a country in recession resents subsidizing a tax-free frivolous lifestyle. All of which is true, but not the whole story. What this new cynicism suggests is that the country may finally be growing tired of the deception with which it has gone along for so many years.

What royalty stands for, more than historical tradition, more than the rule of law or any other time-honoured hokum, is the sacred principle that what you are is more important than what you do. At hundreds of ceremonial dinners and lunches, award presentations and commemorative celebrations, countless citizens who have achieved endless varieties of accomplishment are 'honoured' by the presence of inconsequential persons who condescend to offer their gracious approval. Hands are shaken, prizes are given and congratulations are murmured by people whom we often know to be frivolous.

Anyone who has sat through an embarrassing, incoherent and amateurish speech by a young royal personage and then listened to the gush of reverent gratitude that followed it, will know what it means to be in the presence of a Big Lie. Which brings us back to the question of what exactly we are idealizing – apart from hypocrisy – when we venerate royalty. If someone who has accomplished nothing takes precedence, by virtue of birth or marriage, over the finest artists and scholars, not to mention the most morally courageous and honourable private individuals, what does this say about how we value achievement? True, we escape the dangers which go along with glorifying politicians, but what do we glorify instead? Vacuity? Unearned prestige?

But there is an even more significant lesson in this pantomime: if respect is due to people because of their position at birth, then the obverse must also be true. We would have less difficulty persuading working-class children to take an interest in education if it were not for the apathy and intimidation bred in them by contempt for their origins. Is it really one of the virtuous fixities of British life that nothing you do or know or have can exempt you from the grovelling which is required by royalty?

We are assured that this protects us from a society dominated by money-grubbing vulgarity, as if the only choice were between the Queen and Ivana Trump. But America's obsession with ostentatious wealth doesn't arise simply from the absence of royalty. The United States worships money because the only common thread among its ethnic multitudes is the desire for material well-being. Its history is a quite simple (and short) story of devotion to entrepreneurial capitalism. Britain without a monarchy would be much more likely to resemble European republics such as France, which has not found a crowned monarch necessary to maintain its culture and civilized values.

Indeed, the connection between the present royal family and the survival of culture seems pretty tenuous. Their unapologetic preference for philistine upper-class amusements and middle-brow entertainment deprives them of what could have been a more attractive role.

The Prince of Wales does, of course, take a serious interest in architectural heritage and education. Many of us with tastes and sympathies similar to his have had cause to be grateful for his disproportionate influence. In this respect, he personifies the romantic myth of modern royalists, who see the monarch as having a direct spiritual link with 'the people'. The Prince's remarks often do express the sentiments of ordinary people, and because of his position these remarks are taken seriously, which is all to the good. But why should the views of ordinary people only be taken seriously when a prince articulates them? What we need is not a high-born mouthpiece, but a more confident and articulate populace. And for that we need to plunge wholeheartedly into democracy.

21 January 1992

Major's middlebrow masterclass

Richard Morrison

When preparing for *Desert Island Discs*, the canny politician surely ought to take a masterclass from that great soprano Dame Elisabeth Schwarzkopf. Remember her choice of eight records? Neither do I. But what most Radio 4 listeners recall is that they were (all but one) recordings of herself.

What a superbly focused mind! And what devilish cunning. By eliminating so much of the subjective element from the programme, she offered no hostages to the amateur psychologists, no bizarre quirk of taste whose murky origins might become the subject of voyeuristic speculation. Not for her the 'this is the song the band was playing when my first boyfriend kissed me' approach. Nothing, in fact, to distract listeners from rapt contemplation of the Schwarzkopfian career.

If only our politicians could ascend to this glorious plateau of singlemindedness, what *Desert Island Discs* there might be. Neil Kinnock would have played his immortal *arioso con molto blustero*, 'The Harrowing of Militant', instead of John Lennon's dreary 'Imagine'. Margaret Thatcher might have given us a snatch of her scintillating Handelian *coloratura*, 'Rejoice, rejoice', instead of the Grand March from *Aida*. And James Callaghan would have riposted with his equally audacious and touching swan-song 'Crisis, what crisis?'

In his turn, John Major yesterday would have put together a medley of his most celebrated solo numbers. Throughout the land, pulses would have raced once more upon hearing those rolling Churchillian cadences: 'considerably more optimistic', 'economic convergence', 'oh yes'.

Politicians have generally been disappointingly modest about playing their own hits on *Desert Island Discs*. If there is one lesson to be learnt from a perusal of our present and former prime ministers' musical choices, it is this: you don't get anywhere in politics by having way-out tastes. Modest, solid, middle-brow, middle-of-the-road, middle-aged mainstream music: that is what wins elections.

There has, however, been a brilliant exception to this modest procession: Edward Heath. His choice included the London Symphony Orchestra performing Elgar's *Cockaigne* Overture – conducted by himself.

At the time, this seemed a little pushy. But Mr Heath was issuing a clarion-call to the nation, as stirring as anything in *Henry V*. The whole story is told in his seminal book, *Music: A Joy for Life*: 'As Prime Minister, I wanted the British to regain their former pride and ebullience . . . perhaps the right performance of *Cockaigne* could show the way.'

That may show the importance of music in political life, but how far is political life an integral part of musical choice? Of course, Mr Major selected his records sincerely – he confessed to having started with eighty, not eight. Most desert islanders admit to having pondered their choice for months of sleepless nights. But it is impossible not to review Mr Major's culturally banal list and at least see lighthearted political significance in each and every record. What clarion-call to the nation can realistically be deduced from the list?

MAJOR'S CHOICE

John Major
   'The Best is Yet to Come', sung by Frank Sinatra
   Gershwin's *Rhapsody in Blue*
   'The Happening' by Diana Ross and The Supremes
   Mad scene from Donizetti's *Lucia di Lammermoor*
   Elgar's *Pomp and Circumstance March*
   John Arlott's commentary on Bradman's last Test innings
(1948)

Adams' 'The Holy City' sung by June Bronhill
Popper's *Elfentanz* played by Rostropovich

We may pass quickly over 'The Best is Yet to Come' sung by Sinatra, a splendidly symbolic piece of electioneering. *Rhapsody in Blue* shows the sporting Major: Gershwin's marvellous musical portrait of a conference of Tory women applauding the entry of the young Michael Heseltine. And after that comes the serious vote-winning music.

First there is the appeal to youth, with 'The Happening': a hit for Diana Ross and The Supremes as recently as 1967. A prime minister who certainly knows how to swing. Grey? No way, José.

Then the inevitable appeal to party loyalty and patriotic instinct, set to the strains of Elgar's *Pomp and Circumstance March*, Tory anthem since modern politics began, and now surely a rather weary incantation to the faithful. And just to emphasize the 'ordinary bloke enjoying his pint and his cricket' image, John Arlott's commentary on Don Bradman's last innings in England is also included.

Stephen Adams' stirring Victorian parlour-song 'The Holy City' nods in the direction of Christianity, while the choice of a cello piece by an obscure nineteenth-century Czech composer will reassure the Arts lobby that our leader is (as Shirley Bassey sings in 'Big Spender') 'a man of distinction . . . so refined'.

But what of the Mad Scene from *Lucia di Lammermoor*, that demented passage of scales and trills for operatic soprano and a lone flute? Is this the bizarre, inexplicable choice for which we amateur psychologists have been waiting? Alas, the answer is touchingly mundane, a graceful compliment from John to Norma. She is the biographer of the soprano Joan Sutherland, who is the most famous exponent of the Mad Scene. So with this choice, the Prime Minister emerges as a loving family man.

In Tory Central Office today they will be well pleased with

61

Desert Island Discs. Mr Major's performance is no more calculating than any previous political castaway. Kinnock chose to reinforce his family credentials by playing a tape of his two-year-old daughter singing 'Horace the Horse'. Moreover (and here I must pause to wipe a tear from my eye) he said that, of all his eight records, 'Horace the Horse' was the one he would *most* want.

Mrs Thatcher went to great pains to rebut the innuendo that she lacked a sense of humour. She chose Bob Newhart's classic comic monologue 'Introducing Tobacco to Civilization'. Remarkably, when James Callaghan (who came later) wanted to show that he, too, enjoyed a good giggle, he also chose 'Introducing Tobacco to Civilization'. Had Mrs Thatcher and Mr Callaghan discovered this mutual love of American stand-up comics earlier, who knows what course modern British politics might have taken?

Middle-brow taste seems to be a prerequisite of political success. So wake up at the back of the class, Paddy Ashdown! Whatever came over you, choosing a concerto for two mandolins as one of your desert island discs? And a piece of *Chinese folk music*? Are you utterly determined to see the Liberal Democrats crushed? History should tell you that British leaders pick hymns (Thatcher, Callaghan, Heath, Douglas-Home) and brass band music (Thatcher, Callaghan) and the 'New World' Symphony (Thatcher, Heath).

Mr Major chooses none of these; but then, he is a generation younger. His taste does not veer dangerously away from the middle-brow; it is simply that the middle-brow has moved on. When Heath, Thatcher and Callaghan were in their salad days, middle-brow musical taste meant *Your Hundred Best Tunes* and *Sunday Half-Hour*. Now we have radio stations pumping out 1960s nostalgia and Pavarotti and 'Nige' Kennedy.

With the unerring instinct of a born politician, John Major slips easily into this aural world. His cultural tastes are the tastes of ten million other British people. Nothing too fancy;

nothing too jarring; nothing inaccessible. Consensus tastes, in fact. The boy will go far.

PREMIER LEAGUE

Alec Douglas-Home
    'Roaming in the Gloaming'
    'Alec Bedser Calypso, England vs Australia 1953'
    Mozart's *Magic Flute*
    Gluck's *Orfeo ed Euridice*
    'I sit in the sun' from *Salad Days*
    Handel's *Water Music*
    Handel's *Zadok the Priest*
    'The Lord's my Shepherd' sung to *Crimond*

Edward Heath
    Vaughan Williams' *A Sea Symphony*
    Schubert's Piano Trio in B flat, Op 99
    Trio from Strauss' *Der Rosenkavalier*
    'If I were a rich man' from *Fiddler on the Roof*
    Elgar's *Cockaigne* Overture
    Prisoners' Chorus from *Fidelio*
    Dvořák's 'New World' Symphony
    'Hark the herald angels sing'

Harold Wilson has never been on *Desert Island Discs*

James Callaghan
    Waller's 'I'm gonna sit right down and write myself a letter'
    Chopin's Piano Nocturne in B flat
    Bob Newhart's 'Introducing Tobacco to Civilization'
    'Jesu, lover of my soul'
    Canteloube's 'The Shepherd's Song'
    Bach's Fourth Brandenburg Concerto
    'The day Thou gavest, Lord, is ended'
    'Sunset' played by the Royal Marines Band

Margaret Thatcher

Beethoven's 'Emperor' Piano Concerto

'Going Home', based on Dvořák's 'New World' Symphony

Grand March from Verdi's *Aida*

Bob Newhart's 'Introducing Tobacco to Civilization'

Kern's 'Smoke gets in your eyes'

'Be not afraid' from Mendelssohn's *Elijah*

Saint-Preux's Andante for Trumpet

'Easter Hymn' from Mascagni's *Cavalleria rusticana*

27 January 1992

How I tasted tea and whisky with a cannibal

Joanna Pitman

A Japanese artist who realized a grotesque sexual fantasy when he killed and ate his Dutch girlfriend in Paris eleven years ago has become a celebrity in Japan. He is at liberty in Yokohama. A film about his life has just been released, yet fascination rather than horror has been the reaction.

Amid a complete absence of moral concern, Issei Sagawa has become the subject of prize-winning plays, and bestselling books have been written about him. He tells visitors how Japan's respected dramatists are fascinated by the artistry of his tale, and likes to speculate whether his deed was one of exquisite and pure love, crime redeemed by art.

His 'affair', as he calls it, happened when he was thirty-one, studying literature at the Sorbonne. One evening, he invited his girlfriend to his flat and, having given her a brew of tea and whisky ('to deaden the pain'), he shot her and cut up her body with an electric carving knife. He then ate her flesh, some of it raw, some fried, over the next few days, breaking off between meals to go to a film with his friends and stroll in the Bois de Boulogne.

Finally, seen disposing of a blood-stained suitcase, he rushed home to finish off the last fragments saved in the refrigerator, then gave himself up to the police. Declared insane, he spent three years in a Paris jail until the French authorities sent him back to Japan on condition that he should be confined to a mental hospital.

He was admitted to a Tokyo psychiatric hospital, but fifteen months later his father, a company president, arranged for his release. The doctors discharged him, saying that he seemed normal.

Taking two sturdy friends with me and carefully arranging an appointment soon after his breakfast time, I met Mr Sagawa in the flat where he lives under the assumed name of Shin Nakamoto.

'Sagawa-kun', as he is referred to in the press, welcomed us to his cramped and dingy home with fawning hospitality, displaying an ominous and hair-raising delight at the sight of a foreign female visitor. A desperately self-conscious man (he is well under 5ft tall and has notably undersized hands and feet), he immediately caused considerable alarm by handing round cups of his special tea and whisky brew.

Mr Sagawa had specified in advance that he did not want to talk about his 'affair', but it was difficult to keep him off the subject. 'I still adore the sight and the shape of young Western women, particularly beautiful ones,' he said, his wolfish eyes staring out from behind dark glasses. 'I was a premature and unhealthy baby, I am ugly and small, but I indulge in fantasies about strong healthy bodies. I'm essentially a romantic.'

He still likes to do nude paintings of young Western women. One was a young Dutch model, Ingrid, whom he contacted when he saw her photograph in a magazine. She has now returned to The Netherlands and never knew his real name or anything of his history.

Mr Sagawa likes to dwell openly and almost proudly on his past. 'My fantasy of cannibalism is not crazy. Everyone has fantasies. The special thing about me is that I acted upon mine. At the time I was not well, and it became an obsession, a kind of duty. I regret it terribly.'

One of the most distressing aspects of this solitary man is the fact that he believes he is normal. 'My time in the mental ward was like hell. Everyone else in there was crazy, but the doctors saw that I was not like them, that I was cured. I am normal. I eat an evening meal with my parents every day and spend my spare time painting and weaving.'

Judging by his disturbingly carnal paintings, Mr Sagawa shows no inclination to rid himself of his dangerous passion.

'Cannibalism has been my obsession since I was very young, it is a pleasure lying deep in the human spirit . . . my long cherished desire is to be eaten by a beautiful Western woman,' he wrote in an article two months ago.

While in prison in France he wrote his 'memoirs', recalling the sensations of cooking and eating the body parts – some 'deliciously fatty like raw tuna', some rubbery, and some fried with salt, pepper and mustard.

The book has become a bestseller in Japan and has encouraged Mr Sagawa to write three more, one of which is an anthology of short stories on cannibalistic fantasies. 'That book is a little bit comical,' he said, with a strangely leering grimace. It was time to leave.

25 January 1992

Scandal limitation

Peter Riddell

The first rule of political scandals is that if you are in a hole, do not dig any deeper. Instead admit all and appeal for sympathy. Paddy Ashdown skilfully did this yesterday after admitting a brief relationship with his former secretary more than five years ago. He played a weak hand well.

Mr Ashdown's statement was reminiscent of the similar confession of the Labour Prime Minister also being pressurized by the tabloids in the televised political thriller *A Very British Coup*. He also followed the precedent of Peter Brooke who won the sympathy of most of his colleagues a fortnight ago by apologizing for his ill-judged singing of 'Clementine' on Irish television only hours after a huge IRA bombing.

By contrast, those politicians who seek to obfuscate and deny generally come a cropper. If Richard Nixon had not ordered a cover-up of the Watergate break-in in June 1972, of which he knew nothing beforehand, he might not have had to resign. Similarly it was John Profumo's lying to the House of Commons which forced him out of politics in 1963.

The curious feature of the latest events is not Mr Ashdown's brief adulterous relationship, but how it became publicly known. Violating the oft-breached political rule that one should not put anything down on paper, Andrew Phillips, Mr Ashdown's solicitor, made notes on what his client had told him about the relationship. Nevertheless, it seems to have been appalling bad luck, rather than a conspiracy, that the document was stolen.

Then, to compound the difficulty, when Mr Phillips learnt that the thief was trying to sell the compromising document, he reacted by issuing an injunction last weekend which specifically referred to Mr Ashdown's personal life. In practice, this had the counter-productive effect of alerting the whole of Fleet Street and most people in the political world. The story has been the gossip of Westminster since then. It was simply a question of how long it would take before the full details emerged, given the ingenuity and hypocrisy of many tabloids in evading the injunction.

By bowing promptly to the inevitable, Mr Ashdown may be able to gain sympathy. Only the most sanctimonious in the Commons will criticize what is by any definition entirely personal and private behaviour now several years in the past. There is no shortage of leading politicians, businessmen and even journalists who have had similar brief flings which they would rather not have discussed. Lloyd George, with his semi-bigamous relationship with Frances Stevenson in Downing Street and later, was not the only Liberal leader to have a complicated personal life. And several leading politicians have gone through separations, divorces and remarriages with scarcely any comment.

Coming after this week's other allegations about dirty tricks, the affair may shift attention to the role of the press. David Steel, Mr Ashdown's predecessor, yesterday sought to lead a counter-attack by expressing 'outrage' at the intrusion into privacy entailed in the press's exploitation of stolen documents. The record of the press could become the issue, rather than Mr Ashdown's conduct.

The political leaders, and fellow Liberal Democrat MPs, yesterday argued that the affair is irrelevant to the coming election. That may be, and should be, right, and the affair may be soon forgotten. But some Liberal Democrat MPs from Nonconformist areas in the north of Scotland and rural Wales may be checking closely with their constituents this weekend. Mr Ashdown is potentially vulnerable because he has become so dominant in leading his party from the doldrums and divisions of 1988. To many voters he *is* the Liberal Democrat party, and his high personal popularity underpins its current 15 per cent rating in the polls. If his standing comes in question, it may affect his party, especially since its other talent is thinly spread. Yesterday, revealingly, that shrewd old campaigner Sir David Steel played a more prominent part than he has for a long time.

Mr Ashdown's personal appeal has always been double-edged. To many natural supporters of the Liberal Democrats, his attraction is that he does not appear like a conventional party politician. Unlike John Major and Neil Kinnock, who have been active in politics since their late teens, Mr Ashdown did not make his commitment until he was thirty-five, after a dashing military and intelligence career. He has little of the background or baggage of fellow MPs; indeed, he often slips up when discussing political history. By presenting himself as the outsider in politics, above the two-party battle, he opens himself to the charge of self-righteousness. He is just as committed to chasing power as the other party leaders.

Mr Ashdown always reminds me of Jay Gatsby in creating mystery about his past as he reinvents himself at each stage of his career. But being a buccaneer also has its risks.

6 February 1992

The First Date:
making it watertight

John Diamond

As if seduction wasn't already hard enough, an American lawyer has devised a legal form for both parties to sign before a first date. I'd guess that the document is no more than a series of get out clauses should the date end in pregnancy or a blood test, but I doubt whether that's quite the sort of contract we need in this country. Aids and unmarried motherhood might be a worry for some, but it's the smaller courtesies of first dating that really need to be legally addressed . . .

A Contract between Henry Cripps (*hereinafter* to be known as The Dater) and Caroline Bastaple (*hereinafter* to be known as The Datee).

1: **Notwithstanding** the Arsenal match being postponed, the penultimate episode of *Moon and Son* being a bit of a cliffhanger, or a last-minute pick up at the Two Horseshoes after work on Friday, The Dater and The Datee agree to meet at The Omar Khayyam Tandoori Centre, Ealing W5, at 8.30 p.m. on Saturday (hereinafter referred to as The Date) **always allowing** that The Datee may be no more than 20 (twenty) and no less than 10 (ten) minutes late without incurring penalties under rider 3(i): Emotional blackmail.

2: It is thereby **understood** that *in that* The Date shall take place in order that The Dater may discuss a couple of really quite interesting ideas he's got for the marketing meeting on Tuesday on which he'd like some creative input from The Datee, both parties shall terminate such discussion no later than 3 (three) minutes after the onion bhajis have been served. At this point both parties shall undertake to determine from each other:

71

i: Whether The Dater is still seeing Jennifer from Accounts Pending (*hereinafter* referred to as A Bit Tarty If You Ask Me, But Then Some Men Go For The Obvious Type);

ii: Whether The Datee really stung that fool Nigel in Corporate Holdings for a five course meal at Luigi's, plus entrance to Stringfellows including six large Drambuie and Cokes, plus a cab home and then gave him a kiss on the cheek and left him standing on the doorstep;

iii: How The Dater recalls the very first time he saw The Datee across the photocopying room and even though they didn't speak until the Christmas party, he'd always sort of thought, well, you know, she wasn't like the other girls, she was more, like, *sensitive*.

3: It is hereby **agreed** that at no time during the period of this contract shall The Datee draw attention to the following:

i: The Dater's choice of the second least expensive bottle of wine;

ii: The way The Dater tucks his napkin into his shirt collar;

iii: The Dater's belief that it is only a matter of time before Chris Rea makes it big again;

iv: That The Datee actually has no interest in whether Arsenal should have played Limpar, despite his injury, that afternoon, whatever Limpar is or, come to that, Arsenal.

4: In **consideration** for this and *notwithstanding* that everybody knows who Limpar is, small Swedish bloke, plays up front, The Dater **undertakes**:

i: Not to eat *all* the After Eights which come with the bill;

ii: Not to cause embarrassment to both parties by paying with any credit card that causes the waiter to ask The Dater whether he would mind stepping over to the till for just a second, thus making it clear to everybody in the restaurant that the Dater can't even run to a curry, let alone and *inter alia*, a good bottle of wine.

5: At the termination of the meal The Dater agrees to conduct The Datee to her place of residence, *always notwithstanding* that should The Datee insist on travelling the seven miles home alone, on foot, through a derelict housing estate and a freight marshalling yard, The Dater shall take this as fair notice to quit.

6: *Always provided* that The Datee does not leave The Dater standing on the doorstep (ref: That Fool Nigel, *passim*) The Datee agrees the following:

i: That she shall within 5 (five) minutes of crossing the threshold make it plain, by word or by deed, whether she is any of the following:

a) Not That Sort of Girl.

b) Not That Sort of Girl on a first date.

c) Not That Sort of Girl after a dodgy curry and a warm bottle of Blue Nun.

d) Entirely That Sort of Girl, but not with The Dater.

ii: That at no point during the evening will The Datee introduce The Dater to her collection of soft toys which line her bed and get sulky if he refuses to greet each of them with the words 'How do you do Teddy Nutkin?'

7: Should clauses 1 to 6 above be satisfied it is hereintofore agreed that neither party shall cause the following to be uttered:

i: I don't do this with everyone I go out with, you know;

ii: You will still respect me in the morning, won't you?;

iii: I'd like to stay, honest, but I've got football training first thing. Now, where's my other sock?;

iv: You won't tell anyone in the office about this, will you?;

v: Damn! Look, er, I'm terribly sorry, this has never happened to me before;

vi: Funny, that's not what Jennifer in Accounts Pending says.

6 February 1992

. . . and moreover

Alan Coren

On behalf of the five million Britons who are like me, I wish to apologize to the 55 million who are not. For they are on their own, this week. They will get no help from us. Whatever the depths of their distress or need, our eyes are blind and our ears deaf. Frankly, my dears, we do not give a damn. We are too busy confronting our own fears, facing situations head-on, and generally looking out for good old number one. Or, rather, good old numbers one to five million. And we have been strongly advised not to support others, for the very good reason that both the Sun and Mercury are adversely aspected by Pluto.

Which brings me to an adverse aspect of astrology itself which I had not hitherto considered, probably because I had never considered astrology at all until this morning; when, thumbing through the chaos of the *Radio Times* in search of something else, I inadvertently fetched up against the face of Patric Walker, topping his horoscope column with the knowing smirk of one for whom fate holds no surprises. So I glanced at the Cancer entry, hoping for some such encouragement as 'keep trying, you will find the programme information you are seeking any day now, this week's layout was done by a tall dark stranger who has now gone on a long sea voyage,' but instead received only the advice adumbrated above. And I would have left it at that, had it not suddenly struck me that Patric's counsel, though apparently offered to me alone, had in fact been offered to the entire twelfth of the population born between 22 June and 23 July. This week, five million people were going to confront their fears, face situations head-on, and ignore the pleas of others.

It did not bear thinking about. All those hapless phobics suddenly attempting to pick up spiders, climb the Monument, travel by tube, stroke a Rottie, cross a bridge, never mind the mass of the less manically fearful now doing everything from bursting in on their solicitor to see whether he'd been burgled lately to jamming Yeltsin's switchboard with stammered enquiries about which way he thought Kazakhstan's ICBMs might be pointing; because for those wishing to confront them, there is never any shortage of fears.

Nor any of situations waiting to be faced head-on: all those suddenly reeling bank-managers, all those peremptorily sacked lovers, all those summarily thumped meter-attendants! And all this while the nation's unfortunates find their chance of succour cut by a twelfth; for it is no use, this week, expecting a Cancerian Brownie to help you across the road, or a Cancerian fireman to tug your cat's head from the garden railing. Worse yet, consider the clash when two crab-people meet: simultaneously confronting his worst fears and facing a situation head-on, one such rushes to his dentist, only to have the dentist shriek, 'Clear off, I am not helping anybody this week, as soon as I have conquered my aerophobia, I am facing a situation head-on. I am leaving my wife and flying off to Acapulco with my hunky bank-manager!'

And that, of course, is only the Cancerians. If Patric is to be believed, five million Taureans are about to issue ultimatums to as many unreasonable employers, and five million fraught Librans are poised to concentrate on an affair of the heart. Should they, furthermore, tell these to any of the five million poor saps born between 22 December and 20 January, we can expect real trouble, because for them, as you may have heard, the Sun and Mercury in Aquarius are at odds with Pluto in Scorpio, leading Patric not unnaturally to conclude that minor differences of opinion could well turn into major conflicts. Put another way, if tomorrow's Spurs v West Ham game attracts its likely attendance, anything up to ten thousand Sagittarians and Capricornians may be

75

confidently expected to end up knocking seven bells out of one another.

Not that this is any skin off my nose. Thanks to Pluto's adverse aspect, I am allowed not to give a fig for anyone else. So, just in case you're one of the five million Aquarians currently seeking help with intense personal problems, at least you know where not to come.

7 February 1992

'Twas love on our first date

Bernard Levin

Age signals itself in a thousand ways, almost all of them accompanied by a sneer. On the other hand, wise men learn to dispense with the impossible. I, for instance, have long ago faced the fact that I cannot run a mile in under four minutes, or for that matter in an hour and a half, and the knowledge does not dismay me.

Death, of course, is less trifling. Two of my dearest and oldest friends have been among those who have tiptoed away in the year gone by, and the toll inevitably grows longer all the time, and the years steadily shorter:

> Then many a lad I liked is dead,
> And many a lass grown old;
> And as the lesson strikes my head
> My weary heart grows old . . .

Happily, the years also bring in their merry recollections as well as their gloomy ones, and the further away is the past they emerge from, the merrier they are, however startling the realization of their antiquity.

Will a quarter of a century do? I think it will.

In 1967, I was seeking the ideal pocket diary, and I was failing to find it. They were all either too thick and heavy to be easily accommodated in a breast pocket (I had long been a snappy dresser, the glass of fashion and the mould of form, for whom an unsightly bulge was tantamount to unpolished shoes), or, if sufficiently slim, they provided too little space for appointments, notes and other entries. There was no problem with my desk diary, but I could hardly lug around something getting on for the size of a telephone directory.

Letts were useless in the search, and the Filofax had not yet been born (though I would not have sported the horrible thing if it had – I chortled long and loud when it fell out of favour as rapidly as it had fell in); what was I to do?

I can no longer remember what or who guided my steps to a firm called Day-Timers. I don't think they advertised at all, let alone widely; their telephone number, as I recall, was not even in the phone book then, though I am glad to say it is now. (I might as well give it to you all; they are in the course of moving, because their present premises are once again too small, but only up the street – Kentish Town Road. Try 071-485 5252.)

Anyway, I wandered into a neat office-cum-shop, and ten seconds later let out a scream; actually it was two screams – the first because I had found exactly what I was looking for, and the second because I hadn't invented it.

The place was run (at least I could not see or hear anyone else on the premises) by a couple, whom I subsequently discovered were husband and wife, a Mr and Mrs Elliot, Americans. Friendship soon exchanged formality for first names: the Elliots are Mervyn and Edna. But the friendship has lasted for twenty-five years almost exactly to the day on which I write here.

Before I continue with the friendship, let me explain the trick that solved my problem. The Day-Timer has expanded over the years: you can get desk diaries and all sorts of office helpfulnesses. But what I was looking for took the form of a beautifully neat, spiral-bound pocket diary which gave (and gives) two full pages a day, 6½ in by 3½. But how then is the breast-pocket bulge-problem solved? Simple: the thing comes in a box, wherein are found not one pocket diary but twelve; there is a separate one for every month of the year. (Yes, yes; they *have* solved the subsequent problem of diary-entries for more than a month ahead; at the back of each book there are pages of summarized space for forward planning, months ahead.) Moreover, the whole caboodle comes with an exceptionally handsome leather holder, into which the current month's diary fits; but that's only the beginning – the holder is not just a holder but a wallet and notepad as well: everything a breast pocket will ever need (and there are even smaller, shirt-pocket size ones) comes to the modern man's or woman's hand.

I can still recall in the greatest detail my first time on the Elliots' premises, because their American helpfulness was so much greater than the surliness and ignorance that so many indigenous salespeople offered, and still do. Every question I asked was at once answered; every explanation was clear; the array of items I might be interested in was spread out before me, whereupon the Elliots moved to the back of the store to leave me alone with the choices.

I made my choices and bought the Day-Timer style C21; I paid by credit card. Shortly after I got home, I discovered that I had carelessly left the credit card on their premises; the place was by then shut. The phone rang: it was Mervyn, telling me that the card was safe and sound; he had traced my address and had already sent on the card by registered post. The following morning he rang to make sure that it had arrived.

I was then writing a column for the *Daily Mail*; I told the story and its background to my readers; what I didn't know was that the Elliots had only just set up in business in Britain (they were acting as subsidiaries for the company that had produced the Day-Timer), and my encomium gave them a hearty push.

Twenty-five years have passed since that day; their business flourishes still – they have separated from their parent company to go it alone – and their son now largely runs the business. I send them, each year, my new book, and they send me my annual Day-Timer; this time, when I dropped in, I apologized for the fact that for the first time in eleven consecutive years there wasn't going to be a book in 1991. 'OK,' said Mervyn instantly, 'you'll have to write one twice as long in 1992.'

'We brought nothing into this world,' wrote St Paul to

Timothy, 'and it is certain we can carry nothing out.' I agree, not least because in the very same letter Paul urges his correspondent to abandon his habit of drinking water and try wine instead. But although, of course, the saint is right as to material things, surely his stern admonition was not intended to stretch as far as the words of friendship?

I hope not. It would be horrid to think that some kind of celestial customs officer, after clearing out the pockets of the prospective candidate for Heaven, and confiscating the money and the earthly treasures, went on to demand also my shakehand with Mervyn, and the kiss bestowed on me by Edna. And if he can unbend that far, would it be too presumptuous for me to bring my Day-Timer, too?

10 February 1992

Lumme, was I really counting sprouts?

Lynne Truss

I once heard a very scary story concerning a man who lived alone. I sometimes remember it late at night, and get so nervous that I chew the edge of the duvet. Invited to a friend's house for dinner, it seems, this man behaved in a perfectly normal, outgoing manner until the moment attention turned to the serving of Brussels sprouts – when he suddenly got strangely serious.

'One, two, three,' he said to himself, as he carefully ladled the steaming veggies on to his plate. 'Ha ha, oh yes. Four, five, six, *seven*.' The hosts swapped glances, and shifted uncomfortably in their seats. 'More sprouts, John?' asked the hostess, after a pause. At which their guest made a loud scoffing noise and stood up, violently pushing back his chair so that it rucked up the carpet. 'Look,' he said, 'I've got seven sprouts. And forgive me for having two strong sturdy legs to stand on, but seven sprouts is the number of sprouts I *always have*.'

No doubt there are many married people, too, who have strong feelings on the subject of sprouts. One recalls those famous cases of men murdering their wives (and getting off with a light fine and a reprimand) for serving up the incorrect number of roasties, or putting the cruet on the wrong place-mat. But it is sitting alone in the evening, I am sure, that encourages crankiness: start out with a harmless little tendency towards obsessive-compulsive behaviour, and within a few months of single life you are not only talking to the characters in *Brookside* but also getting dogmatic about vegetable consumption and forming advanced crackpot theories on the nature of evil. Since nobody contradicts you (and the goldfish doesn't care) you easily convince yourself that you are 'on the right lines'.

Take the chap I met recently in a Pasadena cake shop. He seemed normal enough: just a bit over-keen for a chat. But then he mentioned that during his solitary hours he had given a lot of thought to the identity of the Antichrist, and had finally settled conclusively on Richard Branson. Everything pointed to it, he said. There's none so blind as those who will not see, etcetera. I thought he was joking, but it gradually dawned on me that he wasn't, and that moreover he was positioned between me and the door.

'Set in your ways' – that's what they call it when single people start getting things out of proportion. 'Don't get set in your ways.' It means: don't use a protractor when setting the coffee table at an angle to the wall; don't attach so much importance to changing the date on your kitchen calendar that you scoot home from work mid-morning to check you've done it. The image conjured up is of a stupid-looking prehistoric animal sinking in mud and muttering, 'Actually, I always buy the *Radio Times* on a *Wednesday*' and 'I asked for a kitchen towel, and she bought me *yellow*'.

One need only spend half an hour in a supermarket to see where 'getting set in your ways' can ultimately lead. There is a strange urban myth which says that in supermarkets single people strike up impromptu chats over the rindless streaky in the hope of finding a potential mate. In reality, however, they are more likely to start the conversation because rindless streaky has been occupying their thoughts in the evenings.

The trouble, of course, is to recognize when one's own reasonable preferences and quaint pet theories (attained through a painstaking process of trial and error) turn into pig-headed fixed ideas, or even dangerous obsessions. At what point does it 'get out of hand'? I have a nasty suspicion that it is a phenomenon you can never observe in your own behaviour – one of those clever irregular verbs that invariably declines: I have rules about things; You are set in your ways; He thinks Richard Branson is the Antichrist.

I am assuming, I suppose, that a sane live-in partner prevents the escalation of this behaviour – rather as he might helpfully point out that your clothes are thick with cat-hair or that there is toothpaste up your nostrils. But is it worth taking on a live-in partner just for this function? I can't believe it is. Perhaps, instead, there ought to be some tall, supernatural protector for single people (along the lines of Superman) who could spot a burgeoning obsession with his X-ray vision and whoosh into our homes (with a fanfare) to prevent it from getting a grip.

Thus, just as you were preparing your solitary dinner and thinking 'I don't know. Eight sprouts seems too many, yet six sprouts seems too few', he would suddenly appear at your side and dash the whole bag to the ground, releasing you from their terrible influence. 'A close call,' he twinkles (with arms akimbo and a smile reminiscent of Richard Branson's). 'Lumme,' you say, 'was I really counting *sprouts*?' 'It's all over now,' he chuckles, patting you on the shoulder. 'Just don't let it happen again, you hear?'

And as he turns horizontal and flies off through the kitchen door with a cheery salute, you slide down the wall to a sitting position and think – with ample justification – 'I wonder if I'm spending too much time on my own?'.

12 February 1992

83

Sunderland casts off ailing past to win city status

Peter Davenport

Sunderland, the former shipbuilding town in the North-east now better known for its links with Nissan, the Japanese car maker, yesterday became Britain's newest city.

Sunderland beat twenty-two rivals to receive the honour, granted on the personal command of the Queen as a mark of special distinction to celebrate the fortieth anniversary of her accession to the throne.

The new city, population 296,100, has been trying for sixty years to achieve that status and has been turned down four times. Yesterday's announcement means that it will no longer live in the shadow of its more dominant neighbour, Newcastle upon Tyne.

Local dignitaries celebrated with a champagne toast and flag-raising ceremony on the steps of the modern civic centre. They intend to invite the Queen to pay an official visit.

David Thompson, the mayor, said: 'I can hardly believe it. It hasn't sunk in properly yet. The effect on the people of Sunderland will be immeasurable and the impact on the image of Sunderland throughout the world will be invaluable.'

Sunderland, home in the seventh century of the Venerable Bede and, in 1828, of Joseph Swan, inventor of the electric light, was the biggest of fourteen towns formally invited last summer to put themselves forward for the honour of city status. Others also sent in applications.

The Labour-run council based its latest application on the town's contribution to national life, and emphasized its new found prosperity after the despair brought about by the collapse of its traditional shipbuilding industry on the River Wear.

In its formal application it said: 'Sunderland is proud of its past and of the way it has never succumbed to the fierce extremes of economic adversity which have so often been its historic lot. After a decade or so of painful reconstruction, Sunderland's economy and environment have been transformed, an achievement of almost miraculous proportions.'

Nissan's decision to set up a car manufacturing plant on the outskirts of the town in 1984 was the catalyst for economic regeneration. The current workforce is 3,400, due to rise to 4,600 next year when 175,000 cars a year will roll off the production line. By then total investment by the Japanese company will stand at some £900 million. Other firms have followed.

John Nielsen of Nissan said yesterday: 'We are absolutely delighted at the honour given to Sunderland. We can now call it our home city instead of our home town. If we have played a part in the decision to upgrade the status then we are thrilled.' Sunderland has not always enjoyed the best of reputations and it has been the butt of music hall comedians.

Yesterday's announcement came the day after a reminder that life was still far from easy in the area; two miners were killed and six others injured in an underground accident at the local colliery, Wearmouth.

Sunderland, whose motto is 'With God as our leader there is no cause for despair', was ranked as ninth favourite to win the honour, put at 14–1 by the bookmakers William Hill. It beat more fancied towns such as Chelmsford, the favourite at 4–1, Brighton, Ipswich and Milton Keynes. The status of city gives no special privileges or powers and Sunderland's leading citizen will still be plain 'mayor'. Only eleven cities have been created this century, the most recent being Canterbury in 1988.

The other contenders for cityhood were: Blackburn, Bolton, Colchester, Croydon, Dudley, Guildford, Middlesbrough, Northampton, Preston, Sandwell, Shrewsbury,

Southend-on-Sea, Stockport, Telford, Wolverhampton, St David's and Newport in Wales and Armagh in Northern Ireland.

The people of Sunderland welcomed the award. Rose Bell, aged eighty-three, said: 'Some people from down south don't like Sunderland. They think we're all daft. I don't know why, it's a wonderful place to live.'

15 February 1992

Weather forecasts that fail to grip

From Mr Arthur Abeles

Sir, Each night I make up my mind to devote my full attention to the weather report on television.

I put down my newspaper, withdraw from all small chat, listen closely to the description of the struggle between the high pressures and the low, follow the course of wavy lines across the UK and Continent meant to illustrate that confrontation, study swarms of angry little daggers which reflect what the wind is, or will be doing, and finally stare at orange balls partially covered by cloud and often pierced by rain which dot the country.

And then I wonder what it's going to be like in the West of London on the following day.

19 February 1992

From Dr Peter Ayton

Sir, Mr Arthur Abeles's difficulty in understanding the television weather forecast is consistent with a large body of psychological research conducted over several years in Britain, the United States and The Netherlands.

A US survey in 1976 of 236 people, published in *Public Opinion Quarterly*, showed that 70 per cent of viewers telephoned at home immediately after the forecast could not give even one piece of information about what they had heard and seen.

Experimental comparisons involving listeners only in 1985 in The Netherlands, confirmed an equally poor level of recall found for British viewers in 1981. The evidence shows that the abysmally low comprehension scores are not

87

improved by having the message illustrated with a map or by showing a presenter placing and indicating symbols on it.

One might suppose that those with particular motives for viewing would do better at remembering the particular details they need. However, a 1982 Dutch study refutes this notion: professional farmers and recreational sailors did not have enhanced recall for relevant details. Disturbingly, their weather-contingent decisions were no better than would be expected on the basis of their poor levels of recall.

People instructed to focus on information for a particular region have been found to register even less about that area. This can all be attributed to the complex and unpredictable structure of many weather forecasts and the high speaking rate of forecasters.

From the Reverend J. Hemmings
Sir, Arthur Abeles's letter on the local rainfall in the West End of London raises the wider questions of diagnosing national weather patterns and regional bias.

Why is 'weather forecasting' often accompanied by the seemingly retrospective business of 'weather reporting'? Are we to understand that modern technology is more adept at telling us what has been than what is to come?

If Mr Abeles wishes to avoid television's 'wavy lines and little daggers' and tunes to the radio he will find that the forecaster almost always begins the national weather outlook with London and the South-east of England, much to my irritation.

From Mrs John O'Leary
Sir, Mr Arthur Abeles should consider himself fortunate. At least he knows he lives in the South-east.

Here on the Wirral we have no idea what our weather will be. Does the North-west mean this area or 350 miles further north, viz., the north-west of the British Isles? It is a rare weather forecaster who makes it clear.

From Mrs Joanna Purser
Sir, I, too, give great attention to the weather forecasts on television.

Afterwards I go and tap my barometer, take a turn in the garden to note the wind, the sky and the amount of shipping in the bay and then make up my own mind. I am right more often than the weather men.

From Mrs E. J. Blackall Bain
Sir, To determine what the weather in west London is going to be like, I generally wait until the following morning and then look out of the window to see what sort of clothes the people walking across Hammersmith Bridge are wearing and how cold they look. I also check to see whether the buses are using their windscreen wipers. I rarely find much variation between Hammersmith and the West End.

26 February 1992

From Mr M. G. Henley
Sir, I have found that the weather forecasts are much more comprehensible with the sound turned off.

From Mr Zvi Silver
Sir, I suggest that the reason people do not remember anything about the weather forecast is that they are not really interested in the information supplied. What they want to know is, 'Do I need a coat today or should I take an umbrella?'

Proof of this can be obtained by seeing someone look at their watch, then asking them the time. They always look at their watch again because it is useless information and they have not 'filed' it in their brain.

From Mr Patrick Bowen
Sir, Let Mrs Joanna Purser beware of over-tapping her barometer. At Sandhurst in the 1940s there were two in the Old College entrance hall, one above the other. The lower

always gave wild readings. A visiting mother of a cadet asked the RSM why he had two barometers there. 'One is to tell the weather with, madam,' he replied, 'and the other is for the young gentlemen to tap.'

From the Chief Executive of the Meteorological Office
Sir, May I answer some of the points raised regarding weather forecasts on radio and TV? Viewers' difficulties in recalling the relevant information from weather forecasts are similar to the difficulties that most people experience in recalling *any* specific item from lists of detailed information given on TV and radio. This has been established from our own and others' research and therefore we plan and present forecasts in the knowledge of this fact.

In 1990, we split the UK into ten clearly defined regions and introduced consistency into the use of these regions in broadcasts on national radio. We shall be pleased to send any interested listeners a map showing our regions.

Research has also shown that a listener retains information more easily if it is given in a set order. However, this leads to the criticism that weather forecasts are boring. We are trying to strike a balance, using a standard order on most occasions (as on the shipping forecast), but on occasion leading with some other region where there is particularly noteworthy weather.

There is clear evidence that people retain more information when they have a carefully used visual aid in addition to the spoken word: 90 per cent of those questioned in our research stated that they obtained their weather information from TV. But while some people appreciate the displaying of isobars and fronts, others, like Mr Abeles, favour a simpler approach.

It is difficult to please everyone, especially inside two minutes. We will continue to do everything we can to make weather forecasts more easily understood.

4 March 1992

90

Scientists seek Churchill's secret of long life

Thomson Prentice

Scientists are seeking a 'Churchill gene' that may protect people from heart disease despite unhealthy lifestyles. They believe that something in Sir Winston's genetic make-up helped him to reach the age of ninety, although he had almost all the risk factors that lead to heart attacks.

Churchill consumed vast amounts of alcohol, smoked huge numbers of cigars and was stressed by the burdens of wartime leadership and political office. He was short, overweight and aggressive and had been born prematurely, four more ingredients in the recipe for heart disease.

According to some calculations, his daily intake of champagne, cognac and whisky amounted to twenty-two units of alcohol, compared to the maximum of twenty-one units a week recommended by the Royal College of Physicians. Why some people survive to old age against the odds is being investigated by Steve Humphries, newly-appointed British Heart Foundation professor of cardiovascular genetics. 'Winston Churchill is the classic example of a man who survived into very old age despite the odds,' he said. 'His longevity poses the question of whether he was blessed with protective genes.'

Professor Humphries, of University College and Middlesex School of Medicine, central London, is a leading researcher into the hereditary causes of heart disease, especially familial hypercholesterolaemia, which affects about 100,000 people in Britain. About half the male sufferers develop heart disease by the age of fifty-five.

The illness is known to be caused by defective genes involved in cleansing fatty cholesterol deposits from the

91

blood. Researchers can identify those who have inherited some of the defects and provide drug treatment. 'We need to discover why some people are protected against this and other forms of heart disease. The defects are not always passed from parent to child,' the professor said. 'If such genes could be identified in the general population, the information gleaned from them could cast valuable light on how to treat patients at high risk.

'We need to have long-term studies involving perhaps 10,000 healthy men and women who could be followed up to monitor the genetic differences between those who develop heart disease and those who don't.'

But Professor Humphries discouraged the notion that Churchill could be a role model for those who, through scientific advances, might discover they had a genetic defence against heart disease. They would be unwise to tempt fate by over-indulging in tobacco, alcohol or a fatty diet, he said. 'Such knowledge should be the basis for sticking to a healthy lifestyle rather than adopting a dangerous one.'

19 February 1992

Lessons for John Major from the slump of sixty years ago

Matthew Bond

Ten days ago the Prime Minister lifted the pre-electoral temperature a further degree or two by agreeing that 1.25 million public sector workers would receive the pay increases awarded by their review body in full. From doctors to dentists, soldiers to sailors, Mr Major was ordering above-inflation pay rises all round.

The decision to pay these increases was taken with the Prime Minister all too aware of the statistical minefield that lay ahead. Unemployment rising above 2.6 million, house repossessions running at 72,000 a year and, perhaps above all, yesterday's confirmation that Britain's gross domestic product last year fell by 2.5 per cent, the biggest fall since the great depression of the 1930s.

Knowing that such a fall would refocus attention on the most famous slump in history, Mr Major – a stickler when it comes to research – must have been giving the events of sixty years ago serious thought. Indeed, the public sector pay award suggests that its lessons are already being applied.

There is no doubt that in 1931 Ramsay MacDonald would have had an easier time as prime minister had his response to financial Nemesis been to grant real pay increases to public-sector workers. Instead, he ordered big pay cuts for teachers, police and the armed forces, together with a reduction in unemployment benefit.

The results might well have persuaded Mr Major not to follow a similar path. For not only was Mr MacDonald faced with riots among the unemployed, whose benefit was to be cut by two shillings to fifteen shillings a week for men and thirteen shillings for women. Pay cuts of up to a quarter for the armed services prompted a brief but historic mutiny by naval ratings of the Atlantic Fleet stationed at Invergordon, whose daily rate was chopped from four shillings to three shillings. A military victory may have ensured one recent election success, but a mutiny? The Prime Minister must be hoping that pay rises of up to 7.9 per cent, not forgetting that fourth Trident submarine, have quelled any new rebellion. However, deciding what other lessons to draw from 1931 cannot be easy for Mr Major and his advisers. While there are obvious parallels – sliding output and rising unemployment (by July 1931, there were 2.7 million unemployed) – there is one vital difference. The government shouldering the blame for the country's economic woes was a Labour one.

Mr Major will be hoping that the fate of the incumbent government will not provide a further parallel with 1931. Although Mr MacDonald abandoned virtually all of his party's socialist principles, as the economic situation worsened, and in August resigned to form a coalition National Government, the mud stuck. The Labour party disowned Mr MacDonald but it could not disown the recession. At the October election, Labour was savaged; its number of seats fell from 288 to 52.

As the world's economies teetered towards collapse, investors lost confidence in paper currencies, including sterling. In an increasingly unsafe world (by February, 5 million were unemployed in Germany) what they wanted instead was gold, to which Winston Churchill had re-committed the British currency six years earlier.

Sir Montagu Norman – who as Governor of the Bank of England had earlier in the year cut interest rates to a twenty-two-year low of 2.5 per cent – issued warnings that national bankruptcy was near. The decision to abandon the gold standard was taken on 20 September. It prompted a 30 per cent devaluation of sterling, scenes of near-panic outside the Bank and the closure of the Stock Exchange for two days.

Just as Mr Major has had to grow accustomed to having his interest rate policy controlled by the Bundesbank, so the men at the helm in 1931 had become used to outside interference. Indeed, the pay cuts that provoked riot and mutiny were a condition of loans to the Bank of England from the Bank of France and the New York Federal Reserve.

Such overt external interference proved too much for the Labour cabinet, except for Mr MacDonald. Something had to go and Mr MacDonald decided it should be the government. His decision to resign must have been eased by the knowledge that he would remain prime minister at the head of a coalition, with Stanley Baldwin, the Tory leader, as his No. 2.

Then, as now, economic revival was thought to depend on the consumer. In January, John Maynard Keynes broadcast an impassioned plea for the private sector to do its bit: 'Oh, patriotic housewives of Britain, sally out tomorrow early into the streets and go to the wonderful sales that are everywhere advertised. You will do yourselves good, for things were never so cheap, cheap beyond your dreams. And have the added joy that you are . . . bringing a chance and hope to Lancashire, Yorkshire and Belfast.' Provided, of course, that they bought British. Eleven months later, the Prince of Wales lent his voice to the Buy British campaign.

Britain's consumers did eventually respond to their exhortations but, just as Mr Major has discovered sixty years on, far more slowly than the government of the day desired. For those who remained in work, technological advance drove consumer demand. Houses, cars and the new world of domestic appliances created mass markets. From 1934, GDP was back on an upward and buoyant path. Mr Major will bank on history, at least in that respect, repeating itself – but quicker.

21 February 1992

A wrong Royal rumpus

Leader

Was the Queen's tour of Australia her last as monarch of that continent? Her eight-day visit, replete with processions, pageantry and a nostalgic return to the outback she visited thirty-eight years ago, was a success. Yet from the moment of her arrival, the spectre of republicanism hovered over her head, and lingers on after her departure. Hints that Australia may be tiring of its Queen have led to another round of self-examination of the country's identity, ethnic heritage and aspirations. They have set politicians bad-mouthing each other in their inimitable style and given Britain's tabloid press an opportunity to feign outrage at the gall and *lèse-majesté* of bumptious Ockers down under.

The focus of this argument was the speech on Monday by Paul Keating, the Australian Prime Minister. In it he told his Parliament in the Queen's presence that Australia was vigorously seeking friends and allies among its immediate neighbours, just as Britain had sought to secure its future partners in the European Community. (He might have added that Britain then showed little regard for imperial trade preference.) Times had changed, he said, since the Queen first visited Australia, when a population overwhelmingly British in origin still viewed the world through imperial eyes. An 'altogether different generation' now reflected the profound changes in the two countries and the relationship between them.

What with his wife's refusal to curtsey to the Queen, and his familiar gesture in putting his arm around her waist in guiding her through a crowd, Mr Keating was charged with being a latent republican and an ill-mannered commoner, attempting to pre-empt a national debate on the monarchy. There is nothing a politician's enemies like so much as a stereotype to shy at.

All this deserves a robust riposte. Australia's friendly informality is a welcome antidote to the fawning flummery that so often surrounds the Queen in Britain. Media indignation at antipodean uncouthness is ridiculous from a press which delights in uncouth intrusion into the Queen's family affairs. As for Mr Keating's remarks to Parliament, they were moderate, sensible and true. They reflected the changing attitudes and ethnic balance in a country where immigration has diluted the Anglo-Celtic dominance from 90 per cent to 70 per cent of the population, and brought in Lebanese, Greeks, Italians, and more recently Vietnamese and Chinese. The latter's loyalty to the crown, though sometimes fierce, is not bound up with emotive reference to kith and kin.

For the time being, there is little evidence that Australia wants to discard the Queen as head of state. It has long had close ties with the British crown. The previous Duke of Gloucester was Governor-General during the war, the Prince of Wales spent a year at school there and royal visits have been more frequent than to any other country. A hereditary monarch may not be the obvious embodiment of modern nationhood, but there are plenty worse means to the same end. If it isn't broke, why mend it?

On the other hand, even constitutional monarchs 'rule' only by consent. Australians might reasonably anticipate the day when they wish to be represented by a resident head of state, rather than one who lives on the other side of the globe. This feeling was politicized in 1975 by the row over the dismissal of Gough Whitlam, the elected Prime Minister, by Sir John Kerr, the Queen's Governor-General. The status of the monarchy at the time was near absurd.

A change to a republic would not endanger Australia's place in the Commonwealth nor, apart from a twinge of nostalgia, should it alter Britain's warm relations with its fellow English-speaking nation. The Queen, who is surely more robust about such a possibility than her putative champions, is the last person to want to reign where she is not wanted. All that would be required would be a plebiscite. No task force would be sent, no Boston tea party risked, no protest raised.

That Australia and its elected leaders should moot the possibility in the monarch's presence is surely more honest than to do so behind her back. If monarchy cannot defend itself in open court, it can hardly hope to maintain its sovereignty. Such a defence should not now go by default. But Mr Keating should be answered with arguments, not abuse.

26 February 1992

Always behind

From Mr W. R. Smeeton
Sir, Why is it that however expensive the suit or pair of trousers, the first button to fall off is the least used – that for the back pocket?

26 February 1992

From Mr George Lansdowne
Sir, Mr Smeeton asks why the back-pocket button is the first to come off his trousers. Is it because he slouches against the back of the seat instead of sitting up straight?

From Mr R. A. C. Le Cheminant
Sir, Has Mr Smeeton considered the strain on the average back-pocket trouser button when working at a desk? It must be considerably more than the pressure from an overfed stomach on the jacket or trouser-waist buttons.

From Dr P. Glaister
Sir, I frequently lose the button from my trouser back pocket whenever I sit down on a wooden chair with horizontal slats. The button shoots off with immense speed, never to be seen again. The obvious solution is to remove the jacket *after* sitting down, but I always seem to forget.

28 February 1992

From Sean Jeannette, Head Valet of the Savoy
Sir, Whilst I found your recent correspondence very amusing, none of the writers seems to realize the fundamental problem with buttons. It doesn't matter whether people are fat or thin, slouching or not and sit down with or without their jackets on; the problem lies with the buttons, which

are now machine-stitched rather than sewn on by hand.

In the Savoy's valet department, we now sew on as many as fifty buttons per week, 20 per cent of which are back-pocket buttons. The only way to stop this is to hand-sew the buttons on immediately a suit is bought.

4 March 1992

From Mr B. R. Barnfield
Sir, How depressing to read the confession by the Head Valet of the Savoy that that once splendid establishment now admits men (one can hardly say gentlemen) who wear machine-stitched suits. Not only does it admit them; it clearly permits them to take rooms. How ignominious for the valet department to be obliged to repair the consequences of their patrons' parsimony.

From Mr George Carbutt
Sir, I would like to remind Dr Glaister that only potatoes wear jackets. Gentlemen wear coats.

6 March 1992

Schools outlaw sexist jokers

Susan Ellicott

Times were when a teenage boy could twang a girl's bra strap during a maths class and get away with it.

But times have changed, at least in Minnesota. These days, as part of the first programme of its kind in the United States to eradicate sexual harassment in schools, practical jokers face punishments. For snapping a bra strap, a boy would risk a fine, or even expulsion for repeated offences.

'It's kind of graphic,' says Sue Slater, a deputy head teacher at the school district of Lakeville outside Minneapolis. 'But it works.' Before last year, nobody expected to take the issue of sexual harassment so seriously. Indeed, Minnesota used to treat its unruly boys in much the same way as any other state does: they were considered to be predisposed to teasing girls from the day they entered kindergarten until the day they graduated. Besides, the girls on the receiving end of the taunts generally giggled and blushed, even if they were offended. Nobody really thought they minded that much.

Things changed when two teenage girls won landmark lawsuits against their schools for failing to end offensive behaviour by male classmates.

Katy Lyle, aged nineteen, received a settlement of $15,000 (about £8,380) after charging Duluth Central High School for failing to remove graffiti about her that was written on the walls of a boys' lavatory. The scrawled comments called her a 'slut' and linked her name to alleged sexual antics. Ms Lyle asked the school to clean off the writing. Yet it was still there eighteen months later.

Separately, Jill Olson, aged sixteen and in her final year

at Chaska High School, hired a lawyer several months after a friend told her that her name was on a typed list being passed around of the 'Twenty-five most fuckable girls' in her class, ranked in order of sex appeal and looks. Ms Olson had an 'honourable mention' near the top, and she was neither flattered nor amused. 'I felt really degraded,' she recalls with obvious distaste. 'Most people thought it was pretty sick.'

First, Ms Olson asked the school to find out who was behind the list and to let all students know that such behaviour was unacceptable. But, she says, the school failed to come up with any culprits despite a range of suspects. Finally, as the principal decided to drop the issue, Ms Olson decided she could not. She was especially angry that a female dean suggested she was making a fuss over nothing and that it was she, not the authors of the list, who might need counselling.

'All of a sudden something just hit me,' she says, now an articulate twenty-year-old studying telecommunications and Spanish at a local state college. In her view, the incident was just the latest in a long line of intimidation by boys at school which included sexist jokes, sexually-explicit graffiti, and stereotyped portrayals of women in drama skits. 'I don't want to use the word ignorance,' she adds. 'But people are so used to accepting the "boys will be boys" thing that they need the education to understand that certain behaviour is disrespectful.'

She found that her experiences were not unusual. Indeed, in a strange twist that reflects shared stoicism, many of her close friends tried to persuade her to abandon her lawsuit because they saw the boys' behaviour as the standard rite of passage through adolescence and held out little hope of any change. (Britain hardly boasts a better record. In my first week at university, the rowdier members of the men's rowing and rugby teams called out scores out of a maximum ten for the 'freshettes' lined up in the college refectory to take their meals.)

Despite the lack of peer support, Minnesota's human

rights commission sided with the two girls. A panel ruled that their schools appeared to have condoned the boys' behaviour, because they failed to respond quickly to their complaints. 'Naturally, it was upsetting to think that we had fallen short in one family's eyes,' says Nancy Kracke, a spokeswoman for Ms Olson's former school, which denies that it neglected to help the disgruntled former pupil. 'But it made us really examine how we are approaching this subject.'

Stirred by the successful lawsuits, Minnesota has passed a law requiring all senior schools to adopt anti-sexual harassment policies. Among the conditions, which came into effect several months ago, are the posting of rules on prominent noticeboards and the appointment of an official at each school to record in writing grievances by students, male or female. Ms Kracke says, 'We're a mirror of what's happening in society at large.'

Big American firms and institutions in past months have been anxious to show that they do not tolerate demeaning working environments for women after the televised hearings last autumn into allegations of sexual harassment against the Supreme Court judge, Clarence Thomas, by his former assistant, law professor Anita Hill. So topical is the issue that schools in socially liberal Minnesota seem to be competing to prove that they are doing most to help their students overcome the misguided thinking that often leads to sexual harassment charges.

But in a country where 'political correctness' and sexual equality are national buzzwords, few people seem to be surprised that teenage boys are still pulling insensitive stunts. Ms Olson's mother, Susan Strauss, herself a co-author of the state's revised curriculum on sexual harassment, thinks the problem has worsened since her youth. Keen to avoid further negative publicity, Chaska High School has sent a letter to every home in the district about the outcome of Ms Olson's lawsuit and has begun training teachers to recognize potential trouble in their classes.

But teachers have to be realistic about what they can achieve if parents do not set good examples at home. As two exasperated Chaska teachers wrote to their local newspaper, a few excitable teenagers 'will continue to de-pant others just as some of us will continue to exceed the speed limit when no cops are around'. Some schools, including Lakeville High, have set aside blocks of time for workshops that discuss sexual relationships or swap views on what it is like to be male or female and deal with unwanted attention from the opposite sex.

To smooth things along, the state government has even drawn up a pack of tips on how to give three one-hour lessons, including definitions of the differences between harmless flirtation, which does not upset anyone, and harassment, which is unwelcome even if it involves the same words.

Even with the best intentions, the classes are strewn with pitfalls. Often, boys feel that their teachers are 'male-bashing' and call on the girls to lighten up about their behaviour. Older teachers, especially men, sometimes find it hard to deal with an issue of which they were never made aware as youngsters. And, unless they split the anti-harassment seminars with male role models, women teachers are occasionally victimized even as they try to inform those who most need guidance.

This month, two 'particularly obnoxious' boys were suspended from school after they unzipped their flies to embarrass and disrupt a woman lecturer in front of 300 pupils, says Sue Sattel, a former juvenile delinquency social worker who oversees the state's 'sex equity programme'.

Ms Sattel sees a range of potential benefits for Minnesota from the programme. At the very least, she hopes to boost the self-esteem of girls who might otherwise be tempted to ditch courses regarded as traditionally male. More controversially, she predicts that sexual harassment workshops might also prevent some young men from committing violent crimes, including rape, by showing 'another way for a boy to be a man other than being tough and disrespectful toward women'.

Meanwhile, lawyers are still arguing about the size of Jill Olson's settlement and parents in Duluth and Chaska are divided over whether the two girls took a brave stand for their daughters' long-term interests or overreacted to the excusable immaturity of their sons.

28 February 1992

The doctor's dilemma

Leader

Of all the professions, medicine is one of those most reliant on vocation. Training is long, dealing with sickness can be distressing and irregular hours ruinous to family life. Most doctors choose their career by the age of fifteen. Yet many, once qualified, become disillusioned and convey their disillusion through a cantankerous professional lobby. Why the gulf between vocation and reality?

A survey by Isobel Allen, *Doctors and their Careers*, found that of those doctors who qualified in 1981, 46 per cent confessed that they had regretted doing so. Yet once they are in a career built on some six years of study and ten more of training, doctors feel trapped by the desire to realize some return on their investment. Central to this entrapment is the archaic nature of medical education and the stiffened joints of the National Health Service which so dominates the working lives of doctors. Both have developed mostly under the control of the profession itself, though the NHS is now being amended by potentially drastic government reform.

Medical education is among the most conservative of all vocational training. Inspired by Mr Gradgrind – 'What I want is, Facts . . . Facts alone are wanted in life' – students are taught by a mixture of rote learning and ritual humiliation familiar to lovers of 1950s Ealing comedies. Much of what they learn will never be used again. There is little instruction in alternative medicine, in community medicine or in human relations and other skills assumed to be not part of the job.

The sweated labour of hospital training, through which all doctors must pass, benefits neither doctors nor patients and plays a large part in junior doctor demoralization. Yet it is defended by consultants since it suits their more relaxed lifestyle and, in the phrase used to defend so many restrictive practices, 'we had to do it ourselves once'. So punishing is this apprenticeship that many young doctors, even if they had earlier planned to remain on the consultancy ladder, step off into general practice.

At least this means that every doctor has had some experience of hospital work, unlike the bifurcation of lawyers into solicitors and barristers. British general practice is among the finest in the world and continues to offer trained doctors a career free of some of the pressures of high-tech hospitals. Women now make up half of all medical graduates and, as GPs, they can work part-time while having children. For some, this is a valuable escape from the male-dominated world of consultancy, where women still make up just 15.5 per cent of the total. Others want to see the career structure of hospital medicine improved to make it more compatible with family life.

Although the status of general practice has risen over the past couple of decades, those who remain in hospital medicine still tend to look down on it. Over the years, this superiority has been reflected in the flow of resources into hospitals, especially buildings. Current NHS reforms have managed to prise minor surgery out of the hands of hospitals and give it back to GPs. But the profession is structured to defend its status quo: longer-than-necessary training, near intolerable job conditions for those beneath the consultant level, a system of patronage and personal recommendation for appointments, limits on the number of consultancy posts. These restrictive practices protect the prestige and income of consultants, but are good neither for the rest of the profession nor for the patients they serve. Doctors remain reluctant to delegate diagnosis or treatment to paramedical staff, nurses or pharmacists, despite the considerable savings that might result.

How might reform proceed? Education and training must

be modernized. Already, a drop-off in applicants to read medicine is lowering the entrance requirements. Word has trickled down to bright schoolchildren studying science that medicine is not a satisfying profession. More important, that threat to every conservative profession, the consumer in the market place, is making itself felt. Much of medicine has lost its mystique. Television, health journalism, manuals and publicity for alternative remedies are leading to a minor rebellion among patients. Complaints to family health service authorities have doubled in the past decade. Perhaps more significantly, many people have lost faith in conventional medicine's ability to cure all their ills; even the sceptical are turning to osteopathy or homeopathy or acupuncture.

Doctors are thus feeling threatened by alternative medicine (though medical education has not seen fit to meet the threat). But they are being assailed too by politicians. Financial dependence on government has long rankled with doctors but like many so dependent, the drug has become habit-forming. When the NHS was set up, what doctors objected to most was Aneurin Bevan's proposal that the NHS be salaried. But once used to the NHS, doctors, other than those in private practice, lost the spur of competition and relied on a starkly self-centred union, the British Medical Association, to maintain income each year.

Now the government is forcing on GPs and hospitals a new cast of mind, that of making decisions on scarce resource allocation. At the cutting edge of this reform is the fundholding GP. Nothing is more likely to raise the status and thus morale of GPs than this innovation, though this in no way diminished the BMA's hostility to it. Doctors are making their surgeries more convenient and attractive to patients. They are becoming aware of hospital costs. Hospitals, not least the gross oversupply of them in central London, are having to market themselves to GP fundholders who have the power to award them contracts. The consultant now has to return the GP's call, a sure measure of the changing balance of power.

Hospital doctors may feel intimidated by managers, a new breed of hospital animal. These representatives of government are forcing medics not just to make choices – they always had to do that – but to do so in a rational, open way. In a demand-led public health service with necessarily limited cash, not all patients can be treated immediately, or at all. Rational choices on priorities cannot be made without information on the cost and effectiveness of treatment. Whether they like it or not, doctors are having to consider supply, demand and equilibrium price.

Doctors must now accept that patients will shop around. They will take the NHS principle of a second opinion to its logical conclusion. They will want the best doctor, the best hospital, the best medicine. Some will go private, and others may be sent to private hospitals, their treatment paid for by their health authority. Consultants, who have seen their income from the private sector increase enormously in the past few years, will become richer still – as long as they win popularity with increasingly assertive patients.

The doctor of the future will be trained in alternative as well as conventional methods and will be as much a manager and marketer as a medic. Some doctors who shrank from the latter changes when they were first mooted by the health department are now finding, to their surprise, that they enjoy the challenge of thinking strategically as well as clinically. Though others may not yet realize it, this dose of political reform could not only produce a better health service but make a more satisfying profession into the bargain.

2 March 1992

Blowing away saxploitation

Brian Morton

The film *Some Like It Hot* contains one great truth and one thumping misconception. Yes, nobody's perfect; but no, whatever Sugar Kane believed, blondes don't always prefer the saxophone player. Anyway, Sugar's experience tended to confirm the old definition of a gentleman as a chap who owns a saxophone, but never plays it.

There are a lot of unplayed saxophones around – good news, perhaps, for women and next-door neighbours. The sad truth is that the saxophone is a young man's horn – it gets harder to find the puff and the 'lip', and it simply doesn't go with a thickening waistline and slippers. The sadder truth is that many of those unplayed saxes were dumb from the day they were brazed.

The saddest and most shameful truth is that even for those of us who did once play, the saxophone was a great posing instrument, a fashion accessory that built up sexual self-esteem in the pursuit of someone who looked and walked like Sugar Kane.

I can remember exactly where I was when John F. Kennedy tried to kill me. Dunoon, where I grew up, was virtually an American garrison town. I stood on the shore at Holy Loch and watched three US Navy submarines and a depot ship go out to sea. With Cuba coming to the boil, the Americans were keeping a rather meaningless promise to remove South Argyll from the Soviet cross hairs.

The ships were impressive, but not half as much as the tall black sailor who stood in immaculate bell-bottoms and white cap, serenading the departing ships with Honeysuckle Rose played on a straight soprano saxophone. It has been suggested that the impact this made was due to youthful inti-mations of mortality or homosexual panic, but I like to think that the sweet, raw sound had touched an ancestral chord.

Scottish boys of that vintage were coached in chanter, the reeded appendix that represents the marginally controllable part of the bagpipes. Twice a week, a whisky-faced man named McNeill would pace the over-salivating rows in earn-est hope of a new MacCrimmon or Aonghais Dhu, while the drool gathered in little puddles on my desk and I dreamt óf being Sidney Bechet.

It was ten years before I acquired a horn of my own, a leaden Italian tenor that sounded more like a runaway train than like Pavarotti. It was rank with verdigris and smelled of cooking oil. I black-lacquered the body, learnt Honeysuckle Rose and a few bars of Naima, and spent a lot of time cradling it in my window, trying to get Gauloise smoke into shapes like those in Herman Leonard photographs.

There was something about the way Leonard caught Sonny Rollins on his famous Blue Note album cover, all tortured angles and obscure perspectives, that told you the saxophone was dangerous. I liked to think it made me look dangerous, too, so I spent a good few evenings trying to impress a flatful of nurses in the block opposite, until the least Sugar-like of the bunch, a tiny, spherical woman from Kildare, with a sweet face and calves the exact contours of Guinness bottles, cornered me with: 'Oi've seen you practis-ing your trumpet.'

One of the sight-gags in *Some Like It Hot* is the incon-gruity of a woman (or Tony Curtis dressed as a woman) playing a saxophone. At the height of the pre-feminist 1960s, when jazz recovered some of its machismo along with its new-found political credibility, Archie Shepp said that the soul of black Americans was best expressed on the tenor saxophone. He also called the saxophone a sex symbol. It is a peculiarly regressive one – I once liked to think that the mouthpiece and reed, looked at face-on, resembled a suck-able thumb. Dorothy Baker's *Young Man With a Horn* was, of course, a trumpeter, but there was something about his self-destructive narcissism that told you he should have been a sax man.

Old trumpeters are survivors; sax players either don't get old or end up with nothing much left to say. There is something predatory about a saxophone. Watch film of John Coltrane playing a solo with the sound turned down and it looks as if he has been invaded by the thing from Ridley Scott's film, *Alien*; it sounds like that, too.

It is often said that the saxophone is a hybrid of the brass and woodwind families, and that its invention was therefore inevitable. The first part is nonsense, for the saxophone is the only genuinely new, non-electric musical instrument in maybe 200 years. The second is bad design history, for even 'inevitable' evolutions in technology require some conscious intervention. In this case, it was applied by a young Belgian instrument maker named Adolphe Sax, the son of a manu-facturer of serpents and ophicleides, who had come to the attention of the French military authorities after making great strides with brass valve technology.

If Sax did not claim parentage of the first truly modern brasses, he most certainly did with the saxophone. In the spring of 1842, the prototypes made their début in front of a wildly enthusiastic Hector Berlioz, who described their sound as 'full, soft, vibrating, extremely powerful, and easy to lower in intensity', adding: 'It is impossible to misuse the saxophone and thus to destroy its majestic nature by forcing it to render mere musical futilities.' The first of Sax's horns were patented in 1846 for orchestral and military use. Richard Strauss used a group of saxophones to excellent effect in the *Symphonia domestica*.

The collapse in 1871 of the French army, marching to Sax's new horns, was perhaps a symbolic portent, for by the end of the century the saxophone had drifted off into what Harry R. Gee, the instrument's bibliographer, called 'desue-tude'. When it next emerged in Europe, it was as one of the raucous voices in the 'Negro orchestras' that were the rage of post-First World War Paris, and which became the particular focus of the Nazis' hysterical obsession with Judaeo-Negroid subversion of Aryan *Kultur*.

In the process of becoming an icon, the saxophone's extraordinary nature as an instrument has been largely passed over. It is a 'dead' instrument, which calls on the expressive personality of the performer (that is another reason why so many lie unplayed in their cases). The tones possible on a saxophone are curiously empty, as if they are no more than the possibility of tones. Every violinist knows where the treacherous wolf notes lie on his fiddle, those places where the individuality of a particular instrument makes itself known. By the end of his career Coltrane was playing more 'wrong' notes and deliberate mis-fingerings than 'correct' ones. The trouble with the saxophone is that the wolf notes run in packs.

One of the great appeals of the saxophone is the extent to which its varieties constitute a 'family', in which individual eccentricities are more prominent than common characteristics. The unbroken purity of the alto can turn into stormy adolescence; the prosaic tenor has a secret life; the awkward, overweight baritone is capable of unexpected grace. The treacherous soprano can sound like anything from a butch clarinet to some item of Middle Eastern exotica, although nothing like as wayward in tone as the tiny, snake-charming sopranino. At the other end of the scale, there is the bass, once a big-band staple, the contrabass, a huge brute that looks like an oil refinery and produces intestinal sounds of no earthly musical use, and even the sub-contrabass (double ditto). Then there are the country cousins, manzellos, stritches, saxellos, slide saxes, and the once-fashionable C-melody saxes.

Their father is a strange and slightly shadowy figure. In later life, Sax was shunned with a mixture of professional jealousy and the instinctive suspicion reserved for those who seem to have sold their souls to dark forces. A cartoon in the *Saturday Evening Post* was captioned 'Posterity will not forgive you, Adolphe Sax!' His legacy is an instrument that is technologically entire but fundamentally flawed, profound and meretricious by turns, obsessively compelling and utterly galling, beautiful and scaldingly discordant, and, above all, enigmatic. Nobody's perfect.

7 March 1992

A dream in living stone

Melvyn Bragg

Edinburgh was my mother's dream city. We lived about a hundred miles to the south of it, just across the border. The first journey there was by bus after the war. In those austere 1940s, we put our heads up very cautiously. A trip out (the first post-war treat) to another country, to a capital city as far removed from my small market town as Samarkand, was a wild and memorable venture. I remember the floral clock in Princes Street gardens. I remember looking at this wonderful work and being amazed at the size of it, at how it could function in the grass, at the flowers it carried, at the ingenuity of the invention. It was, it is, the dream of a clock. 'This dream in masonry and living rock', is how the city was characterized by Robert Louis Stevenson, one of its most famous sons. The dream goes on.

I arrived in Edinburgh by train one evening recently. It is worth arranging to arrive by train. Even if you fly in, I advise you to hop down to Berwick-upon-Tweed, catch the train and ripple past the fine coastline to burrow into the great plate-glass concourse of Waverley station. Walk up from there, and the high city, the old city, comes into view slowly. Here are the first intimations of the weight of the stone, the crowded congregations of buildings on one side, divided by the rule of a great garden from the spacious façade on the other. And when you reach the ground level of the city, it is like arriving on the stage of a theatre from some depth of waiting-room or cell; there it is before you – the castle floating in yellow light, the medieval fortress on the plug of basalt, a fairy-tale fort, a place of siege and slaughter.

The next morning, I began a circumambulation of the city.

From the window of my hotel bedroom, in the resplendently refurbished, massive pile now known as the Balmoral, I looked out to Arthur's Seat. This is another of that cluster of volcanoes which gives the city its Roman seven hills. It is astonishingly near. Looked at through the hotel window plumb in the heart of a capital city, it appeared little more than a hop and a jump away. Yet it is rock; bare, supported by Salisbury Crags, and often likened in its contour to a lion couchant. It was widely speckled with gorse, the brightness of a heavy daub by Van Gogh. On the top of Arthur's Seat, even early in the morning, were the stick insects, Lowryesque humans, more like Indians in a cowboy film looking down on the wagon train which had drawn into this empty territory. The presence of empty and dramatic countryside reminds you of the danger and the isolation that this place has endured. I knew that, one way or another, I would end my stroll on Arthur's Seat.

They have built a new tourist and shopping centre next to the Balmoral Hotel, jutting on to Waverley station, and it could be much worse. I went in to buy a guidebook. I have been to Edinburgh thirty or forty times since the first visit with my mother: for rugby at Murrayfield, where I saw my first international game; for the zoo on school trips; for the innumerable festivals; to give a lecture . . . I had taken it for granted that over the years I had absorbed enough of the city to be reasonably well informed. Buying a guidebook was a serious jolt. For some time I used that shop as a library, glutting myself on the history of the city, until life beat out art and, clutching what I thought were the most useful of the shorter guides, I blinked my way into the light and saw that they had still not finished healing the Scott memorial.

There it is, rising out of Princes Street like a stone rocket, a fantastical memorial to the man who reinvented Scotland and Scottishness. Under wraps. It seems to be taking longer to clean up than it did to put up. One of my schoolboy treats was to walk up the corkscrew staircase inside. Counting the steps, I would arrive at the top, breathless and lunging for air in the crow's-nest, which gave views across the Firth of Forth where real ships began long journeys across the oceans of the world. Now I see it bandaged like an index finger which has risen from the gardens, wounded for its pains, the ghost of John Knox perhaps pointing out the wickedness of the world's ways.

Over the bridge and up towards the castle. Take steps. Any steps. The Advocate's Close will do. Narrow. Steep. A direct route into the heart of the Old Town. At the top of Advocate's Close, you pop out into the Royal Mile, the name given to a line of five streets; and here you have the heart of the matter.

A few steps up the hill is the castle. This is like a kite. The Royal Mile is its tail, which stuttered down in medieval times, then swelled and thickened. Ornaments and decorations embellished themselves around that slim cord, running down to Holyrood Palace, which brings the Old Town to an abrupt halt. For outside the side gates of the palace is the bare hill rock of Salisbury Crags and Arthur's Seat. Fine buildings interrupt and challenge the flow of the kite tail, none more so than St Giles Cathedral. The might of Presbyterianism exudes from this four-square church in stone, where Knox preached and Jenny Geddes threw her folding stool at a bishop and brought on a riot.

You approach the castle over the Esplanade – a nineteenth-century parade ground peppered with plaques honouring Scottish regiments in battle. There is also a small bronze well which marks the spot at which more than 300 Edinburgh women were burned as witches between 1479 and 1722. The Hell Fire Club and the Centre of Satanic Practices, an ancient building just below the castle, now serves excellent food and satirizes the witchcraft once persecuted and believed in.

The castle is a place for views, for those who love the stories of war, be they male or female, old or young. The guns.

The claymores. The walls. The tales of beaten siege and the once-only retaking of the castle by thirty Scots braves, who scaled the rock by night. Everyone can have that laid on in full technicolor at the Edinburgh Tattoo. Although often mocked by the intelligentsia, which heaves to Edinburgh for the great Fringe, dull would he be of soul who was not stirred by the night-time pipes and drums, floodlit on the Esplanade in the festival weeks, with intimations of Highland Clearances, battles under the sun in countries far away, hopeless defeats and glorious victories. You have to like the bagpipes, of course, and I am told that there are one or two who do not.

Instead of going down the Royal Mile to Holyrood, I walked under the castle walls that wind down to the railway cutting. The path was bordered by long meadow grass, nettles, dandelions, the gentle growth of untended urban parkland. In the gardens below people sit in summer in what we used to call continental fashion, under parasols; a carousel waits for children to be piped aboard by its enticing organ music. You could be in the gardens of many other cities in Europe; one of Edinburgh's claims is, indeed, that it has a truly European face.

Across Princes Street, pocked by some dud modern rebuilding but unchallenged in its strength of line, its commanding façade, I entered another dream. In 1766 a competition was announced for 'the plans for a new town, marking out streets of a proper breadth and by-lanes and the best situation for a reservoir and any other public buildings which might be thought necessary'. The winner was James Craig, aged twenty-two. Over the next fifty years his New Town plan – often criticized as too rigid, too geometrical, too formal – was built very much as he had planned it. Craig himself did not emerge as a great builder (Adam, Playfair and Hamilton were three of the many accomplished architects who carried out the business) and he died bankrupt and forgotten, but the New Town is still a young man's dream of a classic metropolis.

And as you walk through the New Town – with Princes Street to the south and Queen Street to the north escorting the grand gesture of George Street between them with the Rose and the Thistle, symbolic, fetching alleyways, like runners on either side of the stately coach – you realize that this is how Scotland rose again. In stone. In a city. Gone was Bonnie Prince Charlie and the hopes from the Highlands, nurtured by unschooled commanders and raw, doomed, loyal crofting hearts; gone the power of the ancient grudge, for finally the auld enemy had triumphed, and most brutally. Rise again Scotia in the kilts and clans of Sir Walter Scott, in the clear spring of Burns, above all in the Athenian ambition of Edinburgh. Here it is. Outgunning Bath, outgunning London, true to its country, but unafraid to reach up to the Acropolis – Edinburgh triumphant. The New Town was where it staked its claim.

Whether you look at the individual buildings such as the Royal College of Physicians, or at the circles of stone splendour – the twelve sides of Moray Place, the Royal Circus, Heriot Row, Drummond Place – or drift further downwards towards the Forth, you are in a maze of stone determination. These are houses for bankers and engineers, men of industry, doctors, lawyers, publishers, men of commerce and learning. The rectitude of the houses, the severity of the grey stone, the swish of the private communal gardens, the flat, cobbled surface on the wide avenues, the great columns and other classical borrowings . . . it is a monument to bourgeois confidence, and an enduring one.

Back over the bridge and joining the Royal Mile for a downhill stroll, the difference is like being ferried across an ocean. We are back in the kite tail of the castle, a lanky street full of tales. Full of open doorways as well – each a peephole and entrance to a court of stories. This is what most munificently characterizes the Royal Mile – the doorways off it. Called wynds or stairs, but most often closes, these little entrances, no more than doorway size, somehow excite imagination of a festering past. Here were fifty-two brothels on a short tenth of the mile; here were Jacobean plots and literary men at bay; here were seductive encounters and philosophies which teased the world of thought. It is impossible to walk down the Royal Mile without the whole tug and fact of the past coming at you: Lady Stair Close, which in mock-medieval style holds a museum to the great Scottish triumvirate – Burns, Scott and Stevenson; James Court, where David Hume and Boswell lived and Dr Johnson was an ungrateful guest; Carribos Close, where we have a fifteenth-century merchant, a centre of conspiracy and a theatre closed down by magistrates; Bailey Fife's Close; Paisley Close; Milan's Court; Flesh Market Close, which creeps down the steep hill and comes up under *The Scotsman* newspaper.

I do not know what it is that is so potent about this tumult of steep alleyways, led into by a swift hole in the wall through to a courtyard which is often a phalanx of beetle-browed, small-windowed, defence-moulded homes. Perhaps as much as any other city place for messengers; for boys on foot and women in despair or on the game or both; a place which you can sense bred rebellion and harboured rascals; hid knaves, sported cruelly with fools. And it is like the Middle Ages still – even now, when nice shops sell tartan skirts and fudge and you can go to Glens to have your individual bagpipes made.

Holyrood Palace I used as a short cut to make for Salisbury Crags and my late afternoon haul up towards Arthur's Seat. From the Crags you can see the Old Observatory, the New Observatory, Nelson's Monument, a Gothic tower, and the prize which coheres the rather aimless jumble – the Royal High School – rightly thought of as one of the greatest achievements of Edinburgh classicism. It is altogether typical it should be a school which does this. As I pottered along the winding path under the hill and took in more of the breadth of the city I had been to so often, I realized how much more there was to talk about, to learn about.

Edinburgh is a scholarly place: the museums and galleries, the centres of sport and music; the castle, seen from another angle now but still the haughty eagle on the rocks; the New Town almost hidden in the dip, soon yielding to leaf-locked gardens and the sparkling, white sail-flecked Firth.

And now, gasping a little from near the top of Arthur's Seat, a look across to the city, tracing the small passage made through it that day, calling up past visits. I turned and looked out west into the country, into the borderlands – for so long the fighting ground between the English and the Scots, warrior territory – and beyond it the border itself, and beyond that the small town in which I had boarded a bus more than forty years before to set off, pumped full of expectations, for *Edinburgh*!

7 March 1992

Folding papers

Pravda means truth in Russian and *izvestia* means news. The old joke in the days of communism was that there was no *pravda* in *Izvestia* and no *izvestia* in *Pravda*. Nowadays, the danger is that neither of either will even exist, much longer. Freedom has a commercial price. *Pravda* can now say what it wants, untrammelled by the dictates of the communist party central committee. Without the party's cash, however, it cannot keep going. The newspaper that once vied with the *People's Daily* in China for the highest circulation in the world has been reduced to less than a tenth of its former readership, can manage only four pages and publishes only three days a week. Few want to read a paper whose name was once Orwellian newspeak for lies.

Other former Leninist organs are faring as badly. Newspapers such as *Trud* which purported to reflect the interests of trade unions but in fact simply reinforced the party message have seen their circulation down two thirds. The new republics are switching off central television, using the wavelengths for their own broadcasts. Without massive new subsidies, the former state television service will soon be bankrupt.

Some of the old papers, quaintly retaining their communist-sounding names but nothing of the ideology, have managed to adapt to the market: *Izvestia* has a skilled advertising manager and is making a healthy profit; *Komsomolskaya Pravda* has become a radical crusader for the new democrats. A few new papers, especially those focusing on commerce and private business, are doing well. So too are a clutch of weeklies and monthlies, published in English and

122

backed by foreign money, which are tapping the market for glossy advertisements, gossip and picture features so absent from the media for seventy years.

All newspapers in the former Soviet Union are suffering from an acute shortage of paper, distribution difficulties and an instinctive assumption, even among the new democratic leaders, that the press must be subservient to the government. Tolerance of criticism is not yet understood in the fragile democracies of the Commonwealth of Independent States. In Georgia, the wholesale attempt to suppress opposition views was the first sign that President Gamsakhurdia was as much an autocrat as the communists he overthrew. Newspapers and television have in turn not realized that they are no longer on the barricades, where objective reporting was less important than commitment. In a society so politicized, every editor feels he has a mission.

Russia was always a country where the written word exercised peculiar power. Five years of glasnost, spearheaded by the press, have given the media an importance that goes beyond merely reporting the daily turbulent events. Through the truth about Stalin, about social ills, the disastrous Soviet economy, the hypocrisy of communism, the people were in the end set free. Now Russia's intellectual horizons, along with its borders, are narrowing. Price rises, resentment at Russia's cultural imperialism and a distrust of anything emanating from Moscow have combined to limit and impoverish the press and rob television of its power to reach across the CIS's eleven time zones.

The likely disappearance of dozens of newspapers does not yet threaten the new democracy, however. The present ferment has thrown up as many underground and samizdat publications, some frankly pornographic, others racist, all experimental and probably transitory. The greater threat comes from the left and the right, who want to channel the press into old habits of obedience and loyalty.

But so far the peoples of the former Soviet Union have shown no sign of retreating from their new freedom to say and read what they want. The commitment to plurality and press freedom is as crucial as any constitutional guarantee of democracy. It has been said that a free press is preferable to free elections. As long as Russia retains the first, the second seems secure.

11 March 1992

. . . *and moreover*

Craig Brown

My spelling reached a peak of accuracy when I was twelve years old. Grown-ups would ask me how to spell a word, knowing that they could be sure of the correct answer, my 'i's all before 'e's (except after 'c's) and so on. Since then, it has been downhill all the way. Do you spell it 'separate' or 'seperate', for instance? These days, I have to write down the two choices, and still I don't know which to pick.

Recently, I discovered that I have been spelling 'sophisticated' wrongly for at least a year, which is a shame, as it immediately signals how unsophistocated I must be. It reminds me of a childhood friend of mine who fancied himself as an intellectual. Having discovered the word 'subtle', he peppered his conversation with it, and we were all very impressed until one of us discovered that the 'b' is silent.

How important is spelling? Queen Victoria grew tetchy with the Princess Royal whenever she mis-spelt a word. 'I must tell you' she once wrote to her, 'that you have mis-spelt some words several times, which you must attend to, for if others saw it, it might make them think you did not attend to orthography and had not been taught well. You wrote in two letters – appeal and appreciate with one "p".' Sadly, Queen Victoria was herself not absolutely perfect in this regard, sometimes going into 'extacies' and finding things 'schocking' or 'bewhildering'.

As my own spelling steadily disintegrates, I find myself taking comfort from the example of great writers. Many writers of the most elegant prose have been curiously shoddy spellers. John Cheever's recently published letters reveal him as a hopeless speller ('Your magnaminity is overwhelming,' he writes to John Updike). Ezra Pound derived aggressive satisfaction from wanton mis-spelling, particularly when he was writing about higher matters. 'If you are nuvvelizing read JH,' he wrote to one young man, 'no excuse for iggorunce'. The writer Ronald Duncan used to have a letter from Pound hanging in his sitting room. It was written when Pound was in prison, chained to a rapist. 'Terrible – but marvellous xperience' it read. To another correspondent, Pound wrote, 'Keep on remindin' them that we ain't no bolcheviks, but only the terrifyin' voice of civilization, kulchuh, refinement, aesthetic perception.'

Old codger columnists tend to bang on about misplaced apostrophes (our village shop has a permanent sign outside advertising Bana's), but even such a precise writer as Evelyn Waugh never seemed quite sure where to put them, sometimes even – in 'havent' and 'didnt' – forgetting them altogether. Occcasionally, mis-spelling has a grave effect on friendship. 'I have a personal theory', Scott Fitzgerald's daughter has written, 'that one reason Hemingway became so exasperated with him was that Daddy never got his name right.' Fitzgerald tended to spell Heminghway either 'Hemmingway' or (slightly worse) 'Hemminway', whilst even Ernest was sometimes 'Earnest'. His daughter suggests that Hemingway might have felt more tolerant had he seen the scrapbooks, with their headings 'Rivierra' and 'Brittish Critisism'.

Like many poor spellers, Fitzgerald remembered the 'i' before 'e' rule only when inappropriate, so that his friends Theodore Dreiser and Gertrude Stein found themselves addressed as Drieser and Stien. Among his other favourite mis-spellings were 'ect', 'apon', 'definate' and 'yatch'.

Though Fitzgerald was extraordinarily lucky in his editor, Maxwell Perkins, who nurtured and cossetted (cosseted?) him beyond the call of duty, it was bad luck that Perkins' spelling was almost as erratic as his own. This meant that the publication of his first novel was greeted by the *New York*

Tribune with a readers' competition, the winner whoever spotted the largest number of errors. A Harvard scholar won with a list totalling 100, among them the mis-spelling of the dedicatee as 'Sigorney' rather than 'Sigourney'. At least, though, Fitzgerald's spelling did not bar publication; it is said that the TV personality Loyd Grossman was once turned down as a reviewer by a literary editor 'because our policy is to employ only reviewers who can spell their own Christian names'.

12 March 1992

MGN: Forward with Britain

Peter Millar

Encountering the Maxwell brothers together for the first time was most disconcerting; it was as if nature, having realized that Robert Maxwell's entrepreneurial personality was clearly far too large for even his body, had split it between his two youngest sons.

The difference lay in their eyes: Kevin used his as a filter through which he examined the world, retreating when required behind their flat, imperturbable gaze. They were eyes that managed to convey the curious impression of self-consciousness and calculation uncomfortably cohabiting. Ian, in contrast, was all charisma; his eyes flashed with a pale but bright blueness (I wondered if his contact lenses were coloured-enhanced) which marvellously offset his jet black hair. He was, he knew, with an occasional concerned glance at his still trim waistline, a portrait of his father as a young man. Only late at night, in his ninth floor office in Maxwell House, surrounded by strewn papers and still waiting for the satellite call from his father – from the Macmillan headquarters in New York or from the yacht moored off Cannes, or the bedroom of a hotel in Haifa – did I see the same eyes rimmed red with weariness.

No one can doubt that the Maxwell boys worked hard about their father's business: long hours and verbal abuse which few senior managers in other companies would have endured was part of the regime under 'the Captain'. They had other names for him: formally 'the publisher', 'the chairman' or 'RM' as used by other senior functionaries; sometimes, half in awe and half in irony, 'the genius'; or, adopting journalistic familiarity, 'Bob'. Just occasionally, in moments of urgency, they called him 'Dad'.

Officially, Maxwell treated them as employees rather than heirs, but they were privileged ones: they, almost alone, had genuine walk-in access to the throne room. Kevin made most use of it. His office was strategically situated astride the locked double doors that provided formal access to the chairman's chambers; it was possible to go in to see Kevin without going past RM's valkyries. His office, however, also linked through to his father's, so it was possible for Maxwell to retreat to it either to confer privately with his son during a meeting, or through it to gain access to his private lift and escape the building, leaving his guests to stew until some flunky made appropriate excuses.

Ian inhabited an office at the other side of the octagonal tower, with a fine view over the gothic pinnacles of the law courts, a serene calm shattered twice daily by the clattering rotor blades of his father's helicopter landing on the roof a dozen feet above his head. Ian had a pair of his own secretaries, in whom he inspired a loyalty that was to extend beyond disaster. When, after Robert Maxwell's death, the edifice started to collapse, there was a temporary lull as the sons won a breathing space from creditors; there was a marvelling wave of relief from the younger Maxwells' staff, who, like their bosses, had sat around for years wondering when, if ever, they would come into the ogre's inheritance.

Yet in a year of working closely with the Maxwell family, I never saw signs of any feeling for their father other than affection, albeit beneath an often palpable tension. When his father died, Ian certainly was deeply moved. Whatever cynics may say with hindsight, and whatever horrors have been uncovered about Robert Maxwell's business practices, his death left an enormous physical and psychological void in lives lived close to his overweening presence.

It was to escape that presence that his older children opted to live in the United States, a continent away and, therefore, at least out of bearhugging reach. In their father's lifetime, Ian and Kevin, for all the heir-apparent responsibilities seemingly divested on to them, were inevitably thought to be waiting in the wings. They lived under a giant shadow, and who could tell which was the dauphin and which the Prince of Wales?

In the White Hart, the *Daily Mirror* drinking den, hardened hacks who caught a glimpse of Ian or Kevin entering Maxwell House opposite would tug a forelock and make Uriah Heep references to the 'young master'. The brothers occasionally glanced through the window, but they rarely ventured in; fraternization – below a certain level – was frowned upon. Life as a Maxwell, under Bob, meant never being able to say 'sorry'. To those who dealt with him on a daily basis, Ian Maxwell's greatest sin was retelling his father's anecdotes and expecting – as Bob did – the same gust of laughter every time.

When Maxwell died and the theoretical division of the soon-to-vanish spoils allotted Mirror Group Newspapers to Ian and Maxwell Communications to Kevin, Ian began signing letters 'The Publisher' and appearing in his father's multi-coloured bow ties. It was as if the only way to exorcize the ghost was to emulate his fashion sense.

Ian had inherited more than Kevin of their father's gift for tongues. With a French mother it was unsurprising that most of the family professed bilinguality, though it was not always perfect. Ian, however, switched easily into and out of French, and was fond of dropping German phrases into conversations with those who understood them. Kevin, on the other hand, was shy about using other languages, preferring to pass on the role of toastmaster for a delegation from the German publisher, Berliner Verlag, even though he had been involved in its part-purchase. His gift was for doing sums; Ian's was for shaking hands and speaking in tongues.

How far either will now serve them is in the hands of the courts. I am simply glad I never had to take a school report card home to their father.

13 March 1992

Coping with life, from bed
to verse

Valerie Grove

Make light of it if you wish, it's only poetry, and by a woman at that. Wendy Cope's new volume is called *Serious Concerns*, but what do these concerns – love and sex and death – matter in an election-fevered Budget week?

And what do poets know of budgets? They barely earn a crust. A bestselling poet is a contradiction in terms. But of the handful we have – Ted Hughes, Seamus Heaney, Cope – it is Ms Cope who is in danger (because her poems are the soul of brevity and clarity and, though often sad and tinged with malice, full of charm) of becoming as truly popular as Sir John Betjeman. The solemnities of earnest criticism die on the lips, as one male critic found when he wrote in the *Spectator*: 'She is witty and unpretentious, which is both her strength and her limitation.' Upon which Ms Cope seized her pen and wrote:

> I'm going to try and overcome my limitation –
> Away with sloth!
> Now should I work at being less witty? Or more
>   pretentious?
> Or both?

The same hapless fellow said that she 'wrote to amuse'. 'Write to amuse?' she says. 'What an appalling suggestion! I write to make people anxious and miserable and to worsen their digestion.' So much for women poets being a soft touch.

Her first collection, in 1986, was called *Making Cocoa for Kingsley Amis*, a bold move since she had never, at the time, met him, a man not hard to vex. It was I who brazenly rang him on her behalf, to find out what he thought of her stuff. Luckily, he thought it bloody good. He admired her adherence to traditional metres ('She might never have heard of Ezra Pound,' he said approvingly) and, to her amazement, turned up to her launch party.

Six years on, Ms Cope has found fame. She is aired on Radio 4's *Kaleidoscope* and in *Cosmopolitan*, she reads her work aloud in bookshops, where queues form. *Making Cocoa* sold 40,000 copies, and Faber expect *Serious Concerns* to outsell it. The only place to catch her this week, between public appearances, was at the house of her analyst, the appositely named Arthur S. Couch.

Waiting outside Mr Couch's house, I feel a poem coming on myself. I sit in the rain in my familymobile (crumpled crisp packets, homework books trampled underfoot) waiting for the poet. Ms Cope's white Mini (a single girl's dashabout car) is alongside, in the poshest street in Hampstead, where only stars and shrinks can afford to dwell. A burglar alarm rings in the house next door, ignored. I listen to the Chancellor speaking of incentives and consumer demand, and read Ms Cope's lines about lost love and hopeless men.

When she appears she looks wan and anxious, despite her hour on Arthur's couch. The photographer says the light is terrible (it always is) so we go to the garden of Keats's house. In this garden, one spring morning in 1819, Keats wrote 'Ode to a Nightingale'. Today, no songbird 'poured forth its soul abroad in ecstasy'. But there was a carpet of crocuses under Ms Cope's lightly shod feet, until she was firmly told to keep off the grass.

Keats was her favourite poet when she was fourteen and first read 'The Eve of St Agnes', so sexy and beautiful, Madeline lying in the chill moonlight dreaming of love. Keats wrote that in this house, too. Ms Cope is pleased that Sir Kingsley once said that anyone with any feeling for poetry will have loved Keats best at some time. What Sir Kingsley actually wrote was: 'No one who has never thought him the greatest poet in the world, for no matter how brief a period, has any real feeling for literature.'

But this was a 1970 postscript to his 1957 essay in which he had sneered at Keats's 'O Poesy!' attitudes, his bards, pards and Muses, and 'that sugary erotic extravaganza, "The Eve of St Agnes"'' which has inspired countless legions of adolescents to maunder on about lines throbbing with imagination.

But from juvenile enthusiasms crisp modern poets develop, and Ms Cope is adept at parodying 'O Poesy!', or anything else.

Six years ago, she still had her day job as Miss Cope, music teacher in a primary school down the Old Kent Road, in London. She decided that if her book reprinted she would give in her notice, and did. Then the telephone started ringing and, though conscious of her good fortune, she found they wanted too much: could she fly to Leeds each week and read a topical poem on the air? A wise friend told her: never write poems for money. Do other things for money, and write the poems you want. So she did television reviews, which nearly killed all desire to watch television, and only wrote to order on occasion, as in her '19th Christmas poem':

> Big deal. Big chance
> To sell them a rhyme.
> They never publish poetry
> Except at Christmas-time.

Six years strikes me as a long time between slim volumes, but she points out that A. E. Housman waited twenty-six years. She has a thing about Housman (and has already chosen the lines from 'A Shropshire Lad' she wants read at her funeral).

> I think I am in love with A. E. Housman
> Which puts me in a worse-than-usual fix.
> No woman ever stood a chance with Housman
> And he's been dead since 1936.

133

She stipulates, absurdly, that there must be no questions about her private life. But who needs to ask? Like Dorothy Parker's, hers is an open book. See 'Bloody Men', the first poem in the new book.

Bloody Men

Bloody men are like bloody buses –
You wait for about a year
And as soon as one approaches your stop
Two or three others appear.

You look at them flashing their indicators,
Offering you a ride.
You're trying to read the destinations,
You haven't much time to decide.

If you make a mistake, there is no turning back.
Jump off and you'll stand there and gaze
While the cars and the taxis and lorries go by
And the minutes, the hours, the days.

There are several more in the same wistful vein, about men who prove to be not what they at first seemed. 'What we've got in common', Ms Cope says, 'is ambivalence about men.' Her upbringing was in middle-class Bexleyheath, in London, but she was sent away to a Methodist boarding school at seven. At the age of nine she was taken by her evangelical mother to a Billy Graham meeting, and responded to his call. Arriving at Oxford to read history she had OICCU (pronounced Oik-you, the University's Christian Union) knocking at her door to join a Bible meeting. But she soon dropped them. 'When they started praying for the nuns in our college to see the error of their ways, that was the final straw.' Now she avoids all happy-clappy churches, and only goes if she can be sure of hearing Cranmer's prayer book.

She was also, unimaginably, thirteen stone, but a nice doctor gave her speed: in the 1960s, any doctor who gave amphetamines for slimming purposes was regarded as 'nice'. 'I thought when I got to nine stone the world would be at my feet,' she says. 'But it wasn't.' She is still nine stone, and though the world *is* at her feet, she still needs Mr Couch and her anti-nicotine chewing gum, and she frets excessively about what her mother will think, despite being forty-six, quite old enough to do as she likes.

Her younger sister, who joined a female punk band called Moral Lepers and is now a disc jockey in Toronto, has made her escape. (The poem 'For My Sister, Emigrating', says: 'We've grown up struggling, frightened that the family would drown us . . .'). So there is plenty for Mr Couch to deal with here.

The solitary poet misses the companionship of school, and the funniness of the children. 'When I was a young teacher I didn't have a television set,' she once wrote. 'My pupils felt sorry for me. "Miss," said one kindly eight-year-old, "if you got a job, you could save up and buy a telly." I was so touched I didn't have the heart to explain that I had a job already.' From teaching children to be musically creative, she began to write herself. It is no coincidence that so many poets are teachers. Now she travels, expenses paid, to international poetry festivals in Toronto, Tel Aviv, Rotterdam and Macedonia. At workshops and seminars she teaches others to express themselves in poetry, where once she was taught herself. I was struck that all the women finalists in the Arvon poetry competition, won this week by Jacqueline Brown, had either attended writing courses, or tutored them. Ms Cope has both taught, and been taught at, Arvon courses in Devon. She taught poetry in Wales last summer; and this summer will go back, to learn short-story writing. As is evident from the vast numbers of entries poetry competitions attract, masses of people do long to write. You may argue that what we need today is to encourage readers, not more writers, but Ms Cope wishes to reassure aspiring writers that the private process of writing is what matters, not publication.

'I have played the piano all my life. Nobody ever thought I would make a concert pianist, but I don't think playing the piano is a waste of time. Lots of people play instruments and sing, but don't expect to be professionals or stars. But somehow, with writing, people break their hearts to be published, and have this feeling that it isn't worth it unless they are.

'Spare-time pianists have a realistic idea of how good they are: spare-time writers don't. It's as if hundreds of people went in for an Olympic sprint without realizing that the winning time would be in the region of ten seconds. Whereas piano-players know if they can't play a Beethoven sonata up to speed, and just enjoy it at a different level.'

Writing courses are a form of self-help psychotherapy that women especially appear to need, and Ms Cope's success is indubitably to do with being female, but she appeals to men as well. Her male peers admire her for having cracked the trick of having both artistic integrity and commercial appeal; they respect her mastery of metre, and her willingness to use arcane forms, as Parker did too (subtitling her 'Rondeau Redoublé', 'and hardly worth the trouble at that'.)

From 'There are so Many Kinds of Awful Men', in her last book (which echoed Robert Graves's 'Why have so many lovely, gifted girls/Married impossible men?') she now moves on to a more melancholy middle-aged perspective:

> When you're a spinster of forty,
> You're reduced to considering bids
> From husbands inclined to be naughty
> And divorcés obsessed with their kids . . .

So they come and go, the drinking ones, the married ones, the occasional one who is kind, or 'almost human'. When she's let down (again) friends say oh well, you can write a poem about it. At first, she feared that by being psychoanalysed she might become too sane to write. 'But no, luckily I'm neurotic enough to get by.' She still lives alone in South London, with piano and Roger Bear, the teddy (the only touch of whimsy I detect in an otherwise briskly efficient life), portrayed on the cover of her book by Posy Simmonds, reading T. S. Eliot's *Towards a Definition of Culture*.

Does she ever feel she ought to be writing about more important matters in a world full of terrors? Yes. She considered writing of the Gulf war, for instance, when moved by the sight of the retreating Iraqis bombed in their vehicles. 'But I would have felt like a vulture, somehow. I resist writing about something because you feel you ought to. I was very moved, but so was everyone who saw it on television, and if everyone sees it on television, who needs a poem? I don't have a special response.

'I couldn't write television reviews of the news bulletins about Enniskillen or the King's Cross fire. I'm not saying it's better to do what I do. But I do think that human happiness, and relationships, and love, are important subjects.'

Quite. We need all the lightness we can get. As Gavin Ewart said, good light verse is better than bad heavy verse; or any heavy verse, come to that. What is read in quantity matters: if Ms Cope sells, we should know why. What appears trifling (two silly lines on a dead cat) and satirical, like the cricketing metaphor she makes out of *Hamlet*, *Lear* and *Paradise Lost*, is leavened by sombre, moving poems like the one about her late grandmother, ending with 'those last bewildered weeks', reflecting what oft was thought.

Male poets, as she once wrote, she used to imagine were 'mad, bad and dangerous to know'; until she met a few, and found that most of them were 'as wicked as a ginless tonic, and wild as pension plans'. Now she goes further: apart from having invented a painful old soak poet called Jason Strugnell, she mocks the male poets' collective inability to keep accounts, drive a car or read a map, able only to find their way to the bar.

Can they forgive her? It seems so. She was lavishly reviewed by Peter Porter, a poet she parodied before: he called her 'seriously funny and lightly touching . . . much more than a stand-up comedian working in rhyme and metre.'

If today's light-verse writers appear to take themselves too seriously, he said, why not? 'Their work has to be as true to common experience and as memorable as anything more vatic . . .' (Vatic? It means prophetic, oracular.)

Her fellow poet Vicki Feaver, an Arvon runner-up, points out that Stevie Smith insisted that women poets did not have to be kind, or nice, or sweet; but only clear, and fierce. And in touch with life's little ironies. As the Chancellor might have said, nothing matters but death and taxes: it's in the rest of life that sometimes people find a witty quatrain can help them cope.

13 March 1992

One step forward, two steps back

Ginny Dougary

London Transport's electronic voice droned: 'Mind the gap
. . . Mind the gap.' As I was on my way to meet Susan
Faludi, the feminist author, this had a certain thudding
aptness.

Backlash, Faludi's controversial American bestseller, has
been compared to *The Feminine Mystique* and *The Female
Eunuch*, the ground-breaking books by feminists from
another era. The book chronicles the gap between the
American advertising myth of 'You've come a long way,
baby' and the reality: in America the divide between pay for
men and women is widening; nearly 80 per cent of working
women are still stuck in traditional 'female' jobs; discrimination complaints have soared; and abortion is likely to
become illegal in certain states – all of which the author
minds a great deal.

The book has created a stir because of its exploration
of the more insidious myths which invaded the collective
imagination in the 1980s. Myths, Faludi argues, which were
perpetuated and reinforced by a media loop: 'the man shortage' (fuelled by a *Newsweek* cover story which claimed that
a single, college-educated woman of thirty-five was more
likely to be killed by a terrorist than get married); 'the infer-
tility epidemic'; 'the great emotional depression' for single
women; and 'burnout' for career women.

In her opening chapters, Faludi scotches this list with cool
precision, showing how each 'finding' was based on a survey
that was later discredited. In 1986, for instance, bachelors
outnumbered unmarried women by 2.5 million in America.
Some man shortage.

More disturbingly, she goes on to show the way in which film-makers, television producers, magazine editors and advertising agencies all contributed to the myth-making: the barren, single, neurotic career woman of the film *Fatal Attraction* (which had men in the aisles yelling, 'Kill the bitch') versus the saintly, stay-at-home mother; *thirtysomething*, the popular television series in which the only career women you see are the unhappy ones; follow-up stories in newspapers and magazines which assumed that these dramas were telling us something 'real' about everyday life; the proliferation of 'trend' articles in which anonymous, and therefore unverifiable, female subjects spoke of their disenchantment with working life and their unfulfilled longing to procreate.

Faludi's hypothesis is that throughout the 1980s, women's hard-won but marginal gains of the 1970s were systematically eroded. There is nothing new about an anti-feminist backlash. As she illustrates, every time in history that women have tiptoed towards equality, they have been knocked back in a pre-emptive strike, always with the same arguments: 'Equal education would make women spinsters; equal employment would make women sterile; equal rights would make women bad mothers.' As long ago as 1913, Rebecca West said: 'I myself have never been able to find out precisely what feminism is: I only know that people call me a feminist whenever I express sentiments that differentiate me from a doormat.'

In times of economic downturn, a scapegoat must be found. And in 1982, Ronald Reagan, the president of the United States, helped to set the ball rolling: 'Part of the unemployment is not as much recession as it is the great increase of people going into the job market and – ladies, I'm not picking on anyone – because of the increase in women who are working today.'

Faludi emphasizes that the backlash is not a conspiracy orchestrated from a central bureau: 'The people who serve its ends [are] often unaware of their role; some even consider themselves feminists . . . For the most part, its workings are encoded and internalized, diffuse and chameleonic . . . Taken as a whole, however, these codes and cajolings, these whispers and threats and myths, move overwhelmingly in one direction: they try to push women back into their "acceptable" roles – whether as daddy's girl or fluttery romantic, active nester or passive love object.'

One is quite capable of creating myths of one's own, of course, without any assistance from the media. I had expected the Pulitzer prize-winning author of such an impressive first book to be a serious bluestocking; the type that doesn't suffer fools gladly; perhaps a little spiky; and certainly formidable.

The reality is disconcerting. Faludi is an extremely youthful-looking thirty-two-year-old, who positively beams all-American-girl niceness. This mild manner may be a handy smoke screen for her day job as an investigative reporter for the *Wall Street Journal*. The corporate giants who tolerate her infiltration of their organizations certainly seem to have underestimated her, to their cost.

Take her article on the working conditions at Nordstrom, a well-known women's clothing chain in America. The women who worked there, known as 'Nordies', were treated appallingly. When the story broke, Jim Nordstrom, or Mr Jim as he prefers to be called, announced to the press: 'Well, that *girl* ["He was talking about a thirty-one-year-old woman", Faludi tells me with some indignation] simply didn't understand us.'

Faludi was awarded her Pulitzer prize in 1991 for an article on the social consequences of leverage buy-outs. Her subject was Safeway, where a takeover had resulted in the loss of 60,000 jobs. 'My idea was to humanize the story both through the experience of people who had been booted out and those who had remained to work in what was a very different culture with insane productivity quotas,' she says. Inevitably, the piece was punctuated with tales of human loss. One man was sacked on the spot after working at

Safeway for twenty-three years. His misdemeanour was picking up a piece of toast from the deli-counter and forgetting to pay for it. He had spent the previous week at the trial of a man who had murdered his son. Then there was a trucker who was so devoted to the company after many years of service that he would stand up and salute the Safeway trucks. On the anniversary of his job loss, he got a gun and shot himself in the head. The company's response to Faludi's story was essentially the same as Nordstrom's: 'This is a woman invading a man's world and she simply doesn't understand business.'

In 1986, the year of *Newsweek*'s male-shortage cover story, Faludi was a twenty-seven-year-old single career woman. Although she can now talk lightheartedly about the terrorist line's provenance (a woman at *Newsweek* said it as a joke; the rewrite editor, taking it seriously, put it in the magazine and in no time at all it was 'news'), she can still recall her anxiety after reading the story. 'I went from feeling perfectly fine and, as a lot of women do, feeling proud about being able to make it on your own . . . to suddenly feeling guilty and wondering if I'd made a mistake.'

Instead of joining a dating agency, Faludi took a closer look at the Harvard–Yale marriage study on which the *Newsweek* story had been based. 'It turned out that the study had some serious flaws and rested on a shaky methodological base, yet the media did not seem much interested in exploring those flaws. Our culture seemed to want to embrace the result of this study, however erroneous.'

Backlash is the culmination of that initial sure-footed journey towards the truth. Every step of the way, Faludi confronts a sort of official party line that says 'Women are suffering from too much equality', while her research shows precisely the opposite. The official line is reflected in most magazines and newspapers. For instance, 'The feminist mistake', in the *Nation Review*, in which a young law student writes: 'In dispensing its spoils, women's liberation has given my generation high incomes, our own cigarette, the option of single parenthood, rape crisis centres, personal lines of credit, free love and female gynaecologists. In return, it has effectively robbed us of the one thing upon which the happiness of most women rests – men.'

A *Los Angeles Times* reporter writes in *Time* magazine: 'Our generation was the human sacrifice to the women's movement.' A *Newsweek* writer dubs feminism 'the great experiment that failed', and adds: 'Women in my generation, its perpetrators, are the casualties.'

Founding feminists, such as Betty Friedan, warn that women now suffer from a new identity crisis. Erica Jong's independent, sexually liberated heroine of the 1970s bestselling book, *Fear of Flying*, is replaced in the 1980s by an embittered careerist in *Any Woman's Blues*. Its narrator says the book is intended 'to demonstrate what a dead end the so-called revolution had become, and how desperate so-called free women were in the last few years of our decadent epoch.'

And yet, as Faludi makes clear, women are crying out for more equality, not less. 'In poll after poll in the decade, overwhelming majorities of women said they needed equal pay and equal job opportunities, they needed an Equal Rights Amendment, they needed a federal law guaranteeing maternity leave, they needed decent child care services. They have none of these. So how exactly have we "won" the war for women's rights?'

And more . . . 'Women themselves don't single out the women's movement as the source of their misery. To the contrary, in national surveys 75 to 95 per cent of women credit the feminist campaign with *improving* their lives, and a similar proportion say that the women's movement should keep pushing for change.'

The backlash Faludi identifies is an insidious counter-assault, 'a kind of pop-culture version of the Big Lie, which stands truth boldly on its head and proclaims that the very steps that have elevated women's position have actually led to their downfall'. It came about, in part, because of the converging forces of the extreme right and the Moral Majority which swept into centre-stage in the 1980s. The opinions of fundamentalist leaders, such as Jerry Falwell, were echoed by members of the Reagan administration. The Equal Rights Amendment was defeated in 1982; the federal government stalled funding for battered women's programmes, defeated bills to fund shelters and shut down its Office of Domestic Violence, only two years after opening it. And then the media joined in. Suddenly, women were told they should live like Stepford Wives or face a dreadful fate of childless, careerist spinsterhood.

Faludi throws in a few other ingredients which made the backlash such a corrosive cocktail: a lousy economy meant women were a convenient target, particularly as the polls continued to reveal that men saw their role as providing for the family and, in the pre-caring sharing 1990s, it was unfashionable to be concerned about any social injustice, let alone gender politics. 'Feminist anger', Faludi writes, 'is dismissed breezily – not because it lacks "substance", but because it lacks "style" . . . Feminism is "so '70s", pop-culture ironists yawn. We're post-feminist now, they assert, meaning not that women have arrived at equal justice and moved beyond it, but simply that they themselves are beyond even pretending to care.'

They may be provoked into caring if the one gain of the 1970s that we had all assumed was unassailable – women's right to choose an abortion – is overturned in the US Supreme Court later this year, as most observers are predicting it will be. What a triumph for the backlash.

Backlash is dedicated to Marilyn Lanning Faludi, the writer's mother, who jokes about being the book's grandmother. 'She enjoys its success without having had to endure the labour pains,' Faludi says. Marilyn gave up her job as a journalist to please her husband and became a full-time suburban mother. Faludi remembers her ambivalence about the decision. 'She has always been a feminist, even in the deepest slumbers of the feminine mystique. But as soon as the women's movement came round in the '70s, she began to ask questions which ultimately led to her divorce.'

Recalling her mother's unhappiness can still summon painful feelings in Faludi. 'What outrages me about the back-lash now is, knowing how much of a struggle it was for women like my mother to get to the point of being mar-ginally autonomous, to hear young women whine, "I'm not a feminist but . . ." or "We don't really need feminism" . . . I think, if nothing else, what an insult that is to women of earlier generations.'

Faludi's father was ambitious for his daughter, encourag-ing her to become a successful, independent career woman, while denying his wife the opportunity to shine. In the event, Faludi more than lived up to his expectations. She describes herself at school as 'the girl with the glasses'. At the age of twelve, she organized a school survey, on her own initiative, to ascertain how many fellow pupils were in favour of the Equal Rights Amendment and abortion. 'This inspired the animosity of the John Birch Society,' Faludi says. 'The presi-dent of the society attended the next PTA meeting to plant the seeds of discord. My parents were there, of course. She was becoming more and more shrill, when her microphone switched off. She carried on shouting, oblivious to the fact that no one could hear. Mostly everyone thought she was just a tiresome old bat.'

Faludi won a scholarship to Harvard. As editor of the campus newspaper, she was able to pursue the issues that interested her, such as the status of women in the college, and sexual harassment. In her first year, Harvard introduced a grievance procedure for the alleged victims of sexual har-assment. Commendable in theory; in practice it was not implemented. Faludi wrote a story to challenge the authori-ties' failure of nerve and the dean tried to suppress it. Then she identified a professor who had been the subject of a number of serious complaints. 'He used to phone me up in the middle of the night and say, "I'm just an effervescent kind of guy".' He was offered sick leave for six months.

One Ivy League tradition requires freshman-year students on financial scholarships to cook and clean for their peers. The lower-middle classes effectively act as servants to the Boston brahmins. Faludi had the unpleasant task of cleaning bathrooms and lavatories – which takes us abruptly back to *Backlash*. She is reminded of American *Esquire* magazine's 'Tribute to the American wife' in the 1980s, which featured a photograph of a woman, kneeling on the floor, cleaning a lavatory bowl and smiling beatifically at the camera. We both shudder. 'What was kind of depressing,' Faludi says, 'was the photograph was taken by a woman.'

I wonder, in a guarded sort of way, about her personal status. 'I have a boyfriend', she answers, 'and I certainly hope that some day I'll get married and have children. But I do resent the fact that a woman who decides not to have a child has to justify it to a prying world.'

Yet if there is a problem with Faludi's book, it is that she does not acknowledge the very real ambivalence of many working mothers. One American critic had an additional concern: 'Ms Faludi's dark portrait of a new men's movement could also be many shades greyer, tinged with some acknowledgement of mixed male feelings.'

Faludi will get her chance to redress the balance, since her next book will be about men. It will be a challenging assignment for such an assiduous researcher; a constant refrain of *Backlash* is how frustratingly little investigation there has been of men's emotional life. Her bedside reading is a book called *Slow Motion: Changing Masculinities, Changing Men*. So she has started work already? Not exactly. After the publicity hoopla is over, she intends to take a year off. 'There is a story I need to investigate for the *Wall Street Journal* on the abuse of migrant women workers . . .' The girl with the glasses is never too far away.

14 March 1992

146

Glad to be grey

Philip Howard

Old age is something that the British have grown particularly bad at since the 1960s. Other nations revere the old as wise, or endure them as everlasting presidents, or adore them as live-in childminders and household comforters. We bang them coldly away in Stalag-79s to die, out of sight, out of mind, in case they embarrass us by their *memento mori* that to this favour we must all come. Or we bully them with bossy social services. And we patronize them with dreadful sentimentality. If at the age of ninety you can eat a fish finger with a fork in England, they think you deserve a Nobel prize and squeal at you on the soppy Esther Rantzen show. If you survive to your century, you get a telegram from the Queen. And yet the old are people like the rest of us. Any fool can grow old. All you have to do is live long enough. In Britain, growing old is like being increasingly penalized for some crime you have not committed.

The time has come to bring the old out of the closet and discuss the unmentionable topic of old age. Veteran politicians such as Denis Healey and Norman Tebbit, Roy Jenkins and Barbara Castle, pop up continually on our television screens to comment on the election, being put through their hoops by that irascible old buffer in the bow tie, Robin Day. They do it with a style and pungency undreamt of in the bland marketing men's charm of their juniors.

And television sitcom and drama have become much concerned with age from *Till Death Us Do Part* to *One Foot In The Grave*. This month Kingsley Amis's *The Old Devils* has been screened, the last blast of the trumpet of the elderly against the monstrous regiment of youth. The programme can also be interpreted as an awful warning against the demon drink. Seldom a scene flits by without litres of cheap Italian wine being sunk by the women, and assorted stiff brownies and other spirits being swilled by the old boys. Alternatively, it can be viewed as a satire on the unjustified smugness of wearers of the disgusting Garrick Club tie, a bilious mixture of avocado and smoked salmon, and also as a disobliging commentary on the Welshness of the Welsh: a ghastly leitmotif of never say Dai.

But the main message of the book and the programme is that the old have as much right as the young to behave badly. It is Juvenalian, not jolly. A lot of people do not like this theme, finding it unrelentingly bleak. The English are uncomfortable with old age: Amis is furious about it, and frightened, and funny for those with strong nerves. The sensible attitude is that old age is always fifteen years older than you happen to be at present.

When *The Old Devils* won the Booker Prize in 1986, Amis turned up at Guildhall in black tie and brown brogues because he could no longer squeeze his feet into his patent-leather half-boots. One of the concealed blessings of old age is that you stop being embarrassed about how you look. He was seated next to an unknown middle-aged American female whom he took to be a Booker attachment. This was tactless *placement*, though even the Archangel Gabriel would have been a testing neighbour for Amis in the circumstances. After the woman had pestered him for some time about whether he minded her smoking, and whether she could give him a cigarette, she asked: 'Isn't there anything I can do to please you?'

On Sir Kingsley's lips trembled the retort: 'Actually, there is – you see that opening at the far end of the room there, that's called a door, and you can please me no end by going through it and staying out.' He claims, unpersuasively, that he is far too nice and cowardly to have said anything so rude. But in his factional hymn of comic bile to gerontocracy, the rude life is all there. In one of the funniest scenes in the first episode, the unveiling of a pseud modern sculpture to a professional welshing poet thinly disguised under the name of Brydan, Amis gets his own back on Dylan Thomas, whom he considers a very bad poet indeed: 'False, sentimentalizing, melodramatizing, sensationalizing, ingratiating.'

Another advantage of old age is that one can say what one thinks without fussing about what is culturally correct. It is not necessary to be as grumpy about the inevitable process as Kingsley Amis. Few can be as blackly and taste-lessly comic about such things as the humiliations of the flesh and the chilly Atlantic of the double bed, for those who can take black comedy on these forbidden subjects. It is a welcome sign of rude life, to quote Amis's least favourite poet, that he can rage, rage against the dying of the light in such an entertaining way. Give them a bit of time, and the English may come to treat their old, as well as women, and Jews, and blacks, as human beings. They had better, since old age is coming to us all – except perhaps the lucky ones.

18 March 1992

Split causes a big splash among press

Ray Clancy

The world press, especially in Europe, yesterday gloried in the demise of yet another royal couple.

The troubles of the Yorks were not enough to satisfy the European appetite for royal scandal. The marital troubles of Princess Margaret, the Princess Royal and the Prince and Princess of Wales were all included on front pages.

Italian papers revelled in the story, even going as far as to describe the separation as divorce. 'The fairytale of Sarah and Andrew finishes in divorce' said the leading newspaper *Corriere della Sera* on its front page. 'Scandal at the Court' said *La Repubblica* of Rome.

La Stampa of Turin confined its story to an inside page with the headline 'Sarah and Andrew – over to the lawyers' and a subsidiary headline saying 'they divorce out of jealousy' while *Il Messaggero* of Rome appeared to have an exclusive, quoting the Duchess as saying: 'Instead of staying with me, he prefers his helicopter.'

'New divorce in the British Royal Family' said a headline in *El Pais*, Spain's leading newspaper which also said that the story had overtaken the election as the biggest news of the day in Britain. The Barcelona-based *El Periodico*'s main headline said: 'Fergie's Separation Shakes Buckingham'. The paper carried a 1987 photograph of the couple rowing a boat, accompanied by the caption: 'Now they are rowing separately'.

In France, where the republican population hungers after intimate details of other nations' royal families, *France-Soir*, the Parisian daily, declared: 'Sarah and Andrew: the story of a dead love' and went on to say in a front-page article that the Queen is dogged by troubles caused by 'the amorous fiascos of her turbulent family'.

The paper lists the breakdown of royal relationships and tells readers that the Prince and Princess of Wales have separate bedrooms and Prince Edward has neither a woman in his life nor a proper job.

France-Soir also catalogued how the Duchess 'lost 20 kilos to make the English love her and then came the discovery of 120 photos', referring to the photographs found by a cleaner in the London flat that used to be rented by the Texan businessman Steve Wyatt.

There is considerable sympathy for the Duchess in France, where much of the press coverage revolves around her harsh treatment by the British tabloids.

The European press does not hesitate to speculate about the friendship between the Duchess of York and Mr Wyatt as a cause of the marriage breakdown.

In the Belgian daily, *Le Soir*, there was a photograph of the Duchess with Mr Wyatt, describing her 'adventure' with him and suggesting that that was the decisive factor in the separation.

El Mundo in Spain also suggested a romance with the Texan had been the final reason for the separation and described the Duke being involved in a jealous scene. 'Prince Andrew lost his nerve recently, during a dinner at Sunninghill – the residence of the Yorks, near Windsor – when the name of Steve Wyatt was mentioned. The Prince abandoned the dining room, slamming the door behind him,' the article said. The broadsheets and television in Germany virtually ignored the story but the German tabloid press went wild. 'Fergie and Andy Finished!' was the main headline on the front page of the mass-circulation *Bild* which also quoted a psychologist as saying that the couple should not have married because the Duchess was 'far too temperamental for life in a golden cage'.

Express in Cologne called the Duchess a 'scandal noodle' and said that she had now broken the 'matrimonial chains'.

In Canada, where the couple were warmly welcomed on their first major overseas tour shortly after their marriage, it was a case of 'All Eyes on Fergie' as the Ottawa *Sun* put it.

In the United States newspapers carried denials from Mr Wyatt that there had been any romance with the Duchess. *USA Today* described the Duchess as a 'tempestuous, controversial redhead' who is 'walking out on her naval officer husband'.

The New York *Daily Post* describes the royal family as keeping their stiff upper lips firmly shut. 'Andy, Fergie duke the question' the paper's headline said in true brash American style.

20 March 1992

Why I know we will beat Labour

Robin Oakley

Despite Labour's opinion poll lead, John Major is convinced that he chose the right time to go to the country, and that the Conservatives can win. His confidence is based on John Smith's tax plans which, he argues, will assist Labour like a 'draught of poison'.

The shadow budget, says Mr Major, 'seeks to lift the economy out of recession by imposing greater taxation. And it doesn't restrict that taxation to those whom Labour would call rich. The people who are principally hit are middle-class, middle-income earners, typically a senior school teacher in a comprehensive. A GP would pay an extra £1,500 in national insurance alone. These are not people who should have the disincentive of higher taxation.'

Asked why the Tory manifesto itself is not more specifically designed to lift the country out of recession Mr Major replies that it is not necessary. The conditions for recovery are in place. Inflation and interest rates are down, individuals and companies have been repaying debts. America and others are out of recession. Only the 'confidence factor' is preventing investment and that will undoubtedly be restored by the right election result.

Will there, as Labour claims, be more VAT increases under a new Tory government? Or might they extend the range of goods and services it covers? The Prime Minister rules both out. 'We have no plans and no need to increase the impact of VAT. That covers both your points.' The only caveat he enters is a change in law binding all European Community governments.

When challenged on the terse assertion in the Tory manifesto – 'we will maintain mortgage tax relief' – he chooses his words with care. Does that promise last for a parliament? Could it go up?

'I don't think I can give an answer that covers a whole parliament. Whether the Chancellor would wish to increase it over a parliament is a matter that falls to be decided each year. We are committed to the principle of mortgage tax relief to give a good start and assistance to people in the housing market.' But the words allow too for a cut. Does he guarantee continuation of the tax concession at the present rate? 'It would continue in some form. I cannot conceive it would be reduced.'

Asked if his promise to put Britain at the heart of Europe will be realized more fully if he is re-elected, Mr Major lines up with his party's Euro-sceptics: 'A good European is not the man who accepts everything suggested by the EC partners or by the Commission. A good European often says no, just as I said no at Maastricht to the Social Chapter . . . I am not an advocate of a United States of Europe. I am an advocate of a successful Europe of nation states.'

He opposes the Social Chapter's principle of a minimum wage, which Labour would introduce, because of its impact on competitiveness. But if ten of our EC partners can afford a national minimum wage why can't Britain? It is a matter, says Mr Major, of the large numbers in part-time work whom it would no longer be practicable to employ. Many continental politicians, he argues, regret very much that their countries have national minimum wages.

Looking remarkably relaxed and jovial despite a gruelling eighteen hours a day campaigning, he reveals growing scepticism over the single European currency, saying that he is 'very dubious' whether the circumstances will be right for its introduction within the decade. But should the European Community fail to wait for the right economic circumstances, he warns of collapsing asset values in the weaker countries and mass migration to the stronger states.

A 'real attack' on the inner cities' problems is promised over a new five-year term, with urban regeneration schemes, the restoration of derelict land, an injection of capital and the boosting of home ownership. Local authorities, he says, raised rates on companies rather than individuals and forced them out of the inner cities, creating a cycle of deprivation. 'No jobs, just unbalanced communities of people on very modest incomes and people on very wealthy incomes, with none of the adhesion of society.'

If Mr Major's references to 'society' are distinctly un-Thatcherite, confirming the more interventionist tone of the latest Tory manifesto, he does defend her community charge. 'The principle was right but the practice wasn't.' Local authorities pushed up expenditure on the community charge and rendered the system unworkable. 'The community charge was fair when it produced a taxation level that it was credible to expect people on modest incomes to bear, but it was not and it had to be changed.'

Passion is not a word which often comes to mind with the amiable and relaxed Mr Major, who appears to be weathering the election storm with equanimity. But the bite came into his voice when I asked him if he had any regrets, as Mrs Thatcher obviously does, about the decision to take Britain into the exchange rate mechanism. None at all, he says.

Yes, interest rates would have been lower. But the exchange rate would have been lower too. 'As a result we would have been feeding inflation back into the system. People have not taken on board how much I loathe inflation.'

Citing Japan and Germany, he says that countries following hard currency plans have had lower inflation and stronger growth. That is what he wants for Britain. 'We can't run away from problems for ever, letting sterling devalue progressively every time there is a blip in the trade cycle.'

There is no policy for a hung parliament. He is adamant about resisting a Scottish parliament, saying that the constitutional problems raised by two classes of Scottish MP at Westminster would lead to calls for full separation.

And while he 'understands the frustration' of the Liberal Democrats he scorns proportional representation because it would produce weak government. With PR, he says, Britain would never have taken the right decisions about the economy in the early 1980s or the Falklands war. The countries which have it, regret it.

Sitting in his paper-strewn office in Smith Square, I asked if he would contemplate authorizing military action during the campaign either against Saddam Hussein or President Gadaffi of Libya. He would not hesitate to involve Britain in military action against Saddam Hussein during the course of the election campaign. 'Yes, if I thought it the right thing to do. That should not be read as a commitment but if you wish to ask the question and if I thought it was the right thing to do, I would do it.

'Saddam Hussein still has the capacity to make nuclear weapons. He will have to surrender that capacity. The United Nations require it and we, the Americans and the French will make absolutely sure that he cannot proceed with that, whatever it takes. There should be no doubt about it.'

Military action against Libya in support of UN resolutions demanding the handover for trial of suspects in the Lockerbie terrorist bombing is thought to be a less immediate prospect. A further UN resolution imposing sanctions is expected to precede any use of military force.

John Major said he had rejected calling the election after the Gulf war, when the Tories led in the polls, because it would have been 'immoral and a cheat'. He ignored November because he was determined to conduct the Maastricht negotiations and because he wanted the replacement for the poll tax on the statute book before facing the electors. At New Year he decided that it had to be April. Any later, he reckons, and a country driven near distraction by the phoney election would have been up in arms.

Despite the fact that no government party has increased its poll standing during a general election campaign for forty years he remains confident. All over the world, even in India, he says, people are reducing high taxation. 'Only the British socialist party wants to put taxation up.'

20 March 1992

Pakistan crowned champions

Alan Lee

There could be no excuses. This time, there was no possible injustice. England did not win the World Cup final because they did not deserve to.

The cup was won, for the first time, by the volatile and inspirational men of Pakistan. More particularly, it was won by Imran Khan, who has planned for this moment for two years and who never lost faith that it would happen, even against the improbable odds that confronted him early in the tournament.

It was then, amid the battered morale of players on the very brink of elimination, that Imran invoked the leadership ploy of risking all when there is nothing left to lose. He told his men to behave like cornered tigers. Only he and his players know how the address was delivered, but the world now knows its effect.

Pakistan, clumsy and clueless in the early rounds, needed to win five successive games to take the cup and they did so with ever-increasing conviction. Yesterday, they touched heights that few countries reach. The fickle gifts that decorate this team were produced on cue and the effect was like the synchronized opening of parcels on Christmas morning.

Imran and Javed Miandad, the lord and his lieutenant, batted with the good sense born of five World Cups together. Later, they hugged animatedly, aware that their structured stand of 139 had influenced the game every bit as much as Wasim Akram's consummate all-round performance, Mushtaq Ahmed's beguiling leg-spin and Inzamam's stunningly confident strokeplay.

Against such a performance, even the England who began

158

this tournament with method and momentum would have struggled to cope. The England who sustained themselves yesterday on the pickings of memory were thoroughly out-played. The margin was only twenty-two runs but the defeat was heavier. 'It was,' as Graham Gooch confessed, 'pretty conclusive.'

Gooch could be excused for wearing his most sorrowful expression last night. The hurt of losing his third World Cup final was plain. England did their best. It just was not the best to which we had become accustomed until the tour bandwagon lost a wheelnut or two in Ballarat and suffered punctures in Wellington and Albury that were never adequately repaired.

To win yesterday, in a state of reduced confidence and poorly concealed fatigue, England needed their leading players – Lewis, Botham and Gooch – to summon one final show. They did not have it in them.

Gooch and Botham began cup final day on the front pages and in the television headlines for walking out on the official banquet.

By the time they walked out together again, this time to open England's batting, the game had taken an ominous turn.

Imran won the toss and chose to bat, having been informed that Robin Smith, although declared fit, had not been included by England. 'The toughest decision I have ever had to make,' Gooch said.

Derek Pringle, who missed the previous two games through injury, did return – and it was just as well. Not only did he take two wickets with the new ball and another in the final over, he bowled so tightly that only fourteen runs came from the bat in his ten overs.

Others were not so miserly. Lewis's final four overs were caned for forty-two, Botham conceded six an over and Illingworth five. All this after Pakistan had lost two for twenty-four and then stood at only seventy at the halfway point and 125 with fifteen overs remaining.

Imran had a plan, however, and he carried it through to perfection. Although Miandad, now struggling with a back injury, was out to a violent reverse sweep and Imran joined him four overs later, the platform had been solidly laid for Inzamam and Akram, who then put on fifty-two in six overs.

England had looked like chasing no more than 220, very attainable on a good pitch with a fast outfield. Instead, they set off in a more pressurized pursuit of 250 – a target that was still more remote after a tempestuous start against Akram's darting inswing and Aqib's varied outswing.

It was now that Brian Aldridge, the New Zealand umpire, gave two dubious decisions – one inflaming the Pakistanis, the other dispatching Botham muttering thunderous expletives inside his helmet.

Botham plainly thought he had not hit the ball from Akram that brought his end. The posturing Sohail, who had already been fined once for his behaviour in this tournament, was fortunate to escape further censure for first prancing in front of Botham, pointing him to the dressing-room, then firing some uncomplimentary words at Stewart after Aldridge reprieved him for what looked a plainer deflection.

Stewart did not linger, however, and when Mushtaq, having confused Hick with a top-spinner, left him floundering with a googly and very much leg-before, England were sliding.

The mortal blow was the end of Gooch, top-edging a sweep against Mushtaq, whom Imran later admitted was almost sent home prior to the tournament, so badly was he bowling.

Lamb and Fairbrother restored hope in a stand of seventy-two, but back came Akram to provide the memory of the match. One ball swung in to Lamb, then jagged away to hit off-stump; the next cut viciously in to bowl Lewis off an inside edge. Game over, despite Fairbrother's pluck.

At the end of it, the Pakistani players flung themselves down in prayers of thanks and Imran mounted the rostrum with pride in his step and smile.

He dedicated the triumph to the cancer hospital in Lahore, his abiding obsession. The fund-raising will go on, he said, and, because cricket is so important among the moneyed of his country, he must go on playing.

That means he will be back in England this summer, more sobering news at the end of a deflating final day for Gooch and his men.

PAKISTAN

	6s	4s	Min	Balls
Aamer Sohail c Stewart b Pringle	4	0	0	20	19
Edged ball moving across from leg				
Ramiz Raja lbw b Pringle	8	0	1	36	26
Playing back and across his crease				
*Imran Khan c Illingworth b Botham	72	1	5	159	110
Drive to deep mid-on				
Javed Miandad c Botham b Illingworth	58	0	4	125	98
Left-handed sweep to backward point				
Inzamam-ul-Haq b Pringle	42	0	4	45	35
Cross-batted swipe				
Wasim Akram run out (Stewart)	33	0	4	31	18
Impossible last-ball single				
Salim Malik not out	0	0	0	1	1
Extras (lb 19, w 6, nb 7)	32			
Total (6 wkts, 50 overs, 212 min)	249			

Ijaz Ahmed, †Moin Khan, Mushtaq Ahmed and Aqib Javed did not bat.

FALL OF WICKETS: 1-20 (Ramiz 8 not out), 2-24 (Imran 1), 3-163 (Imran 67), 4-197 (Inzamam 27), 5-249 (Akram), 6-249 (Malik 0).

BOWLING: Pringle 10-2-22-3 (nb 5, w 3) (8-2-13-2, 2-0-9-1); Lewis 10-2-52-0 (nb 2, w 1) (6-2-10-0, 2-0-20-0, 2-0-22-0); Botham 7-0-42-1 (w 1) (4-0-17-0, 3-0-25-1); DeFreitas 10-1-42-0 (7-1-25-0, 3-0-17-0); Illingworth 10-0-50-1 (one spell) Reeve 3-0-22-0 (w 1) (one spell).

INTERMEDIATE SCORES: 10 overs: 26 runs; 20: 49; 30: 96; 40: 170.

ENGLAND

	6s	4s	Min	Balls
*G A Gooch c Aqib b Mushtaq	29	0	1	93	66
Diving catch at deep mid-wicket				
I T Botham c Moin b Wasim	0	0	0	12	6
Edged away swinger to wicketkeeper				
†A J Stewart c Moin b Aqib	7	0	1	22	16
Drawn forward to away swinger				
G A Hick lbw b Mushtaq	17	0	1	49	36
Beaten on back foot by googly				
N H Fairbrother c Moin b Aqib	62	0	3	97	70
Skied towards square leg				
A J Lamb b Wasim	31	0	2	54	41
Beaten playing forward to leg cutter				
C C Lewis b Wasim	0	0	0	1	1
Ball cutting back from off				
D A Reeve c Ramiz b Mushtaq	15	0	0	38	32
Skied to deep extra cover				
D R Pringle not out	18	0	1	29	16
P A J DeFreitas run out (Salim-Moin)	10	0	0	13	8
40-yard throw from deep mid-wicket				
R K Illingworth c Ramiz b Imran	14	0	2	9	10
Skied drive behind bowler's wicket				

Extras (lb 5, w 13, nb 6) 24

Total (49.2 overs, 213 min) 227

FALL OF WICKETS: 1-6 (Gooch 3), 2-21 (Gooch 7), 3-59 (Gooch 23), 4-69 (Fairbrother 2), 5-141 (Fairbrother 40), 6-141 (Fairbrother 40), 7-180 (Reeve 13), 8-183 (Pringle 0), 9-208 (Pringle 14)

BOWLING: Wasim 10-0-49-3 (nb 4, w 6) (5-0-21-1, 2-0-9-2, 3-0-19-0); Aqib 10-2-27-2 (nb 1, w 3) (7-2-15-1, 3-0-12-1); Mushtaq 10-1-41-3 (w 1) (8-1-29-2, 2-0-12-1); Ijaz 3-0-13-0 (w 2) (one spell); Imran 6.2-0-43-1 (nb 1) (1-0-9-0, 4-0-20-0, 1.2-0-14-1); Aamer 10-0-49-0 (w 1) (one spell).

INTERMEDIATE SCORES: 10 overs: 32; 20: 66; 30: 108; 40: 165.

Pakistan won the toss and elected to bat.

Pakistan won by 22 runs.

Man of the match: Wasim Akram.

Umpires: S N Bucknor (West Indies) and B L Aldridge (New Zealand).

26 March 1992

Tory faithful cling to
Maggie's Ark

Matthew Parris

In a few days, someone is flying to America. She has had time to canvass only for the Tory hopefuls she likes best. A UK map showing the constituencies visited would chart what Mrs Thatcher regards as dry land: hilltops of sanity poking their heads into the Thatcherite sunshine while the rising vapours of compromise lick all around.

The ex-Prime Minister's campaign voyage has been a fastidious progress from beacon to beacon, a Thatcher visit bestowing the lady's Good Housekeeping seal of approval. Departing a rally in support of her soulmate, Michael Forsyth, in Scotland, Maggie's Ark sailed south. Watchmen on the bridge peered through the Majorite mist . . . was there *any* dry land left in England? Yes, upon the hills of Cannock and Burntwood, home of her friend Gerald Howarth, she went ashore yesterday and then onwards . . .

'Land ahoy!' It was North Warwickshire, an Ararat of no-nonsense Toryism awaited the blessing of her landfall: the domain of that dry young prophet of fiscal rectitude, Francis Maude.

Mr Maude is thirty-something with a majority of two thousand and something. An honourable man, an intellectual, and honest, but not one of nature's baby-kissers, Mr Maude is already financial secretary in the Treasury. He has ahead of him a highly promising career . . . or not. It depends upon the voters.

It depends, for instance, on the electors of Shustoke, a village near Coleshill, where I caught up with him canvassing on a bitter afternoon. It was 2.30. Maggie's Ark had already been sighted on the horizon, and radio messages received.

163

Mrs Thatcher was to come ashore at Coleshill at five. 'Mr Maude', his office told me, 'will be canvassing until three. At five he will be awaiting Mrs Thatcher.'

And from three to five? 'He will be preparing himself for Mrs Thatcher.' I had visions of the thin and ascetic-featured Mr Maude in a hairshirt in the Coleshill churchyard, being birched by monetarists for two hours, in preparation for the honour of her touch. First, though, there was Shustoke to be canvassed. I followed Mr Maude from house to house.

'North Warwickshire' sounds blissful. In fact, it is a land of electricity pylons and humming power lines: old pit villages overshadowed by cooling towers and skirted by 1950s dual carriageways. In the night you can hear the roar of the motorways, never far, and always the orange glow of Birmingham in the western sky. Brick houses, mostly detached, are china-dog and porcelain-horse territory. Neither rough nor poor, North Warwickshire is not quite smooth and not quite prosperous.

Its electors are not really socialists and not quite Tories. 'He says he voted for the Social Democrats last time, and the Liberals the time before that,' reported one of Mr Maude's door-knockers as Mr Maude himself approached the house. 'He says he votes whichever he thinks is best for the country.'

'Good of him, a kind concession on his part,' smiled Mr Maude thinly, his face completely blue with cold. At the next house an old gentleman *would* be voting Tory – out of sympathy. 'I heard you on the wireless. Clare Short was yelling at you,' he said. 'She's a big woman.' But it was time for Mr Maude to prepare himself. He left.

I found a café in Coleshill in which to prepare myself. In the streets of the town, for fully an hour before she was due, the people of Coleshill began to gather in knots, preparing themselves.

Whispers ran round. 'What's she doing?' 'Where's she going?' 'Why's she coming?' Labour supporters gathered in huddles to oppose, a sense of solidarity and purpose missing since November 1990 returned to their lives. She swept up in a black Jaguar. Francis Maude was waiting to lead her to the door of a new home in which a newly married couple were to dwell. She was to meet them.

Crowds pressed at the barricades. 'I'm not a Tory at all,' whispered the lady next to me, 'but she's – well – *someone*, isn't she?' Mrs Thatcher, in a navy-blue suit with white piping, like a sea captain's uniform, bore down on her. 'How *are* you? This is my *fourth* constituency, and *everyone* is in good heart . . .' She passed on, still talking.

'It's like the Queen,' said the lady beside me. Francis Maude stood in the doorway, smiling and wringing his hands.

28 March 1992

It's a grate life here if you don't weaken

Libby Purves

I think I have found a new career. More than found one: I will have founded it. I am going to set up as the world's first consultant psychotribologist.

If you are a good, solid back-page reader, you are already a jump ahead of me, crying 'Yes! we need psychotribology now!' Last week, this newspaper introduced plain tribology to a wider public on the occasion of the Institution of Mechanical Engineers' new War on Wear campaign. The word comes from the Greek 'tribein', meaning 'to rub', and is the study of things which rub against each other, which grind and squeak at one another's hostile surfaces and throw off shavings of swarf. If we could lubricate them better we would save energy, prevent mechanical breakdown and be £1.5 billion a year richer. So that's tribology: oiling the wheels of industry.

And psychotribology? Well, you know already. Just look around you, at the way your colleague on the left keeps sniffing at his Vick inhaler, and the one on the right is rearranging her drawerful of neat little paisley-patterned boxes marked PAPERCLIPS and PERSONAL. Psychotribology has to come. After all, if £1.5 billion a year is being lost through squeaky ball-bearings and incompatible cogs, how much more is being wasted on the capacity of human workmates to rub each other up the wrong way, present jagged and damaging surfaces, and generally get up one another's noses?

What is the point of installing an expensive new executive, finely engineered at Insead and Harvard Business School, if he is going to waste half his energy grinding horribly against the rough surfaces of his ex-works 'basically, I'm a barrer-boy' managing director? Why take such trouble polishing job descriptions for a new PA, only to offer her up to a departmental head with a personality like coarse sandpaper and a work pattern designed by a committee of Heath Robinson and Jeffrey Bernard? On the other hand, why waste your time on an anti-harassment code if the tolerances of your employees are all equally crude, and the girls fouler-mouthed cogs than the boys?

Actually, I suspect that a good three-quarters of sexual harassment cases are due to nothing but poor psychotribology. When a doctor accuses a partner of public fondling, or a woman erupts with fury at being consistently called 'sweetheart', it is not straightforward sex warfare. There can be antipathies stronger and less rational than any mere passion. Stray phrases betray it: 'She had an unfortunate manner', 'He had always thought he was too good for the job'.

Sex itself is a squeaky wheel: sometimes the very presence of a nubile woman workmate – whose Lycra bodysuit is, in fact, a statement about having lost 12lb, not about sexual rapacity – can deeply infuriate men whose own lovelives are a bit ropy and who come to work partly in order to *stop* thinking about Lycra and pouting lips. If they harass her, it could be that her very presence is – tribologically speaking – harassing them first. It is no excuse, but it is an explanation.

And remember, just as you can be chivalrous and loving towards a direct rival with whom your gears mesh smoothly, so equally can you fall into a frenzy of hate about a quite innocent colleague. For all kinds of weird reasons: because she has a silly accent, because she always wears four-inch spike heels, because she keeps on agreeing with you and saying 'Well, this is it'. Or because his shoes squeak *on purpose* (we are not in rational areas here); because he has a deep, annoying, masculine Freemason sort of laugh that makes you want to assault him with a crowbar; because he has pictures of three grinning kids on his desk and you are having an access battle over yours. Add a habit of tunelessly humming 'Abide with Me' under the breath, a hot summer's afternoon and a frustrating meeting and you have all the ingredients for a good Agatha Christie stabbing any day.

Except that violence rarely breaks out. The people concerned merely squeak and grind and grate against one another, sending acrid fumes of resentment across the office. Whenever Personnel tries to investigate, everyone says through gritted teeth 'No – very good worker – can't complain'. It is the hate which dare not speak its name.

And what will the psychotribologist do? Why, lubricate them, of course. First with drink: I will take the grinding gears out separately for lunch and winkle out of them what particular way of laughing Nyah-nyah-nyah on the telephone, what deliberate inability to change the paper in the fax machine has brought on this helpless enmity. The next step is to move into that office myself for a week, and guarantee to be so annoying that everyone will unite in detesting me. I have a particularly good line in singing 'Ya picked a fine time to leave me, Lucille' under my breath, and my reminiscences of convent schooldays have brought deskmates to their knees in days. After I go, nothing will ever seem so bad again.

I shall charge a great deal for this service.

30 March 1992

168

The man who saved Labour

Patricia Hewitt

At a private dinner earlier this year, Neil Kinnock was being pressed by a group of businessmen worried that Labour in government would abandon its pledges. With great force, he leant towards them and said: 'You people know what it's like to take over a bankrupt company and turn it around. In 1983, I took over an unelectable party. I've spent nine years making it fit for government. And I haven't come this far to throw it all away once we're elected.'

I first met Neil Kinnock during the 1983 campaign, when he came to speak at an election rally in Leicester, where I was a Labour candidate. Typically, in that shambolic campaign, it was his second speech of the evening, his fourth of the day. His voice had almost gone, but not the anger and passion which culminated in his eve of poll speech, 'I warn you'.

Last Thursday night, the anger and the passion were just as strong, the voice just as strained. But in nine years, the party – and the man – had been transformed.

The party which elected Neil Kinnock with a rapturous majority in October 1983 had no idea what it was getting. It had forgotten his conference speech two years earlier, when, as education spokesman, he refused to commit himself to restoring 'the cuts', warning instead that if everything Labour said about Mrs Thatcher's government were true, then the problems Labour would inherit made easy promises impossible. The party ignored the implications of his campaign against Tony Benn and the abstention in the deputy leadership contest in 1981.

The man whom Labour elected nearly nine years ago

detested those who preferred the purity of opposition to the hard choices of power. Unshakeably from the Left, he had no time for the posturing of the Left's factions. He set out to win the power needed to implement Labour's principles, never to choose between power and principles. Last Wednesday night, home in his Islwyn constituency, he was still urging the British people to 'vote your values'.

As he transformed Labour with singleminded ruthlessness, he was often on his own. Sometimes, in the privacy of his office, he would admit to longing for a colleague who would offer him the unquestioning loyalty he had given Michael Foot before 1983. Instead, he had to construct his own majority.

He inherited a shadow cabinet most of whom had voted for a different leader. He won their respect, and gradually transformed the shadow cabinet by appointing the 'young, gifted and Kinnockite'. He inherited a National Executive Committee bitterly divided between Right and Left. He set about building alliances and marginalizing those who were irreconcilable. With his devastating attack on Derek Hatton in Bournemouth in 1985, he finally sloughed off the hard Left, in the constituencies as well as on the NEC. And even then, it was Mr Kinnock who had to lead the gruelling work of seeing through the expulsions and, later, reforming the constitution to provide for a saner way of doing things.

As Labour's opinion-poll lead crumbled before the 1987 election, and we faced a campaign in which the only issue seemed to be whether Labour or the Alliance would take third place, he knew that all the changes had not been enough. It was his campaign in 1987 – and above all, his speeches – which saved Labour from extinction.

After nearly nine years in the most thankless job in British politics, Neil Kinnock has discovered in himself a steeliness and courage which perhaps even he only guessed at. He has taken everything the tabloids could heap on him and his family, and come out stronger. He has borne with immense dignity the jibes of Oxbridge columnists at his Cardiff education and the whispering campaign of colleagues who, when times were tough, told journalists that it was time for him to go – but never said it to his face.

Once, when the sneers were particularly malicious, Dora Gaitskell walked along from the Lords to the office under Big Ben, to tell him: 'I travel on the buses and that's not what people say about you there. Don't take any notice of what the others are saying: they're just snobs.' Only recently did English snobbery give way to respect for the man he really was.

A few days ago, I reminded Neil Kinnock of something he said nearly nine years ago. 'We may not manage it. But we'll give it everything we've got. And if it turns out to be impossible, we mustn't blame ourselves.' In 1992, it turned out to be impossible. Nothing that he or anyone else could have done would have withstood the avalanche of fear which engulfed Labour last Thursday.

Neil Kinnock took Labour from the edge of extinction and transformed it into the voice of modern European social democracy. He has discovered in himself the strength which would have made him a good and probably a great prime minister. But this is no obituary, and Neil Kinnock's voyage is not ended. Whatever he chooses to do, he will be there, using all his force in the great task of winning support for the values in which he and millions of British people continue to believe.

14 April 1992

Time to get tough in Ulster

Conor Cruise O'Brien

The replacement of Peter Brooke as Secretary of State for Northern Ireland looks like signalling a change of priorities in the province. Throughout his tenure, Peter Brooke put the quest for a political solution first and security second. The right priority is the other way round, as Mr Major may have been persuaded by the IRA bombs in London just after his electoral victory.

The political solution Mr Brooke so diligently sought – a compromise between Unionist and Nationalist parliamentarians – is almost certainly unattainable, and certainly incapable, if temporarily attained, either of providing Northern Ireland with stable government, or of ending or even reducing the violence. Remember that the Anglo-Irish Agreement was supposed to bring about 'the isolation of the men of violence', yet after more than six years under the agreement, there is a higher level of violence than there was before 1985. The IRA is now more capable than it was before of striking repeated blows at the heart of London, and the blows are getting heavier: one of last week's bombs was reported to be the heaviest ever exploded by the IRA. The kind of agreement Peter Brooke was looking for would have had no more beneficial effect than the Anglo-Irish Agreement has had.

Sir Patrick Mayhew is best known in Ireland for obdurate replies to various nationalist demands in the security field. The Dublin press registered 'deep dismay' at his appointment, but Sir Patrick's unpopularity with the Nationalists will ensure for him a measure of popularity with the Unionists. And after all, in Northern Ireland last week, 56 per cent voted for parties supporting the Union (including the Conservative candidates), whereas only 33 per cent voted for the Nationalists (SDLP and Sinn Fein).

I believe John Major really wishes to strengthen the Union between Great Britain and Northern Ireland, and that he has appointed Sir Patrick Mayhew for that purpose. If so, Sir Patrick's first year as Secretary of State should run something like this. On arrival, he will make a speech expressing the government's determination to uphold the United Kingdom of Great Britain and Northern Ireland, and to defeat terrorist conspiracies of all descriptions.

Asked about the Anglo-Irish Agreement, he will say that it remains in being, and that he hopes shortly to attend a meeting of the Anglo-Irish intergovernmental conference. Asked about the 'Brooke talks', he will say that he will be happy to preside over a continuation of these, assuming that all constitutional parties so wish. He will make it clear that whether the talks are to succeed or not is a matter for the parties themselves. If they succeed, well and good. If they fail, he will continue to govern Northern Ireland as before, but with enhanced emphasis on security.

As his first important initiative, he will place on the agenda of the intergovernmental conference the Irish Supreme Court's insistence that 'reintegration of the national territory' is a constitutional imperative. John Major will then privately let Albert Reynolds know that unless the Republic abandons this stance, the Anglo-Irish Agreement may not survive. That intimidation will probably be enough to bring about a referendum amending the offending articles of the Republic's constitution.

Such moves will tend to dissipate the widespread impression that Britain is really anxious to disengage from Northern Ireland. That impression more than anything else boosts IRA morale and incites the terrorists to keep up the killing.

In the field of security, Sir Patrick will make known to the security forces that the government has in mind, for certain contingencies, the introduction of selective internment, on an even-handed basis for both sets of paramilitary god-fathers, and that the security forces are to be ready to apply internment at short notice. Internment could then follow immediately on the next major escalation of paramilitary violence.

The SDLP will not be happy about the new course. But the Secretary of State can make two things clear to them. First, that he is bound to resist all attempts at progress towards their ultimate objective: the dissolution of the Union. Second, that as long as they remain at best neutral between the security forces and a particular group of terrorists, the extent to which the Secretary of State can be guided by their advice on security matters is limited.

If things move that way, as I hope, a lot will be done to stabilize the United Kingdom of Great Britain and Northern Ireland. Stability is in the interest not only of Unionists, but of all the peoples of these islands. For the disintegration of the Union would be accompanied by civil war in Ireland similar to the Serb-Croat conflict, beginning in Northern Ireland and spreading to the Republic. Mainland Britain would also suffer from that conflagration on its doorstep.

However things work out under Sir Patrick Mayhew, the change of tack and of priorities is already clear. Interviewed as he arrived in Belfast on Monday, he said that the government was determined 'first and foremost' to defeat the terrorists. He also emphasized that Northern Ireland is part of the United Kingdom at the wish of the majority of its inhabitants. These are new notes, both welcome and salutary.

15 April 1992

Rock and the charity bankroll

Peter Barnard

On 11 June 1988, a young singer-songwriter appeared at Wembley stadium in the charity concert for Nelson Mandela, which was televised around the world. The singer, an American, had been enjoying marginally more success in Britain than in her native country but she was still largely unknown. Twenty-one days later, on 2 July, the singer became a household name. She had an album at number one in Britain and 'Fast Car', a single taken from the album, was at number five. A month later, in August, the album reached number one in the United States (where the concert had been shown live) and 'Fast Car' was at number twenty. Tracey Chapman had arrived.

There is a cynical view that charity concerts do as much good for the performers as for the charities. That is not true, but it contains a grain of truth. Tracey Chapman's career would have taken off at some point but there is no doubting that some acts have cause to be grateful, after the event, for the enormous selling power of charity rock shows, a phenomenon which has recently achieved the status of a durable fashion.

Easter Monday will see the biggest manifestation of this fashion since, and perhaps including, Live Aid in 1985. Wembley Stadium is again the venue and the concert, in memory of Freddie Mercury, the Aids victim and lead singer of Queen, will raise countless millions of pounds for Aids charities.

Ironically, the power of these events to sell records and raise money is also illustrated in the career of Queen. The band had released a 'greatest hits' album in 1981 which sped to the top of the charts and was still in the lower reaches of the top 100 by the time of Live Aid. At that concert, Queen and Mercury played a set of stunning intensity, the performance of the night. Within days the greatest hits album was back in the higher reaches of the charts and was to stay there for two years.

Monday's Wembley event is a concert whose bill looks as if it has been taken from a rock *Who's Who*: Queen, David Bowie, Roger Daltry, Def Leppard, Guns 'n' Roses, Elton John, Annie Lennox, George Michael, Mick Ronson, Seal, Spinal Tap, Lisa Stansfield, Paul Young and a satellite appearance by U2 . . . the list goes on. The compilation of that list indicates the sophistication of rock charity productions. Charities have learned that a mix of styles is vital, hence everything from heavy metal to ballads, young chart stars to middle-aged superstars. And if big names are so willing to do this kind of work for nothing but their hotel and travelling expenses, how do seeming unknowns get on to these bills. Zucchero? Who he?

A huge success in Italy, but unknown almost everywhere else, Zucchero is on the Wembley bill as a means of tempting the Italian television networks, in which aim it has succeeded. Italy is one of more than seventy countries taking the television feed, either live or for broadcast within twenty-four hours. The final worldwide television audience is estimated at half a billion.

Harvey Goldsmith is promoting Monday's spectacular but there is another, less well-known key player. He is Kevin Wall, forty-year-old president of Radio Vision, which claims to have 80 per cent of the world business in marketing concerts for television. The Mercury concert has involved most of Radio Vision's twenty staff working full time on the project for three months.

Mr Wall operates from an office building on Hollywood Boulevard in Los Angeles, directly opposite Grauman's Chinese Theatre. This is where the real success of a charity concert is planned and measured. 'Usually these projects start with a charity organization coming to us,' says Mr Wall, whose company handled part of Live Aid and has negotiated television deals for Amnesty International. 'In this case Queen Productions contacted us. My first question is to do with the purpose: is it to raise money or to raise awareness, or both? With this concert it's both.

'So I have to strike a balance between revenue and exposure. Fox TV is taking the show in America and there are other, smaller pay-TV networks. They will pay around $250,000 [£141,000] and whereas Radio Vision would normally take 25 per cent, with a charity we take perhaps 10 or 15 per cent, to cover costs. We do it as cheaply as possible without killing ourselves as a company.

'It's roughly true to say that you have thirty-five or so countries where selling the television rights makes money for the charities and beyond that you are breaking even, but of course in those places raising Aids awareness is the key benefit.'

Whereas big markets like the US, Britain (the BBC is showing Monday's concert live) and Japan pay well, others pay very little or nothing. Eastern European countries, such as Bulgaria, Poland and Czechoslovakia, have little money, in some cases not enough to cover the cost of a satellite link. But the chance to reach big populations means that the organizers will pay for links out of other income. The most dramatic illustration of the balance between money and awareness is Russia, which will take Monday's concert. Russia has no money; what it does have is 100 million people with television sets.

The bottom line purpose of the Wembley event, as opposed to its televising and marketing opportunities, is at least to have ticket sales pay for the production costs of the concert. Monday's show sold out in six hours. Those costs include everything from the stars' hotel rooms to subcontractors handling lighting, sound, seating, security and myriad other functions, most of which are carried out at cost.

There are vital, if half hidden, benefits from television. Within the countries which take the show, television companies are encouraged to set up domestic credit card hotlines so that people can contribute to their own Aids charities while the concert is on screen. And television companies often contribute the profits from commercials, or advertisers pay airtime fees direct to charities rather than to the television company.

In one respect the relationship between rock music and Aids charities is an uneasy one. For all the publicity about Aids victims within the industry, rock's image is still rooted in the macho, heterosexual ethos that helped launch Elvis Presley, Buddy Holly, Eddie Cochran and other icons of the mid-1950s. The recent libel case won by Jason Donovan was in part a demonstration that rock's morals are still essentially conservative. Items of female underwear tossed from the front rows to the feet of male singers signify that this is still a world in which men are men and many women are, if not grateful, then at least willing participants in a symbiotic relationship which stars jeopardize at their peril.

Most big names have until recently been notable for their absence from Aids campaigning, at least overtly. A few, including Elton John and George Michael, have supported Aids fund-raising for a number of years and Aids charities talk of their 'courage' in doing so. Only since the late 1980s, when Aids began to be perceived as a heterosexual problem, has the rock industry begun casting aside its image obsessions and started to make Aids campaigning the centre-stage cause that it is now.

Even Queen have not been notably associated with the cause before and Mercury's affliction became public knowledge only in the days just before his death. Clearly Queen were too big to need fear a backlash over Aids and there was no reason for Mercury to make a private matter public before he did. But rock as a whole was for a long time reluctant to take the stage against Aids with anything like the enthusiasm it demonstrated over hunger.

Nor are a few phone calls and the rental of a stadium any guarantee that the fans will roll up to help the cause. More than one Aids charity has caught a cold by trying to organize rock events itself, hence the marked increase in the use of professionals over the past few years. Usually charities have fallen victim either to bad timing or too narrow a base as regards the appeal of the stars.

In late 1990, one of the biggest Aids charities, the Terrence Higgins Trust, put on a show called Life Serenaids at the Brixton Academy in London. It starred Marc Almond and Everything But The Girl, which outsiders might have thought would be enough to draw a crowd. The show lost £10,000 and taught the trust a lesson. Other Aids concerts have had to be cancelled.

'Concerts are the least cost-effective area of fund raising when charities try to run them themselves,' says Francis Cox, special appeals fund raiser for the Trust. 'Part of the problem is that they are terribly labour intensive and you never know how successful they are going to be. The planning takes a long time and in that time a lot can go wrong. In the case of the Brixton concert, we started planning it at the beginning of 1990 but by the time the show went on the recession was just beginning to bite. We couldn't get the numbers.'

That uncertainty contributed to the Trust having to make redundancies last year when its forecast income fell short of its forecast expenditure, but it will benefit from Monday's concert. Indeed it has already received a seven-figure boost from royalties donated by high-street record retailers when Queen's biggest hit, 'Bohemian Rhapsody', was re-released immediately after Mercury's death.

Aids charities can also benefit from obtaining the video copyright on events. Hysteria 3, re-broadcast on Channel 4 last week, is a comedy show run every two years. It is the brainchild of the actor-comedian Stephen Fry and viewers who switched off when the credits rolled will not have noticed the most significant credit of all: 'Copyright Terrence Higgins Trust Enterprises.' This gives the television and video copyright to the trust, a significant boost to the £100,000 received in telephone pledges during Hysteria 3.

That is part of the reason why the first move Queen Productions made when it planned Monday's concert was to set up the Phoenix Trust, a one-off organization designed solely to handle the income from Monday's concert. By the time it is wound up, Aids charities around the world will have made amounts that would be unimaginable through any other form of fund raising. If a minor side-benefit is that another Tracey Chapman rises to fame next week, nobody suffering from Aids will be heard complaining.

15 April 1992

Frankie Howerd

Obituary

Frankie Howerd was born to be funny. His forlorn, elongated face, like a bloodhound that had mislaid its bone, the expressive bushy eyebrows, the loose, uncoordinated limbs plus a lightning wit, sustained him for almost fifty years as one of our foremost post-war comedians. His secret was that he appealed to all sections of society. His bawdy one-liners, his ability to extract sexual innuendo from the most innocent-seeming remark with a purse of the lips or a lift of an eyebrow, were guaranteed to convulse countless fans. And time and again, throughout his switch-back career, he was taken up or 'rediscovered' by a new generation, including the more thoughtful who saw something deep in his shrewder side-swipes at life.

Howerd's highly-strung insecurity as a stand-up performer was with him all his life and showed itself in a nervous stammer on which he quickly learned to capitalize. Many of his enduring catch phrases quoted nationwide were the result of this hesitancy. They were delivered as imaginary interruptions of some joke or humorous narrative: 'Ah yes . . . Well . . . No, lis-sen! . . . No, don't laugh . . . titter ye not . . . it's wicked to mock the afflicted . . .' and so on. And if the joke didn't get the laugh he anticipated, he would draw himself up in mock high dudgeon and roar: 'Please yourselves!' At other times, he would exhort his audience to loosen something and enjoy a good titter. 'Let us not go home titterless,' was another of his cries.

On stage, Frankie Howerd, a long time favourite of the Queen Mother, was a comic of the old school who believed that the well-tried lines were those best loved by his devoted audiences, although they were usually sprinkled with new material being given a trial. It was a different story with radio, at which he excelled, and also, to some extent, his solo appearances on television when he would go to infinite pains to ensure there was fresh material.

Nevertheless, he had his favourite jokes. Typical was the one about two young mothers with new babies who meet on the street:

'One mother looked at the other's baby and said, "Oh isn't she small." And the other mother replied, "Oh, well, you see, I've only been married a fortnight!"'

Frankie Howerd was born Francis Alick Howard – he was later to change his name to Howerd – the eldest son of Sergeant Frank Howard, Royal Artillery. The actual year of birth was a secret confided only to his passport. He and his family moved to Eltham, Kent, when his father was posted to Woolwich, south-east London. He was educated at Gordon School and Shooter's Hill Grammar School and as a tall, thin, shy thirteen-year-old he became a Sunday school teacher. He first became interested in showbusiness when he successfully starred in his church dramatic society's production of Ian Hay's *Tilly of Bloomsbury*.

His ambition to go on the stage stayed with him in spite of a disastrous RADA audition, and he bided his time working as an office clerk until he was called up for the war in 1940, training as a gunner. He was to sum up his stock-in-trade at that period of his life as, '. . . born of natural shortcomings and weaned on necessity during those years at Shoeburyness.'

He failed to get into the entertainment corps ENSA (Entertainments National Service Association) or, as another war-time comic Tommy Trinder once described it, Every Night Something Awful, but ended his war service, after the cessation of hostilities, running a concert party touring north-west Germany. On demobilization, and with the unwavering encouragement of his mother and his sisters, he persevered as a funny man until in 1946 he was squeezed on to the bill of a revue at the Sheffield Empire as 'Frankie Howerd, the Borderline Case.'

He began to develop his uniquely individual style of narrative or what he called his 'one-man situational comedy' rather than the conventional reeling off of a string of unrelated jokes. The first of his catch phrases also emerged: 'I was a-mazed!' . . . 'Not on your Nellie!' and 'What a funny woman!' And when referring to his supposedly deaf piano accompanist, 'Poor soul – she's past it!'

At this stage, he achieved national fame on radio in the popular *Variety Bandbox* where yet another of his phrases, 'Ladies and gentle*men*' was born. He was soon topping the bill of the still flourishing variety theatres and in 1949 he appeared at Buckingham Palace; the following year he was on the bill of his first Royal Variety Performance. Recruiting Eric Sykes and Galton and Simpson – who later wrote *Steptoe* and *Hancock's Half Hour* – as his scriptwriters, his career took off and remained airborne for much of the next decade with more radio, annual pantomime and trips abroad entertaining the troops, including one to Korea in 1952. He starred in films like *The Runaway Bus*, *An Alligator Named Daisy*, *Jumping for Joy*, *The Ladykillers*, *Further Up the Creek* and *Watch It Sailor*.

Frankie Howerd was not the world's greatest ad-libber and relied heavily on his scripts so that an appearance on the popular quiz show *What's My Line?* proved disappointing. But a television revival of *Tons of Money* proved successful and he scored a West End triumph at the Prince of Wales Theatre in 1953 starring in the revue *Pardon My French*, which ran for 759 performances. In 1955, he starred as Lord Fancourt Babberley in *Charley's Aunt* at the Globe, followed two years later with another stage winner playing Bottom in *A Midsummer Night's Dream* at the Old Vic.

But his ever-shaky confidence was sapped in 1958 when the lavish and costly musical *Mister Venus* closed in London after only seventeen days and recovery was not helped when he suffered a painful riding accident soon after. There followed the first of the slumps that were to occur during his career when in 1960–62 he counted himself lucky to land a pantomime booking. Things brightened in 1963 when a new generation discovered him on the television satire show *That Was the Week That Was*. It was said that the producers wanted him as an exhibit of the last of the old music hall comics. Instead, the canny Howerd outwitted them by putting together a cracker of an up-to-the-minute routine and stole the show. He landed the roles of Prologus and Pseudolus in the hit American musical set in ancient Rome, *A Funny Thing Happened on the Way to the Forum*, which ran in the West End for two years. During that time he kept his name in front of the wider public with two radio series and the occasional television special.

He starred on Broadway in 1968 at the Ethel Barrymore Theatre, as John Emery Rockefeller in *Rockefeller and the Red Indians*, and in the early 1970s appeared in pantomime at the London Palladium. More films followed including *The Great St Trinian's Train Robbery* and *Up Pompeii*, which was a spin-off of his *double-entendre*-laden television series in which he played the mournful slave Lurcio. At first the leery nod-and-a-wink innuendoes caused some protest but his saucy music-hall delivery won over the more prudish viewers and it became cult viewing, running to two series, both repeated. The even broader sequel *Whoops Baghdad* was less successful. He was never afraid to experiment outside his field; he even tried opera, playing the drunken jailer Frosch in *Die Fledermaus* at the London Coliseum in 1982 as well as taking roles in Gilbert and Sullivan's *Trial by Jury* and *HMS Pinafore*. He played a number of Royal Command performances and was made an OBE in 1977. In 1986, he starred in a revival of *A Funny Thing . . .* at the Chichester Festival and in the West End.

Frankie Howerd was accident prone. In 1987, he fell while walking in the countryside, injuring his leg and a surgeon warned him he might have to spend the rest of his life on crutches. He once fell from the balcony of his hotel while admiring the view. In the 1990s, he became the darling of the new generation of alternative comedy fans in another resurgence of his fluctuating career. He was persuaded to do a show at Barking town hall, which he found packed with young people eager for his autograph, and last year he made a rap record which climbed the pop charts.

A lifelong bachelor, Howerd was a close friend of the film actress Joan Greenwood for many years and was engaged in his adolescent years to a girl he first met at school, although it came to nothing.

Frankie Howerd was a complex personality nursing a mixture of doubts, some depression coupled with a powerful sense of ambition and deep philosophical integrity. He took his humour seriously and had put together a fine collection of books on the subject at his Kensington home. Beneath the insecurity that troubles many stand-up comedians because they dare to presume to amuse an audience on their own, Frankie Howerd enjoyed his success. Once asked for his favourite memory he replied: 'It hasn't happened yet.'

20 April 1992

Change, and its effect on the pocket

Neil Lyndon

Money has been much on my mind this week. If you are in any doubt whether you should consider yourself middle-aged, take a sure rule from me. You may know with categorical certainty that you have descended to your place among the crustaceans of midlife when you catch yourself saying, 'Thirty years ago, a man would have had to work for a month to pay for that.' It has been that kind of week.

A youth from the village has taken to coming to this house at the weekend to clean my car. He charges £3 for the wash and 50p to muck out the interior – a job from which Hercules himself would have shrunk after my son and his mates have been in the car for an hour with their gums, chocolates, crisps, drinks, toys and vile delight in foul air. I give him the work on the same principle that I always give lifts to hitch-hikers if they have got enough brains to place themselves in a spot on the roadside where I can safely stop. The principle is that, having been in that spot myself, I will always give a hand to those I find there today. When I was seventeen, I spent Saturday mornings making a grimy mess of the wings and panels of Morris Minors, Vauxhall Crestas and Singer Gazelles for five shillings a time.

After my youthful double had finished the job last weekend, he explained that he would want to come, in future, on Sunday mornings. On Saturdays, he is going to be working in Woolworth in the local market town. I was beside myself with pleasure: my doppelganger had come to life. 'My first holiday job was in Woolworth,' I exclaimed. I thought I detected a minimal rolling of his eyes as he saw another hoar-laden anecdote approaching.

'I was fifteen,' I said. 'When the manager gave me the job, he said the pay would be £5 for a five-and-a-half-day week and I gasped aloud. "Yes", he said sternly, "it's a lot of money, isn't it; and you'll have to work bloody hard to earn it".'

'Five pounds a week,' said the youth, obligingly. 'Good heavens: I thought my pay was bad and they're paying me £2.75 an hour.'

He went off whistling with his bucket and my money. I retired to the kitchen to scratch my puzzled old head over a cup of coffee.

If he worked, as I did, a fifty-five hour week at Woolworth and they paid him £2.75 an hour he would earn £151.25. That's thirty times the amount I was paid in 1961. Is this a true reflection of inflation and the decline in the value of money in the period? Or is a better guide to be drawn from the difference between the amounts we earned for car-washing? His £3 is twelve times my charge for the same job (I didn't offer an interior service; too much like hard work).

It seems possible, though I'd be grateful if we kept this to ourselves, that he is undercharging. Another possibility, far more comforting, is that I was overcharging for my services. His hourly rate at Woolworth is slightly unfavourable compared with the £3.50 he can earn in about three quarters of an hour on my car. My hourly rate at Woolworth was one shilling and nine old pence. By that measure, dear old Mrs Harnden should have been paying me, at most, two and six for the smears I left on the bonnet of her Morris Minor; and if she is still in this world to read these words, I imagine that she will be feeling, rightly, that she was skinned.

These calculations and comparisons may be head-spinning, confirming the uneasy feeling that we have been living through a Ruritanian era of tinpot finance, but they include some degrees of measurable reality. If you want to lose all feeling for the value of money, try spending a week with a nine-year-old.

On a single day's excursion with my son last week we got

187

through more than £70. In the morning, we went bowling: three games, £13.20. We went for lunch in a fast-food dive: two small pizzas, two large soft drinks and a single serving of garlic bread, £15.25. We bought a pair of trainers, nothing flash: £24.99. We went to see *Hook*: £6 for the tickets and £2.50 for drinks and popcorn. Add parking, petrol, crisps and drinks at the bowling alley, sweets along the road and you've topped £70.

Thirty years ago, a labouring man would have to work for a month to earn £70. I would have had to work for three-and-a-half months in my holiday job at Woolworth. My young doppelganger would earn that amount in half a week. Even allowing for the effects of decimalization and the Wilsonian deception of a depreciation which would make no difference to the pound in your purse, this colossal inflation must still be counted bewildering for those who have lived through it.

My son does seem able to retain some feelings of prudence in the face of this madness. 'I don't like you to be spending all this money,' he says, and means it. I don't like it either. The treats, I tell myself, are modest, the shoes essential. If I can't take my boy out for a day in his holidays and give him his idea of a good time, I tell myself, there is not much to be said for working at all.

I tell myself that I am doing nothing more than my own parents did for me when I was nine, though we travelled by bus when we went to see *The Pyjama Game*, ate our lunch in the Odeon Cafeteria and dreamt not of bowling alleys and foot-high cartons of popcorn. None of these admonitions and reassurances from self to self provides much comfort. It still feels like a hell of a lot of money demanded by an insanely extortionate world; but that, I guess, is how it must feel to be middle-aged.

21 April 1992

188

Benny Hill

Benny Hill's humour was drawn from a number of sources, including music-hall and the silent cinema. He excelled both in mime and in clever word play. He also made great use of outrageous characterization, employing all the worst and funniest of national traits from cross-eyed Orientals to belligerent Bavarians and could transform himself at will from a bashful choirboy into a lascivious lout. He was the first British comedian really to harness the facilities of television to advance the art of comedy beyond the music hall stage without resorting to the dependence on the strong story-lines of the modern cinema. He pioneered the visual techniques of split screens and multiple appearances, playing all four members of the *Juke Box Jury* panel in one innovative 1961 take-off and in another taking fifty parts in one comedy playlet.

In essence, Benny Hill animated for the small screen the bawdy tradition of the seaside postcard, with its jokes about bottoms and bosoms and hen-pecked husbands leering at pretty girls displaying their suspenders and stocking-tops.

He was often criticized by the more po-faced sectors of society for vulgarity and the 'sexist' nature of his sketches, falling foul of the Broadcasting Standards Council and Mrs Mary Whitehouse and her campaign to clean up television. Nor did his penchant for scantily clad girls endear him to some of the more ardent feminists. He argued cogently, however, that in his sketches it was the men who lost their dignity rather than the women. Benny Hill never swore. Nor did he chase the girls in his sketches. The girls chased him. Whatever his critics said, for much of the viewing public both at home and abroad he was, year after year, just about the funniest man on television. He eventually became something of a cult figure in America and was revered by many of his showbusiness peers as one of the all-time masters of visual comedy, alongside Chaplin and Laurel and Hardy.

Benny Hill's persona was that of plumpish man with a moon face, a mischievous grin and the bearing of an overgrown schoolboy. The dirty joke and the rude rhyme were an essential part of his act, although they were usually conveyed by innuendo. The audience was left to pick up the double meaning while Hill protested wide-eyed innocence that anyone could misinterpret what he was saying. Hill was a master at leading his audience into naughty thoughts before ending with a perfectly innocent line. 'Two bishops in a bed. Which one wears the nightdress?' he would ask, then add: 'Mrs Bishop.'

He was a talented impressionist and one of the first comedians to make a feature of sending up other television shows. He also evolved his own comic characters, among them the lisping impresario, Fred Scuttle; Mr Chow Mein, the Chinaman with an accident-prone grasp of the English language; and the black-wigged madrigal singer, Herbert Fudge. Hill took great delight in word play, showing great originality in his use of tongue-twisters and outrageous puns. But he believed that television humour should be primarily visual and many of his sketches were entirely without dialogue, comprising a non-stop succession of gags speeded up by the camera and delivered to tinkling piano accompaniment after the style of the silent film.

Hill wrote his own scripts, at first in collaboration with Dave Freeman and later alone; he composed the music for his shows: and he was virtually the director as well, spending hours on one routine to perfect its pace and timing.

Benny Hill was born Alfred Hawthorne Hill of working class parents in Southampton. His interest in showbusiness may have come from his father, a former circus performer. After attending Taunton School – where he was taught English by Horace King, later Speaker of the House of Commons – he left early, and was a weighbridge clerk in a coal yard, served in Woolworth's and became a milkman. In his spare time, he played the drums in a dance band. While still only sixteen he was a property boy and played small parts in a touring revue, later becoming stage manager. He got his first chance to appear on stage at the East Ham Palace. The comedian's stooge failed to appear one night and Hill went on in his place.

He developed as a performer in troop concerts during the Second World War. He joined the army in 1942, serving for five years, the last of which he spent appearing in 'Stars in Battle Dress'. After leaving the army he went into variety, a tough but invaluable training ground. In a summer show at Margate he was straight man to Reg Varney, the cockney comedian later to star in *The Rag Trade* and *On the Buses*. In the immediate post-war years, he made more than 200 broadcasts, performing on such shows as *Midday Music Hall*, *Starlight Hour*, *Anything Goes* and *Henry Hall's Guest Night* as well as at least one Royal Command performance. Early television success came when he was chosen to compere a Forces show from the Nuffield Centre in the early 1950s. He was an immediate success with viewers, and within two years he had been given his own series, winning his first television personality of the year award in 1954.

Benny Hill was shrewd enough to realize that television performers can easily be over-exposed and outstay their welcome and he deliberately restricted himself to a handful of shows a year. In doing so, he risked the opposite danger, that the public would forget him, but this never happened.

Once he was established his style and his routines varied little but he had an unfailing grasp of popular taste and even when he had been away from the screen for a long period he was able to pick up exactly where he left off. In addition to writing his own scripts he composed comic songs, several of which became hits, in particular 'Ernie (the Fastest Milkman in the West)'. The show's finale was almost always a speeded-up chase sequence in which Hill was pursued by a mêlée of women in varying states of attire, police, irate husbands and assorted animals and children, to the accompaniment of the Benny Hill theme tune.

Between 1968 and 1988 he made about 70 of these one-hour productions for Thames Television. The programmes were rarely out of the top ten ratings, winning the Bafta best comedy award in 1971, and were enormously popular worldwide, being transmitted in such unlikely places as Angola, China and Russia. During the 1970s, Hill was one of the few British comedians to be successful both in America and Europe. Compilations of sketches from his television shows were screened from coast to coast in the United States and enjoyed huge ratings.

Thames Television, however, was eventually cowed by the anti-sexist lobby into dropping the comedian from its schedules. He was distressed by this snub. Recalling the moment, he said it happened at 10 a.m. and he was out of the building by ten past. After more than twenty years it would have been nice, he added, to have had a 'pat on the back'. He was later to remark that in one 'alternative comedy' act on television he had counted ninety-one swear words; yet he would get into trouble simply for: 'looking at a girl and saying: "Oh her dumplings are boiling over!"'. During the following three years Hill made only one television programme – for American audiences.

Early in his career, in the 1950s, he appeared in two West End revues, *Paris By Night* and *Fine Fettle*, but he then abandoned the theatre completely. In the 1960s, he was in several films, among them *Those Magnificent Men in Their Flying Machines*, *Chitty Chitty Bang Bang* and *The Italian Job*. Like other television comedians, though, he had less impact on the larger screen. In 1964, he made a single excursion into Shakespeare, playing Bottom in a television production of *A Midsummer Night's Dream*.

Unlike many fellow comedians Benny Hill never appeared

192

to be weighed down by the responsibility of being funny. He enjoyed his craft, was a perfectionist in its practice but avoided taking himself too seriously. He was a cultivated man with wide interests. He travelled extensively and spent much time in France, speaking French with ease, as well as some German and Spanish. He had a reputation for being unfailingly courteous and caring. He never married and did his best to keep his private life private. In response to perpetual enquiries, resulting from the fact that he was so often surrounded by pretty girls, he said he had had three serious attachments and in each his proposal of marriage had been rejected.

Despite being one of the highest paid entertainers in Britain, Hill lived simply. He had a London flat and a modest house in his home town of Southampton. He never owned a car and did his own shopping in the local supermarket. His passion was travel and wherever he went he was on the look-out for some quirk of human behaviour that could be worked into a gag for his next show.

22 April 1992

Fitting the cosmic jigsaw

Arnold Wolfendale

Of the physical sciences, astronomy is unique in its popular appeal, and within it cosmology stands supreme. Just how did the universe start? How did galaxies form and stars, and planets and . . . ? No one who has looked at the sky on a dark moonless night can fail to be moved by the vastness and beauty of the heavens or not want to know more about it. Hence, the excitement at this week's announcement by Dr George Smoot in Washington that the Cosmic Background Explorer Satellite has detected evidence for the birth of the universe in the form of huge ripples of matter at the universe's edge.

To understand the significance of this finding, we need to know how it fits into the now conventional Big Bang theory of the origins of the universe. According to this theory, some 15,000 million years ago a 'big bang' marked the start of both space and time. After some very early mischief, which we still do not understand, the light nuclei formed – mainly hydrogen and helium – but it was not until some half a million years after the Big Bang that the temperature had reduced enough for the nuclei to capture electrons and form atoms. Later, these atoms clumped together to form 'clouds', from which the galaxies grew.

The Big Bang theory received great support in 1964 with the discovery by Arno Penzias and Robert Wilson at the Bell Telephone Laboratories of the so-called 'cosmic microwave background' – radiation at a temperature of nearly three degrees Kelvin, and the birth of observational cosmology stems from that time.

This low-temperature radiation glow – the embers of the

Big Bang – should have within it the imprints of tiny enhancements of radiation showing the hot spots on which galaxies were to form much later on. It is these imprints that our colleagues in America claim to have found. Many theoretical cosmologists confidently predicted they were present, but it must be admitted that some had almost begun to despair because of the difficulty of seeing them (their magnitude corresponding only to about one part in one hundred thousand).

The main difficulty has been in distinguishing the observed signals – previously detected mainly by radio telescopes – from effects due to cosmic ray electrons wandering about in our own galaxy. My own research group showed that some previous hints could be explained in this way, and the effects went away when new observations were made.

The virtue of the latest results is that they have been made at higher frequencies than can be used from the ground, and where the 'cosmic ray foreground' can be guaranteed to be small. Nevertheless, there are other hazards which have to be taken into account, most notably the effect of dust in the space between the stars. This dust is warmed by starlight and can mimic the sought-for effects if one is not careful. My first inclination was to be very sceptical about the results, having been brought up on the Russian cosmologist Lev Landau's dictum 'cosmology is often wrong, but never in doubt'.

Dust really is a menace, and Dr Smoot's comment about the presence of 'ripples' of wispy clouds worried me mightily, not to mention the fact that the claimed detection is on the edge of their limit of detectability. However, having received a message from an old student who worked with me on the dust problem and is now a member of the Cosmic Background Explorer team, I am rather happier. He tells me that the results pass all the tests. Nevertheless, great care is still needed, and it is a pity that there has been such a great flurry of publicity about the results before the scientific community has had the chance to go through them thoroughly. This will certainly need to be done.

What should our reaction be to the discovery if, as seems likely, it is correct? A sense of perspective is necessary. The Big Bang theory was so well developed in other ways that it would have been more exciting, in one respect, if the small signals had not been present. We should regard the observations as providing another piece of the cosmic jigsaw which is allowing us to evolve 'a theory of everything' (everything, that is, in the material world – I see nothing to militate against the existence of God in any of the work that has been done; the reverse, perhaps).

Among astronomers, the hunt will quicken for the dark matter which seems to account for some 95 per cent of the mass of the universe. I would regard the identification of whatever 'particles' are responsible for this missing mass as just as important as this week's findings – perhaps even more so.

A related, and fascinating, question concerns the fate of the universe. Will it expand forever, or eventually return to a 'Big Crunch', from which perhaps another universe would grow, and so on? The simplest Cold Dark Matter model, which the present work supports, suggests that the universe is so finely tuned that it will come back, but only after an infinite time. Cosmology will not cease to fascinate.

25 April 1992

Painter bursting with exhilarated despair

Richard Cork

The first time I met Francis Bacon, for an interview in the early 1970s, I approached his South Kensington mews with trepidation. Would I be greeted by a writhing, turbulent figure, so obsessed with his own neuroses that conversation proved impossible to sustain?

My anxiety could hardly have been more misplaced. Charming, convivial and wonderfully eager to talk, he greeted me enthusiastically at the top of his steep, narrow stairs. Preparing at the time for his immense retrospective exhibition at the Grand Palais in Paris, he was prepared nevertheless to spend the whole morning ranging inexhaustibly over art and literature, from Velázquez and Proust to Rembrandt, Greek tragedy and T. S. Eliot. Stimulating, often provocative and above all intensely energetic, the conversation continued over a bibulous Soho lunch and terminated tipsily in the ramshackle Colony Club.

I realized, on that bacchanalian day, just how much this animated man relished life. Far from viewing it with depressive morbidity, he savoured his defiantly unconventional existence with boundless zest. The same gusto animates his paintings. Isolated the figures may often be, but they are far from limp or defeated. At their most dynamic, they fill the entire canvas with protesting howls. But even when simply sitting on a chair, accompanied by one of the sinister shadows Bacon favoured, these solitary men have a tense, coiled dynamism that counters their awareness that each of us is, in the end, alone.

Bacon himself claimed that he looked on life with 'exhilarated despair'. The horror is there all right, as well as the violence that erupted in the world on so many occasions during his lifetime. But Bacon's awareness of man's capacity for bestiality is offset by his stubborn belief in grandeur.

Viewers who recoil from Bacon in disgust are unable to grasp the more positive aspects of his art. But they are a vital part of his towering achievement. Bacon set great store by accident when painting, and his finest work is galvanized by an exuberant sense of risk. An inveterate gambler, he loved to surprise himself in painting as in life. The many canvases he destroyed throughout his career testify to his impatience with predictability. In Bacon's greatest canvases, his impulsive handling of paint has an astonishing eloquence as he pummels, caresses, obliterates and coaxes the pigment at will.

At the same time, though, Bacon has a passion for order. His compositions are always calculated and refined, playing off the convulsive figures against areas of flat, semi-abstract colour. He liked immaculate painting, and the tormented passages in his work gain enormously from their contrast with the clean, plain areas surrounding them.

Bacon's superb finesse, coupled with an instinctive monumentality, counteracts the depressing aspects of his world. Indeed his exhilaration seems all the more persuasive precisely because it is pitched against the confinement and vulnerability of the human condition. Bacon's assertion of a resilient vigour could not be more hard won. And in some of his most impressive pictures naked figures close on one another with extraordinary erotic forcefulness, as if trying to combat their former isolation.

Bacon will be remembered, not only as the finest British painter of his time, but one of the most outstanding artists anywhere in the late twentieth-century world. With his death, painting suffers an incalculable loss. When we met for the last time a few months ago he told me that he hated the thought of death, before pausing and then brightening with a defiant cry: 'Shall we have some champagne?'

29 April 1992

Moving scenes as Alice and the crew break into showbiz

Paul Heiney

In one mad burst of frenzied activity involving much mooing, plaintive bleating, and disgruntled grunting, the entire scene changed. It is as if a curtain has been rung down on the first act of a spectacular rural musical, and during a brief interval an army of stagehands has moved the scenery and revolved the seasons from frost to cow-parsley in a moment.

First on stage for Act II were the cows. With the grass and clover well on its way to knee-height, it seemed time to bring down the curtain on their winter season in the farm-yard and offer them a wider touring engagement.

The cow and the bullock have had several seasons at pasture, but the calves were born only at the end of September and so they are new players at this grazing game. Show business has always advised strongly against working with children and animals, and since the children in my particular extravaganza are animals as well, you see how daunted I feel.

So I called on the help of Farmer White and his team of lads to act as assistant stage-managers and ensure the cattle tripped lightly in the right direction, and not down the lane heading for the main road.

I gave the cue by opening the gate. The cattle shot through like first-nighters diving for the reviews. They pranced along like a fat red ballet chorus, conducted by our waving hands and flailing sticks. Farmer White charges for his services by the hour, and I guess that when we reached the meadow, such was their speed that the whole operation would have netted him about three pence. He would do well to learn the box-office trick of charging by the head and not by the length of the play. On arrival in the meadow, the confused beasts started to tune up with a relentless throaty moo. They seemed displeased, but unsure why.

Then it was the turn of the sheep to play the tragic scene, and with some justification. I had decided to wean the larger young lambs from their mothers. This is distressing for all concerned; not only do you leave behind a pitifully bleating lamb, you also have a cross ewe on your hands who has been both deprived of her offspring and put on the worst grazing on the farm in order to dry off her supply of milk. She, too, bleats as if her world has come to an end. But you can never be certain whether it is the maternal separation or the lack of a good dinner that has caused most offence. The bad temper seems to last only a day or so and then life returns to normal; but it is a truly moving scene while it lasts.

Alice, the Large Black sow, made only a cameo appearance in this drama, having declined all major roles this year. She and her litter merely walked across the stage from the confines of the sty to the field of clover where she will hold her summer season. She wants to be alone.

But the least pleased on the entire farm is our matinée idol: our pure-bred Dorset ram. He is a muscular, well-endowed chap who in another life might have been a Schwarzenegger or a Stallone. Boy, has he got charisma! Of course, he'll tell you that he is but a humble bit-part player who 'just got lucky', but no one is fooled. The performance he gave at tupping time last August will be long remembered.

So you can imagine his distress when I singled out an old ewe from the flock and pointed her in his direction. This sheep is more than thirteen years old and has produced twin lambs every season except this year, so we think she is past it. But we are fond of her and so she is going into retirement and will spend her final days providing company for the ram, who might otherwise fall into the depths of gloom, deprived of his bleating, swooning audience. He has to be kept away from the flock of breeding ewes, you understand, until August, when we hope he will give another spirited rendering of the performance he has already made legendary.

But I can tell he is not happy. He feels that if he is going to be shut up with any starlet, it ought to be something more like Madonna than Mollie Sugden.

It has to be said the old ewe does not have the box-office appeal she once did. Her fleece is rough, her teeth unappealing. The ram's bleat has a rough, offended edge to it. He seems to be saying 'I simply can't go on.'

But I have told him that the show *must* go on, because in farming it always does. It is a long-running drama and the intervals are too few, and too short.

16 May 1992

Are you listening to me?

Jonathon Green

I am perhaps seven. Visiting my Aunt Ann. Lots of clanky jewellery, and a somewhat dated (it is, after all, 1955) Veronica Lake wave. Generally acknowledged as the 'glamour puss' of our 1950s family, Aunt Ann is a bridge nut, about to depart for an evening's play. Well tutored in good behaviour, I offer a nephew's felicitations: 'Good luck, Aunt Ann.' Forget Veronica Lake. What we have here is raging Bette Davis. 'Never,' she positively spits with venom, 'never, *never* wish a card player good luck!' Aunt Ann storms out. I shudder to this day.

Only sporadically can I recycle the advice my parents, doubtless with best intentions, showered upon my growing head, but forty years on my aunt's snort of fury is etched across my memory. And never, never, *never* have I wished a gambler good luck since.

'We can't form our children on our concepts,' pronounced Goethe two centuries ago; 'we must take them and love them as God gives them to us.' But goodness me, how far from such ideals are most upbringings. We just cannot keep our hands off the next, or even the next but one, generation. Lord Chesterfield, endlessly writing to his son, told him: 'Advice is seldom welcome; and those who want it the most always like it the least,' while the social reformer William Cobbett dignified the meddling thus: 'It is the duty and ought to be the pleasure of age and experience to warn and instruct youth.'

The first parental advice, if we take literally the concept of 'God the Father', is of course the Ten Commandments. It may be that Adam and Eve hunkered down for the occasional serious chat with Cain and Abel but, as we well

202

know, the boys didn't listen. But the Decalogue, what a perfect paradigm for future parental caveats. All negatives – don't do this, don't do that, keep your hands off the other – with just the single positive: honour thy mother and father. And generation after generation, they have been at it ever since.

Scriptwriter Jurgen Wolff has taken it upon himself to amass a wide-ranging compilation of advice. His own family treasured a simple saw: 'Don't shoot your wife', an *aperçu* that followed from his grandfather having done just that, albeit with an air rifle. Quite what retribution followed was not recorded, but the family never forgot.

The Deity aside, authority figures, parental or otherwise, just cannot resist giving advice to the young. Indeed, the older they get the more prolix and unwavering becomes their determination to pass on guidance. As the aphorist Logan Pearsall Smith, the most confirmed of bachelors and thus immune to any familial snares, suggested, 'to deprive all people of their bogeys is as brutal as snatching from babies their big stuffed bears'. Sometimes the advice does have a degree of folksy charm. As one of Mr Wolff's correspondents recalls: 'My gran believed that, like wood pigeons', a human mate should be for life. Her advice to couples contemplating marriage was always the same: "If one's not enough, then forty ain't too many!" Thus, with only one chance to get it right, gran would advise the girls never to trust a man who carried a purse and to remember that kissing a man without a beard was like eating an egg without salt.'

Inevitably, much of family folklore tends to be amusing, if not downright absurd. Jumbled proverbs, recycled pieces of massively tendentious information, and cussedness are all potential sources. But they can be serious, too, and as Mr Wolff points out: 'There is a kind of connection and communication in families through these sayings, especially the serious ones. Often they get used when other communication isn't so good. Using these slogans was a way of showing that somebody cared or was trying to help. One woman offered me the advice her father had given her as a girl. And while the advice itself was somewhat mundane – boys are only after one thing, or something like that – she said in the postscript: "This was one of the only times in his life that my father managed to say anything personal to me at all. And it stuck in my mind".'

Still, fractured communication aside, the best memories remain the funny ones, many of which contain at least the germ of practicality. 'My mother always said, "Every time you go to the shops buy a four-roll pack of toilet paper. You never know when there'll be a snow storm." At one point we had fifty-one rolls in the house.' Good practical stuff, as is the oft-repeated adjuration 'Always wear clean knickers in case you have an accident', although a more worldly variation was sent to Mr Wolff: 'Always wear clean knickers, you never know when you're going to be seduced.'

The subject on which we all genuinely need advice, and the one that in most families is the hardest to elicit, is sex. Aside from the clean knickers dictum, there were a number of strategies for sidestepping grim biology. 'Mother's sex advice didn't involve any rude bits or diagrams. She just believed in "lock up your daughters" and kept us in liberty bodices and ankle socks until we married. We also knew that men whose eyebrows met in the middle were deceitful.' Another mother (it is always mothers; even with their sons fathers seem consistently reticent here) offered: 'Take a good look at his toothbrush. If you don't like its appearance, think what his mouth's going to be like when you're kissing him.'

The nuns in an Essex convent of the 1950s counselled girls: 'Imagine there's a 5ft circle around your body and on no account let a man come within it.' Another girl received the terse admonition: 'Use your knees.' Older women, in older fashions, were equally militant: 'Always have a hatpin handy.'

Not all advice, of course, is so earnest. Nor does it necessarily come from such close quarters. The opinions today's teenagers treasure are less likely to come from the much discredited family, but from the disinterested recommendations of strangers, especially if they are famous. 'Children begin by loving their parents,' pontificates Oscar Wilde; 'after a while they judge them; rarely, if ever, do they forgive them.' Forget toothbrushes, this is what the young appreciate.

So, too, the stars of fiction. Damon Runyon's punter Obadiah Masterson, better known as The Sky from the size of his bets, recalled what his father told him as he left his Colorado home town: 'Son, no matter how far you travel, or how smart you get, always remember this: Some day, somewhere, a guy's going to come to you and show you a brand new deck of cards on which the seal is never broken, and this guy's going to offer to bet you that the jack of spades will jump out of this deck and squirt cider in your ear. But son, do not bet him, for sure as you do you are going to get an earful of cider.' And, Runyon adds, The Sky follows this advice and never gets any cider in his ear although another bet, that St Louis is the biggest town in the world, proves less fortuitous.

In the end, as we find with so much advice, parental or otherwise, the world of 'My mother said I never should . . .' runs hand in hand with good old double standards. 'Don't do what I do,' says the aged one, 'do what I say.' Either way they probably will not listen, even if some of it does meld into the subconscious. I, for instance, seemingly in common with thousands of others, find it hard to throw my belief that 'you mustn't go swimming for two hours after you've eaten, because your arms and legs will suddenly become heavy and you'll sink like a stone'.

In the end, one turns to the American president Harry S. Truman, who summed up his attitude to any communications as: 'If you can't convince them, confuse them.' In the realm of the young, Truman offered this: 'The best way to give advice to your children is to find out what they want and advise them to do it.'

12 May 1992

Is Boris good enough?

Michael Binyon

A year ago a burly, silver-haired engineer from a remote village in the Urals became the first democratically elected leader of the world's largest country. The wonder is not that Boris Yeltsin, against all the political odds, broke with communism, challenged the Soviet leader, faced down an attempted coup and survived; the wonder is that after a tumultuous year which has seen prices rise to at least thirty times the old rate and inflation approach 1,000 per cent, he still enjoys a popularity rating of around 50 per cent. The worry is that he has become indispensable. While he remains in the Kremlin, there is an even chance that Russia will successfully negotiate the transition to full democracy and a market economy; if fate, a coup or a heart attack removed him now, the outlook would be bleak indeed.

Mr Yeltsin's first year in office has been dominated by the two issues that defeated Mikhail Gorbachev: the transition to a market economy and the nationalism that is pulling apart the fragile Commonwealth of Independent States. Unlike Mr Gorbachev, who was paralysed by the spectre of chaos thrown up by reform plans and unable to commit himself to any alternative, Mr Yeltsin has taken a bold, radical position and largely stuck to it. Even before the collapse of the Soviet Union last December, he had decided that communism could not be dismantled slowly; Russia had to break free from it as rapidly as possible. His first step was therefore to outlaw communist cells and party meetings in factories – a step that infuriated the old guard and arguably speeded up the plans of the August conspirators. After the coup, he decided to outlaw the entire party – a popular move which appears to have survived a legal challenge by the hardliners trying to reconstitute the party.

Breaking free from communist economics meant picking a government untainted by the half-hearted attempts at fudge and reform under Mr Gorbachev. Passing over senior, experienced economists, Mr Yeltsin chose as his deputy the man who has taken Russia's biggest gamble in opting for immediate deregulation of prices, Yegor Gaidar. At first Mr Yeltsin was reluctant to trust his government to an unknown, baby-faced academic and his twenty-member team of free market theorists. It took the threat of a parliamentary revolt by Democratic Russia, Mr Yeltsin's main base of support, to clinch the appointments in November.

Since then Mr Yeltsin has kept his nerve and his faith in the team, even when the price rises in January threatened hardship for millions and led to hyper-inflation. He has also stuck by his commitment to privatization, deregulation and the eventual convertibility of the rouble. He has taken Russia into the International Monetary Fund, invited in its experts and analysts, and broadly accepted their painful prescription of tight money, an end to subsidies, realistic energy prices and austerity. And he has stood up to his conservative critics, especially in the Russian Parliament.

Nevertheless, Mr Yeltsin has not been able to force through a hostile Parliament key elements of his Government's programme including privatization, a law on bankruptcy and, most importantly, a commitment to give back land to the people and farms to private ownership. He has had to rule by emergency decree, lending weight to critics' accusations of dictatorship. Nor has his support for the Gaidar team been politically blind. Faced with a groundswell of criticism over inflation, unemployment and bankruptcies, he has recently circumscribed Gaidar's radical zeal, sacking a liberal oil minister, bringing three old-style Soviet ministers into the cabinet and postponing full liberalization of energy prices. He has also begun to bite the Western hands attempting to feed him, criticizing the IMF and insisting that Russia will not bow its head to foreign bankers.

His tactics reveal a political shrewdness underestimated by his enemies and in the West. Former President Nixon was one of the few to recognize a fellow master practitioner. Like Khrushchev, he said, Mr Yeltsin concealed beneath an oafish peasant exterior an extremely sharp intellect. Like a powerful tsar, Mr Yeltsin has deliberately kept himself aloof from the daily battles between Parliament, still dominated by conservatives, and his Government. He will not expend his political capital, nor be the lightning rod for the anger generated by every clash. The big test came in April, when opponents attempted to censure the government, slow down economic reform and limit Mr Yeltsin's power. Rather than argue out his case in public *ad nauseam* as Gorbachev used to, Mr Yeltsin made himself almost invisible, encouraging squabbles among frustrated critics and appealing over their heads to the broader public. The mood turned against his opponents. His cabinet and his reform programme survived.

When under siege, Mr Yeltsin has shown resolution: no Russian has yet forgotten his address to loyal followers from atop a tank during the August coup. He came out with fighting talk also when the Right was mustering its forces to exploit popular discontent in winter, warning that he felt the 'hot breath of fascism' on his neck. He also knows how to exploit his popular support. He has travelled extensively around Russia as president to take stock of the mood. He has insisted on seeing the worst, on cutting through the trappings of office, on bluff talk and emotional rallies. Two weeks ago, faced with mounting despair over unpaid wages, he brought a second plane with him on a visit to the Mongolian border, loaded with 500 million roubles in cash, and joked that no one should now doubt his word.

Mr Yeltsin has had to deploy all his shrewdness over the other issue that has dominated his presidency: the tense relations between Russia and the other republics, and in particular the acrimonious and potentially disastrous quarrel with Ukraine. The focus of the dispute has been the unified armed forces of the CIS, and in particular control of the Black Sea fleet. In angry language touching almost on demagogy, Mr Yeltsin insisted at first that the fleet was Russian and that Russia would defend its interests. But Mr Yeltsin and Leonid Kravchuk, the Ukrainian leader, both know that they cannot afford an escalation of the quarrel.

On the need to preserve unified armed forces, Mr Yeltsin has reversed his position. He now accepts that the CIS command has virtually ceased to exist – except in the control of nuclear weapons – and has agreed to the establishment of a Russian army, with himself as Commander-in-Chief, and a Russian defence minister. He has also accepted that the Black Sea fleet will be split between Russia and Ukraine.

Mr Yeltsin insists that he has not turned his back on the CIS, and that he still believes in close economic and political cooperation, especially with Kazakhstan and the rest of Central Asia. But he has taken a tough stand on quarrels between Russia and its former fellow Soviet republics. Despite his early support for Baltic independence and condemnation of the bloody Soviet crackdowns there, he had resisted Baltic demands for an earlier withdrawal of Russian troops. He has also thrown Russia's moral weight behind the Russian-speaking minority on the east bank of the Dnestr in its resistance to the Romanian-dominated government in Moldavia.

More difficult has been Moscow's response to nationalist demands for the myriad of restless ethnic groups within the sprawling Russian federation. Here Mr Yeltsin's tactic has been a lofty magnanimity. Knowing how dependent the various autonomous republics are on Russia, he has happily conceded the principle of subsidiarity, and avoided confrontation with volatile groups such as the Tartars and the Chechen-Ingush. His patience has paid off: he managed to negotiate a new federation treaty that was in the end accepted by all, and disillusion with the more extreme

Nationalists is already apparent in such fiefdoms as Chechen-Ingushetia.

Mr Yeltsin's skill has been to rally the support of two quite contradictory groups: the liberals who believe communism made Russia cruel and the nationalists who believe communism made it weak. Maintaining the support of both has been crucial to his relations with the outside world but he has not wanted to appear the darling of the West at the expense of accusations of selling out Russia's interests. He made his debut on the world stage at the United National Security Council summit in January, where he established cordial relations with Western leaders – especially John Major – but he has not flaunted these back home.

Mr Yeltsin is likely to be a difficult guest at the Washington summit. And last-minute haggling over arms control details, together with some familiar accusations of American bad faith, will only help him at home, especially with the suspicious military. The advantage is that whereas Mr Gorbachev was able to present an acceptable image of the Soviet Union to the West, Mr Yeltsin can sell pro-Western policy to Russia.

Much of what leaves the West still wary of Mr Yeltsin is precisely what gives him strength at home: his emotional, impetuous nature, his risk-taking, devil-may-care attitude. Russians see in him one of their own: a warm, extravagant man, brave, reckless and with peasant shrewdness. Mr Yeltsin has adequately carried out the ceremony of office, but clearly is not the smooth practitioner Mr Gorbachev was. He has left diplomats floundering and his own officials embarrassed when he has disappeared inexplicably from view and cancelled meetings – with James Baker, the American Secretary of State, for example – without any notice.

Two big questions hang over Mr Yeltsin after a year in office. The first is his health. He is, without doubt, a hard and frequent drinker. Russians are indulgent of his infamous binges, though accusations of public drunkenness are becoming more and more a liability, not least because of the ammunition they give his critics. Despite considerable physical stamina, he has a history of heart problems, and has already suffered a heart attack. A combination of drink and overwork could provoke a fatal one.

The other question is whether he is in the end sufficiently committed to reform to lead his country to the New Jerusalem. There is no doubting his Pauline conversion from totalitarianism to democracy and acceptance of the will of the people. But Mr Yeltsin's inevitable need to trim to political realities, his reversion to some old ways and personalities from the past, his understandable reluctance to preside over the ruin of Russian industry in the cause of greater efficiency and IMF demands all raise questions on whether he can keep up the pace and zeal of reform.

He understands, as Mr Gorbachev did not, that the country cannot mark time or it will slip right back to the bad old ways. He knows that he probably has less than a year to show some results. He also knows that public tolerance of rising crime rates, falling production, food shortages, unprecedented corruption and the flashy stink of new money being earned by the privileged few will not last much longer. Russian anger may turn ferociously against him.

For the moment, he is a vital symbol of democracy and reform, a figure whose authority is indispensable to a country that has only ever made real progress under benevolent despots. But is this enough to rescue Russia from its past?

15 June 1992

Can the soft-cover turn away wrath

Victoria Glendinning

Who is this? His lazy eyelids drooped 'further and further until his irises looked like two moons sliced by clouds . . . Those low-slung eyelids could give him an exhausted look.' It sounds like Salman Rushdie, who cannot show his face in public, but whose face is familiar to the world. It is actually Gibreel Farishta, versatile star of the Hindi 'theological' movies in Rushdie's novel *The Satanic Verses*: 'It was part of his persona that he succeeded in crossing religious boundaries without giving offence.'

Rushdie himself did give offence, even though his, too, is a movie-universe of transformation, dream and fable. It was the movies, Rushdie has written, that made him a writer. *The Wizard of Oz*, seen at the age of ten, was his 'very first literary influence'.

The film fed his fantasy and amazed him with its 'joyful and almost complete secularism'. But it is the risky playfulness of scepticism, not rank disbelief ('too certain, closed, itself a kind of belief'), that makes for tension in *The Satanic Verses*, plus the consequent swings between self-distrust and megalomania, conformity and outrageousness, idealism and disillusion, the dream of home and the dream of leaving. 'When a man is unsure of his essence, how may he know if he is good or bad?'

The willingness to say the unsayable, to use the oldest stories of all to show 'how newness enters the world', as a film-maker says in the novel, is what gives *The Satanic Verses* its smell of fresh blood. 'Fiction is fiction. Facts are facts,' says the film-maker. Re-read three and a half years on, *The Satanic Verses* seems startlingly self-referential and autobio-

212

graphical, and frighteningly prophetic. In a writer's imagination, past, present and future, like fiction and fact, bleed into one another.

Where there is no belief, the novel asserts, there is no blasphemy. Yet hubris, and blasphemy punishable to death, are central topics. Rushdie, already a migrant from his place of birth, is freeze-framed in a worse exile since the fatwa. 'Exile is a soulless country,' he wrote in the novel. 'In exile no food is ever cooked; the dark-spectacled bodyguards go out for takeaway. In exile all attempts to put down roots look like treason: they are admissions of defeat.'

To write a book, says the novel, is to make a Faustian pact in reverse: 'Dr Faustus sacrificed eternity in return for two dozen years of power; the writer agrees to the ruination of his life, and gains (if he's lucky) maybe not eternity, but posterity at least.'

Much of the novel seems now like a commentary on what happened to its author after it was published, and why 'From the beginning, men used God to justify the unjustifiable.' To read *The Satanic Verses* today, knowing what we know, is a weird experience.

'There's not been a huge run on it,' said the young sales-clerk, wrapping up the paperback for me in the Corner Bookstore on the corner of Madison Avenue and 93rd Street in New York. 'Not like the hardback. People who never bought a book came in for that, making a moral decision.' It was the same story at Barnes & Noble and at Brentano's, downtown. The paperback is on sale, and it is moving. (The initial print-run was 50,000. Two weeks later, 175,000 copies were in print.) The gold, black and red cover is suitably defiant: *The Satanic Verses: The Paperback*, as one would say, 'The Movie' (and who will make that, and when?).

But the paperback publication was not perceived as a critical event. The *New York Times* Book Review for 12 April merely listed its appearance, in second place, in its 'New & Noteworthy' paperbacks column. New York bookstores do not generally display paperbacks in their windows, and they have made no exception for this one. Nor do they hide it away; it's there on the shelves under 'R', in the normal way.

Here in Britain, where the risks to staff are greater, the bookshop chains allow individual shops to make their own decisions. Waterstone's Deansgate branch in Manchester, for example, has a prominent display near the till, while Waterstone's in Nottingham will take orders but is not stocking it.

I chanced to be in New York the week the paperback came out both in Britain and in America, after months of rumours, denials, negotiations and fears of renewed demonstrations. It is published from an address in Delaware (and distributed in this country) by The Consortium Inc – a group which remains anonymous for security reasons. The dedication to Rushdie's estranged wife Marianne has been replaced by one 'to the individuals and organizations who have supported this publication'.

The book's downbeat reception in New York may also be for security reasons. But not entirely. Friends working as publishers, academics, authors and journalists there all told me much the same story, which goes like this: most people who wanted the book had already bought it in hardback. American memories are very, very short. The Rushdie story is an old story, therefore it is a dead story.

The American ethos is that you look out for yourself, tote your own gun if necessary. There was no public perception, when Rushdie was in the States recently, that he should have official protection, nor was there any equivalent of a minister for the arts to give his visit official endorsement, even had it seemed politically desirable. American foreign policy (like Britain's, unhappily for Rushdie) favours closer ties with Iran. 'Guess we haven't helped much,' said the sales-clerk at the Corner Bookstore.

In fact, Rushdie not only spoke at Columbia University but was interviewed by Charlie Rose on his popular CBS television show. But Rushdie's American constituency, although ardent, is narrow. When the hardback came out, the protests of the Pen Club, an international association of writers, and the writing community were directed chiefly at bookstores that were unwilling to stock or display it; the contrary views of Muslim fundamentalists in the US did not involve book-burning, personal violence, or large demonstrations.

'If Rushdie had been a Sikh . . .', said a *New Yorker* writer; and 'If Rushdie had been a New York Jew . . .,' said a leading publisher, the implication in the latter case being that under different circumstances the Black Muslims might have been out on the rampage.

The Black Muslims are a social-protest organization of African-Americans, barely recognized by orthodox Islam. The fundamentalist presence in America may, however, become more strongly focused.

A brand new mosque is a portent. The mosque – the first purpose-built one in Manhattan, astonishingly – is financed with Saudi money and widely seen, politically and architecturally, as a big statement. To a Londoner, accustomed to the imposing mass and the dazzling golden dome of the mosque in Regent's Park, it seems a very discreet statement indeed.

On 96th Street and Third Avenue, it is no higher than the run-down flat-faced apartment-houses, zigzagged with fire-escapes, which surround it. Dwarfed by newer apartment blocks, it looks squat, faced with polished pinkish-grey marble, set in a small patch of what will be a garden, with its minaret beside it.

Yet the far more open presence of orthodox and fundamentalist Islamic communities in Britain did absolutely nothing to prepare us for the response, either in Iran or here, to *The Satanic Verses*. The indigenous British deal with otherness by not seeing it, or by reinventing it in not-us terms, which is precisely one of the themes of *The Satanic Verses*.

The book is reputed to be the most unread bestseller in

the Western world apart from the Bible, which, if true, has a certain piquancy. I was not among those who found it unreadable.

Not for many years will it be possible to make a purely literary judgment on the book, because of all that has happened – notoriously to Rushdie, but to us as well. I was totally ignorant, when I first read it, of the sacred stories of the Koran and of Islamic culture.

The first important thing to have come out of the *Satanic Verses* débâcle is the erosion of British ethnocentricity and of our shocking ignorance of the nature and content of one of the world's most potent religious systems, which is also one of the world's most potent political systems.

We are still ignorant, but not so pig-ignorant. I thought, when I first read the book, that although pedants in seminar rooms might tease out the tangled mythologies, literary allusions, double identities and so on, the ordinary reader could simply lie back in the channel-hopping, split-screen technicolor pleasure of ideas, jokes and images, and enjoy it – or think of England, which is, after all, one of the novel's chief concerns. I read *The Satanic Verses* in the way that a child reads *Animal Farm*.

You do not need a degree in Islamic studies to know what gave or gives offence to the fundamentalist in the street. You only have to know what he knows, or was told. The Prophet Muhammad appears under his devilish other name, Mahound.

The Satanic Verses themselves are those in the early part of the Koran which exalt, as do passages in the novel, the three powerful goddesses who are the daughters of Allah. These verses were later repudiated and expunged, since Allah is the One God. The other main cause of offence is a whorehouse where the women assume the names and identities of the wives and concubines of the Prophet.

There is more, but we'll leave it at that. ('And do not pursue that of which thou hath no knowledge': Koran xvii.)

216

It is worth mentioning, however, that the 'blasphemous' bits of the story happen in dreams, and in a dream-city; that Islamic poetic literature has traditionally provided a haven for deviations from and even attacks on the literalist religion of the orthodox; and that fundamentalist Christianity is much more explicitly caricatured in the novel, in the person of Eugene Dumsday, the crazed bore on the plane that crashes.

American Islamic fundamentalists don't burn books. They have become Americans. They drive taxis. Many literati in the States have stories about white-knuckle rides with Arab-American drivers whom they have conscientiously engaged in conversation on the subject of *The Satanic Verses*. The best/worst cab driver story was told to me by the British writer Jeremy Treglown. He has been in Austin, Texas, home of the Humanities Research Center and the Mecca, if I may so call it, of British literary biographers.

'What is the difference,' asked the black cab driver, 'between Elvis Presley and Salman Rushdie? Salman Rushdie is really dead.'

Ha ha ha. Not so. I would quote back to Rushdie the question put to Gibreel in *The Satanic Verses*: 'What kind of an idea are you? Are you the kind that compromises, does deals, accommodates itself to society, aims to find a niche, to survive? Or are you the cussed, bloody-minded, ramrod-backed type of damnfool notion that would rather break than sway with the breeze? The kind that will almost certainly, ninety-nine times out of a hundred, be smashed to bits; but, the hundredth time, will change the world.'

You may be that one in a hundred, Salman. You are one in a million.

16 May 1992

Returning to the leaves of history

Eluned Price

Many of the flowers and shrubs we take as common or garden – winter-flowering jasmine, Japanese anemones, varieties of rhododendron, chrysanthemum and cherry – are comparatively recent immigrants, owing their introduction to the intrepid explorations of Robert Fortune, a Victorian Scottish plant-hunter.

His story bears all the hallmarks of an eminently repeatable drama-documentary. He left school at the age of twelve, rose quickly through the ranks of under-gardeners to the Chiswick gardens of the Horticultural Society, the Harvard of career horticulturalists, and by the time he was thirty-one was chosen as the society's envoy collector to China. Attacked by pirates aboard a Chinese junk, and racked by fevers that almost killed him, he went where no Briton had gone before, roaming hills and islands, Chinese graveyards and the walled gardens of potentates and mandarins for a tiny primrose or a spotted laurel.

Five years after this first trip, he went back for more, this time disguised as a native, a horticultural Lawrence of Arabia, for the clandestine collection of tea plants for the East India Company.

There is more. There are tales of lost manuscripts, burnt letters, and among Fortune's descendants, lost relatives. Next week at the Chelsea Flower Show, Alison Durie, his great-great-granddaughter, will be hoping to find someone who can help to solve these mysteries when she and her classmates, horticultural students at Writtle Agricultural College, Essex, mount an exhibition of Fortune's flora and travels.

Fortune was born in September 1812 at Blackadder, near Kelloe in Berwickshire, and attended school at the nearby village of Edrom. He left to work as a garden boy on Morde- dun, the Buchan family's Kelloe estate, where his father had risen to hedger. After some years there, he braved the perfectionist employ of William McNab at Edinburgh's Royal Botanic Garden. Two and a half years later, McNab recommended Fortune as superintendent of the Horticul- tural Society's (later the Royal Horticultural Society) Chis- wick hothouses, and only a few months after his appointment, Fortune was commissioned by the Society's Chinese committee to mount its first expedition to China since the Treaty of Nanking, which marked the end of the Opium Wars and the beginning of China's openness towards foreigners. However, the welcome extended only to the treaty port areas. The Chinese committee furnished its collector with a basic kit of thermometers, hygrometers, a spade, trowels and a life preserver. Fortune requested fire- arms and was refused. He wrote to the society: 'I think [you] are perfectly right in the majority of cases – that a stick is the best defence – but we must not forget that China has been the seat of war for some time and that many inhabitants will bear the English no goodwill . . . A stick will scarcely frighten an armed Chinaman.'

Fortune embarked on the *Emu* on 26 February 1843, with a Chinese dictionary, a fowling piece and pistols. It was just as well. Towards the end of the first expedition, he was returning in a junk to Chusan when they were attacked by pirates. As E. H. M. Cox writes in *Plant-hunting in China: History of Botanical Exploration in China and the Tibetan Marches*: 'Fortune, at the time, had a severe bout of fever, but with no other Europeans to help him he dragged himself on deck, bade his own crew take cover behind the bulwarks until the pirates were close enough, then stood up and raked the deck of the pirate junk with a big double-barrelled fowl- ing piece. He drove off pirates on three separate occasions without turning a hair.'

He was paid a salary of £100 a year and given £500 for expenses, to be detailed with each letter home to the Society, together with receipts. 'You are required to keep a very detailed journal of all your proceedings,' read his contract, 'noting daily your observations . . . You will write home at every opportunity, numbering your letters consecutively (and sending them) in duplicate.' All this, presumably, in between fending off pirates and avoiding shipwreck twice.

The Society had very little idea of what Fortune might collect or where: 'The Council do not feel able to determine what ports you should visit, or in what directions you should conduct your researches.' The list of plants, 'for which you must enquire,' the society informed him, comprised a mix of the potentially commercially valuable and the botanically exotic, derived from hearsay. 'Camellias with yellow flowers, if such exist . . . The lilies of Fokien, eaten as chestnuts when boiled . . . The peaches of Pekin, cultivated in the Emperor's garden and weighing 2lb . . . Peonies with blue flowers, the existence of which is, however, doubtful.' He was to find 'the plant which furnishes rice paper . . . The canes of commerce and the varieties of bamboo and the uses to which they are applied.'

The Society's concerns were clearly not those of the disinterested botanist, indulging in horticulture for horticulture's sake. Among the first items on Fortune's list for his early trip were tea plants, which leads one to think that the East India Company may have partly funded the expedition as a preliminary trip before going to the expense of a full-blown expedition.

Between 1843 and 1860, Fortune made four expeditions to China, Japan and Formosa (now Taiwan), two specifically commissioned by the East India Company. 'Their aim was to break the Chinese tea monopoly and generate their own,' says Andrew Boorman, lecturer in horticulture at Writtle Agricultural College. 'Until Fortune returned with live plants, research on tea growing possibilities in India was a hit and miss affair, based on a few seeds and odd cuttings. China and Japan, in contrast, had perfected the breeding of tea varieties for specific flavours and aromas.'

On his first tea trip in 1848, this time in the luxury of a steamship, Fortune achieved immediate success, exploring the best green-tea districts inland from Ningpo, and the black-tea areas near Foochow. So successful was his disguise as a native (pretending to be from one of the northern provinces, to account for his height) that a friend in China failed to recognize him. In 1851, he sailed for Calcutta with 2,000 plants, 17,000 germinated seedlings and six expert teamakers.

Fortune's success depended partly on his use of the wardian box or case, a sealed mini-glasshouse invented by Joseph Ward in 1829, which, until Fortune's enterprises flourished, was used mainly as a terrarium and fashionable conversation piece. 'He was the first collector to use the box,' Boorman says. 'It eliminated prior dependence on seeds and made it possible to transport cultivated varieties that don't come true from seed, as well as species from the wild.'

Fortune's findings are taken for granted now: *Rhododendron fortunei*, discovered, as he described, with Scottish eyes 'in a romantic glen' and now parent of some fifty hybrids: *Skimmia reevesiana*, mainstay of the garden centre, and *Weigela*, now infelicitously renamed *florida* and growing in British hedges and gardens alike. He found it in a mandarin's garden near Ginghae, 'loaded with its noble rose-coloured flowers . . . the admiration of all who saw it, both English and Chinese.'

So everyday have Fortune's plants become, that they have been given common names. Bleeding heart, Dutchman's-breeches or Lady in the bath is *Dicentra spectabilis*, a ferny perennial 2½ft high. There is also the winter honeysuckle, *Lonicera fragrantissima*, which perfumes our gardens with tiny cream trumpets, Fortune's winter-flowering *Jasminium nudiflorum*, speckling sunshine on leafless branches, and the Japanese anemone, carrying its delicate pink or white cupped stars on tall slender stems in late summer and early autumn, which we owe to Fortune's discovery in a Chinese graveyard.

Fortune wrote four books of his explorations – splendid examples of Victorian travel writing, but thin on personal detail. It is said his widow burnt all his letters. A memoir by his nephew, James Marshall, survives, as do a few letters to the Horticultural Society. 'The missing link is a manuscript biography written by William Gardner, a botanical scholar,' Durie says. 'We are trying to trace Gardner's widow and the two daughters of his grandson, another Robert Fortune, a London barrister, who might remember tales about him.'

16 May 1992

Gods of the back pages

Bryan Appleyard

The odd, frantic and artificial issues of sport have never seemed more urgent and resonant. Something has changed about our relationship with games. There is deep symbolism in the spectacle of John Major in bliss at Lord's. There is national unease at the clockwork facility of Nigel Mansell's five Grand Prix wins. Nick Faldo's year off form has disseminated anxiety. And, of course, there is the tragi-comedy of Gazza's knee finally convincing the Lazio doctors: comedy because it is Gazza, tragedy because of the certainty that something else clownishly awful will go wrong. Everybody talks about these and other sporting things almost every day. Partly this is because the dramas of sport provide one of the few universal mythologies, small-talk material to fill awkward silences. The more elevated claim – once made by old American sportswriters in sub-Hemingway prose – is that sport is like life, a highly-coloured version of the conflicts, failures and triumphs that we endure daily. Sport is the heroic catharsis that reconciles us to our humble destiny. It is democratic, secular drama.

But there was always something tweedily, pipesuckingly academic about this idea. It was liberal wishful-thinking which compensated for the wilful refusal of the working classes to flock to opera by insisting that soccer *was* their opera. The idea spawned some high-flown prose about George Best as a 'whirling, Biblical pillar of fire', but it never felt right, and these days it is quite unsustainable. The whole point about sport now is that it is completely unlike anybody's life. Sport has taken off into a mannerist realm of

223

fantasy and myth. And, oddly enough, it works. In this form, sport is worth talking about again.

There are two versions of this myth: the global and the local. Tennis, golf, motor racing and athletics are fully globalized sports. Each is played by a closely-knit oligarchy of Marvel Comic superheroes who seem to dwell in an entirely unreal, personality-free zone. Nobody in his right mind wants to identify with – or even talk to – Becker, Agassi, Mansell or most of the Identikit athletes who will be streaking about Barcelona; and nobody expects them to do anything but play their games.

The point about such people is that they are obliged to be utterly professionalized. Their myth is that they are working at the limits of what the human body can do, and any awkward intervention of mind, spirit or character will only get in the way. Even their nationality is suppressed, except during those weird and dull competitions in tennis and golf when they are asked to play as teams. In the midst of a howling media circus, they are expected to display a passionless, colourless, monastic devotion to their discipline.

This ideal is, to a large extent, commercially inspired. All these sports are laden with sponsorship for global products which, like the superheroes themselves, can be distinguished only by the subtlest variations. Who can really tell Pepsi from Coke? And is there really much difference between a Nike and a Reebok training shoe? The point is that the product, like the sportsman, is a blank sheet upon which the marketing can be written. By partaking of the product we are supposed to be partaking of some fragment not of the hero's personality – he does not have one – but of his physical superiority.

Of course with heroes like John McEnroe there is a kind of madness, or with Ayrton Senna a kind of artistry, which breaks through all this and, indeed, none of the stars could conceivably be as one-dimensional as they appear. But the myth of supremacy prevails, and children buy the shoes.

The local sporting mythology tends to focus on team

sports. Boxing is the exception. Probably because of its distinctive working-class and ghetto associations, and because of the human significance of the idea of a man-to-man fight, boxing has retained a requirement for personalities. We shall not see Nigel Mansell doing pantomime, but Frank Bruno does.

Football is the sport in which the new mannerism has most fully taken hold. It is now *de rigueur* for smart, powerful men to acknowledge with arch shyness a passion for some football team, the more obscure and incompetent the better. This is more than just radical chic – the self-conscious embracing of working-class culture – it is an implicit boast that the man in question is human enough to turn away from the blandly global and embrace the small, local and culturally rich.

Football has risen to meet the challenge by becoming a brazen parody of itself. 'I'm pleased for him,' commented Spurs manager Terry Venables of the closing of the Gazza deal with Lazio, 'but it's like watching your mother-in-law drive off the cliff in your new car.' Football managers were always supposed to say stupid, meaningless things by accident; now they do it on purpose.

And Kenny Dalglish, because he has a reputation for being taciturn, has become absurdly, grossly taciturn: 'Speedie had a clear shot at goal. The referee has given the penalty, we took it and we scored.' Dalglish's words are as flatly descriptive as possible, but, coming from a legend, they seem laden with depth and soul.

Such localization makes football the last realm of the shamelessly politically incorrect. The need for the game to advertise its local roots makes national and racial stereotyping quite acceptable. African players in the World Cup were portrayed as happy black men, in a way that in any other field would have had the commentators dragged before the Commission for Racial Equality. All South Americans are described as highly skilled but emotional and untrustworthy, and every Scot, one need hardly point out, is little and fiery.

Both the globalization and the localization signal sport's attempt to dramatize and intensify itself. It is no longer required to be like life as it is lived; now it must be like some mannered, extreme ritual of conflict. And this ritual is cleansing and good. John Major likes to advertise his love of cricket because it displays his ability to escape from the terrible dullness and pragmatism of politics into something bizarre, wonderful and entirely acceptable. There would be fewer votes in a picture of him kneeling in church.

And perhaps that is the real message. Sport is taking on this role because nothing else does. Perhaps, after the wars and the great explanatory belief systems, there might only be boredom – were it not for the physiological intricacies of Gazza's right knee.

27 May 1992

Bankrupts who built a city

Simon Jenkins

A load of nonsense has been talked about the financial collapse of Canary Wharf, both by its defenders and by its
detractors. Any London historian could see that from the
day it was planned, this project would fall victim to the
oldest law of the property jungle: that cities grow not from
the profits of speculators but from their bankruptcy. Canary
Wharf tests the law to destruction. It depended heavily on
the personal backing of Margaret Thatcher, including a huge
distortion of public spending on London transport, not on
any market-led demand for property in the East End.
Canary Wharf would 'create its own property market', its
publicists declared, a sure sign for the wise investor to fold
his tent and vanish into the night.

Le patron mange ici is a sound maxim of the restaurant
business, and not a bad one in property too. Most of the
designers, sponsors and even tenants of Canary Wharf did
not eat, live or in many cases even visit the wharf before
blowing their money and their peace of mind. In conversation, I found few had the slightest idea where they were
going. They had no idea of the *genius loci* of Poplar. In the
face of a grand idea, the *genius loci* could go to the devil. If
their staffs revolted when they saw the place, more fool their
staffs.

Yet London has always been thus. Canary Wharf is only
the latest in a long and noble line of London's great speculations. My own favourite was that of the outrageous Nicholas Barbon, first of the great seventeenth-century
developers to 'leap ahead of the market' after the Great
Fire. Not for him the genteel terraces in back gardens of

227

old suburban mansions, built by such grandees as Leicester, Berkeley, Bedford, Jermyn and Grosvenor. Barbon was convinced the new city would move west not east. He lived in Fleet Street, dressed flamboyantly and bribed, cajoled, sued or intimidated any owner who did not sell to him. He pulled houses down overnight if owners resisted. Thus Essex House and Buckingham House gave way to streets of the same name, and Red Lion Square was built against the violent opposition of benchers from Gray's Inn.

Barbon's most notable speculation was Downing Street. It was so gerry-built that Government architects have had to restore it over and over again ever since. As Mrs Thatcher encouraged her friends the Reichmann brothers in their Docklands dreams, she might have reflected on the fate of the builder of No. 10. By 1698 Barbon was bankrupt, and he died crippled by failure. He left one characteristic instruction to his executors: that nobody should pay a single one of his debts.

Where Barbon led, others followed. The Adam brothers designed and built the Strand Adelphi, which in its day was as stylish and risky as Canary Wharf. When it duly went bankrupt, the brothers pleaded for a Government lottery to rescue it (David Mellor to imitate?). The nineteenth century saw wildly gyring building cycles: 1815–25 saw Regent's Street and Regent's Park rise to glory and most of its builders go spectacularly bust. Park Crescent was supposed to be Park Circus, but the lessee went bankrupt. To the west, Blashfield was ruined trying to build Kensington Palace Gardens for the then Crown Commissioners, and went off instead to manufacture terracotta.

Of the three men invited to build over the marshes of Belgravia and Pimlico – Smith, Cundy and Cubitt – only Cubitt emerged solvent. Cubitt's two vast mansions at Albert Gate (one now the French embassy) were known at the time as Malta and Gibraltar, because the public thought they would 'never be taken'. Where villas should have dotted sylvan St John's Wood, modest terraces appeared. The miles of stucco-land that rose across Kensington and Brompton west of the 1851 Great Exhibition were swiftly littered with crashed builders, 'India widows' shorn of their savings, and the eyeless hulks of half-finished Italianate blocks.

Nowhere saw such ruination as the Ladbroke estate in Notting Hill and Notting Dale, precursors of Canary Wharf in testing the viability of the suburban new town. Planned by James Weller in the 1820s as a *rus in urbe* to rival Regent's Park, the estate saw a century of disaster. Building did not start until the 1850s and destroyed more builders, bankers and small savers than any other London neighbourhood. Trollope had great fun at their expense. The Ladbroke speculation did not truly realize its social ambitions until the gentrification of the 1960s and '70s, a century later.

So does this just mean that Canary Wharf is far ahead of its time? Possibly, but how far is what will concern the receivers. Like the best London developers, such as the Bedford and Cavendish estates, the Reichmanns understood that quality of building and a sense of neighbourhood integrity are vital to attract nervous tenants to a new part of town. Their Cabot Square is pleasant and no expense has been spared on public spaces. Sadly, the developers were too greedy to keep densities low and to leave in place the serene expanses of dockland water: the docks have been reduced to mean canals. The overpowering blocks look the more bleak and lifeless when underoccupied.

But the Reichmanns' biggest gamble was to defy the law of the property market: that location is everything. Canary Wharf is not like Adelphi or Ladbroke or West Brompton in the history of London speculations. It is vaster and wilder than any before. These speculations ran with the grain of the city's growth. Sooner or later they were bound to fill up. For reasons that baffle geographers, most cities develop westwards, towards the setting sun. London always has. As existing tenants break contract and flee to more convenient locations, Canary Wharf could stand empty for decades.

Here was a rare lapse in Thatcherism's free-market faith. Over a billion pounds of public money was poured down the well before it was sealed, a folly of misplaced enterprise.

Visiting Canary Wharf in its early days, I assumed that when the banks had written off their losses, the poor would colonize it. First the Irish and then the West Indians saved Notting Hill from becoming a ghost town. Perhaps the Nigerian and Zairean exiles now occupying other towers on the Isle of Dogs will move into its great trading floors, setting up communities of squatters in its foyers. As in the hotels of the Costa Brava discarded by tourists and now colonized by north Africans, there is always a market for shelter.

Or perhaps creepers and vines will cover Canary Wharf like Angkor Wat. Children might play in its halls and East End gangs roam its piazzas. Or perhaps both will happen. Canary Wharf is a solid development. Physically, it will outlast the downturn in the economic cycle and be ready for a new dawn. For the moment, the inclination is to say 'Look on my works ye mighty and despair', but London would not be London without an occasional Ozymandias.

30 May 1992

Failure of Maastricht treaty could revive de Gaulle's Europe vision

Anatole Kaletsky

General de Gaulle was right. Denmark, Britain and the other peripheral trouble-makers should never have been admitted into a Europe trying to forge an 'ever closer union'. If the Irish and French referendums clearly approve the Maastricht treaty, this unspeakable thought will remain safely repressed in Europe's political subconscious. The Danish debacle will prove a storm in a teacup, and there will be huge profits for the brave investors who bought last week when the whole world was selling gilts, Spanish, Italian and ecu bonds. But if the Danish vote stirs up anti-Maastricht feeling in Germany and France, the consequences could be more dramatic than anything politicians are willing to discuss aloud.

At the very least, the exchange-rate mechanism in its present form would cease to function. Although the ERM existed for twelve years before Maastricht, it only became a system of permanently stable exchange rates from 1987 onwards, and it was repeatedly challenged by markets until the prospect of monetary union appeared on the political horizon. The long run-up to Maastricht, and not just the signing of the treaty itself, was what convinced investors European exchange rates might be permanently fixed, transforming devaluation-prone ecus, lire, pesetas and pounds into high-yielding bargains. If the goal of EMU were now abandoned, ERM's credibility would revert to its state in 1987, not in 1991.

But how serious is the threat to Maastricht? Given the

recent record of opinion pollsters, it would be rash to antici-pate the results of the French referendum that will probably make or break any attempt to salvage the treaty. But for investors who have to anticipate such events, three rarely mentioned points seem worth noting. First, there is 'real-politik'. Whatever the Treaty of Rome may say about unan-imity, the idea that Denmark could ultimately override the self-interest of the great powers of Europe is absurd. In fact, the European foreign ministers have already stumbled on a plausible approach: simply to ignore Denmark.

Only when every other country has formally ratified is Denmark's signature required to put the Maastricht treaty into effect. The first practical step agreed at Maastricht does not need to be taken until January 1994, with the creation of the European Monetary Institute. Until then, EC officials could continue to prepare for union precisely as if the treaty were already in effect. A second Danish referendum could be held any time after the ratification by all the other EC countries was completed. By then a new question would be perfectly justifiable, given that the other eleven countries would have formally agreed to create a European Union. For example, the Danish people could be asked: 'Do you want Denmark to withdraw from the European Community when it is renamed the European Union?' Even in Denmark, to ask this question will probably be to answer it.

Provided the other EC countries genuinely want a Euro-pean Union, therefore, Denmark alone will not stop them. The real issue is whether the German parliament uses Den-mark as an excuse to back away from Maastricht. For all the huffing and puffing in the press and opinion polls about 'giv-ing up' the mark, the German position, in turn, will probably depend on whether the French people confound President Mitterrand and all the pundits and vote 'non'. This raises the second rarely mentioned issue. Why should the vote in Denmark catalyze anti-Maastricht feeling in the rest of Europe, especially in Germany and France? Denmark has long been the most anti-federalist country in Europe, and even there the margin was hair-splittingly close. Furthermore, the Danish vote was not just a vote against Europe. It was also a vote against the extreme deflation suffered by the Danish economy as the price for monetary convergence. It may be only subliminal, but the Danes must realize that, apart from their farmers, they have not done particularly well out of Europe and have done particularly badly as a result of the ERM. Danish inflation has converged to the German level and below. But the cost, in terms of unemployment and lost output, has been appalling. Denmark, in fact, has had the slowest growing economy in continental Europe for the past four years and has suffered a collapse in the property market that makes the situation in London look like a boom.

In France, by contrast, the impact of the ERM has also been a dire one and the much-vaunted victory over inflation has been won at an unacceptable cost. But there is one huge difference between the French and Danish attitudes to ERM and EMU. For France, the whole point of EMU is to give the French government an influence over European monetary policy, which is denied it in the present German-centred structure of the ERM. In France, EMU is quite clearly seen as a salvation from the excessive rigours of monetary convergence; for the Danes, it is more of the same.

More fundamentally, the concept of European union has a historic resonance in France and Germany that is hard to imagine in places like Britain and Scandinavia, which have remained on the sidelines of Europe for a thousand years. From Charlemagne, through Napoleon and Bismarck, to Hitler, the entire histories of France and Germany have been about creating pan-European empires and unions. The history of Britain, by contrast, has been about colonizing the new world and avoiding permanent entanglements in Europe. It seems less likely, therefore, that the French or German people will react to the idea of a federal Europe with the same visceral suspicion and hostility as Britons or Scandinavians.

This leads to my third observation. If France and Germany reject the Maastricht treaty, it will be because many of their people and politicians want a tighter federation, rather than a looser one. Already this desire has been manifested in the Franco-German military corps created against the wishes of Britain and most Nato countries. But if Maastricht collapsed, the Franco-German co-operation would probably accelerate, of Britain especially in monetary policy. A subgroup of countries, including Germany, France and Benelux, might well move even faster towards monetary union than agreed at Maastricht.

The main question for the inner monetary core of Europe would be which other countries to admit. There would also be no question of 'cohesion funds' to transfer resources from the richer northern European countries to poorer southern ones as a reward for joining the monetary club. In fact, far from bribing new countries to join, this club's membership policy would be 'strictly by invitation only'. The main condition the Bundesbank would lay down for membership would be for far more centralized control over fiscal policy from the Euro-federal level than in the Maastricht treaty. For Britain, these fiscal criteria would almost certainly preclude membership, not because the government would be unable to meet the guidelines, but because it would refuse to submit its tax and spending policies to European control. In Italy, by contrast, a fiscal straitjacket for the local politicians would be welcomed by central bankers and voters, and even by the politicians themselves. Oddly enough, if Maastricht failed, the inner core of Europe might look remarkably like the community General de Gaulle had in mind.

8 June 1992

Man-made champion of the American dream

Jamie Dettmer

Steve McElroy was Ross Perot's blue-eyed boy. He had access to the Texan billionaire whenever he wanted. But his relationship with the man who wants to be the next American president turned into a test of nerve. A hero one moment, in a flash he became the enemy.

McElroy, a young inventor from the state capital of Austin, found out how it feels to oppose Perot and receive the full weight of his displeasure. In Texas, where Perot has made his imprint, there is nothing so remarkable about that, except that McElroy withstood the bullying that followed, and faced Perot out.

America is afire for Perot since he led President Bush in the opinion polls, but the country is still struggling to make him out. Could he be the most dramatic winner of the century, or will Americans revert to type by November? What should they believe of the stories that show him as courageous patriot and Machiavellian manipulator, as international action man and local maverick, as business genius and narrow-minded nit-picker? Even Perot admits he is a man swathed in myths. I went to Austin and the Perot power-base city of Dallas, and found people like McElroy whose first-hand accounts tell the tale of the man who wants the White House.

McElroy's crime was to refuse to relinquish a royalty interest in a product he and Perot were developing. He had written to Perot in 1988 for help in marketing a biodegradable one-size-fits-all lid for cups and small food containers, called Total Top. Within a few days of sending the letter, McElroy, then twenty-nine, was being ushered by security guards to the seventeenth floor of Perot's dark-glass skyscraper in north Dallas. He passed a bronze bust of Abraham Lincoln, a series of signed Norman Rockwell prints depicting an idealized America, and an early American flag.

'World-class idea,' Perot announced to the inventor, as he poured out aphorisms such as: 'Young man, you have to go out and collect scars in life before you can be successful.'

Their partnership went relatively smoothly for a year, although McElroy realized that 'there would always be a fine line between pleasing and displeasing' the prickly Perot. Suddenly the billionaire ordered that one of his executives should become the president of Total Top, and that McElroy should convert his 5 per cent royalty interest into stock. Perot was furious when the inventor refused. McElroy was denied access to Perot and, with his lawyer, was made to sit facing five unsmiling attorneys, as Perot ranted at him over an intercom.

'He became increasingly exasperated as I refused to accept his do-it-just-because-I-say-you-should argument,' McElroy says. Perot asked how much it would cost to buy out the inventor. McElroy momentarily silenced the intercom by suggesting Perot should sell *his* interest.

In the days that followed, Perot sought to confuse and intimidate McElroy into submission. He refused to sell, then offered to toss a coin for the company, and finally agreed to sell his interest if McElroy could come up with more than $500,000 within four days. When McElroy was on the verge of concluding a partnership with another business, Perot called off the transaction and agreed to the original partnership terms. 'Frankly, I enjoyed dealing with someone of his calibre. It was exhilarating,' McElroy says. 'I didn't find his behaviour offensive. I respect him as a doer. He is like a whirlwind.'

And Perot has certainly put the wind up Bush and Bill Clinton, the Democrat contender. There is obviously an element of voters using the opinion polls to express disillusion with the political choices. But such is the momentum swelling behind the outsider that everyone from Capitol Hill to California is taking the prospect of President Perot seriously.

He is in tune with the mood of the voters. He says he can fix things, and Americans, tired of the recession and exasperated with old political squabbles, want to believe in him.

What nobody knows is whether he would be a brilliant leader or a disastrous one. Perot is an outrageous self-publicist, and has said little about his policies. He says people should judge him on his principles, and has declared that he would bar homosexuals and adulterers from top White House jobs.

He made his fortune from the computer business, and he has used his money to finance lobbyists and to make contributions to the politicians of both parties. While he knows how to manoeuvre in the world of politics – he has twice been investigated by Congressional committees – his own direct experience is limited to two appointments given to him by Bill Clements, his friend and then Texas governor, in the late 1970s and 1980s.

Perot is as Texan as the next man in Dallas or Houston or Texarkana, the town of his birth and childhood, in his ability to mix myth and reality. He partly acknowledged this a few years ago, when he said: 'I'm not a living legend. I'm just a myth.' He is a short man at 5ft 6in, but he has lived up to the image of the archetypal go-getting Texan. But then, as the Texan politician Sam Rayburn was fond of saying, how tall a man is has little to do with his height.

Perot has said that if people want to know about him, they should read *On Wings of Eagles*, the book written by Ken Follett, the British author, recording the derring-do of a private commando team hired by Perot to free two of his employees from a Tehran jail. Follett was employed to write the book by Perot, who had editorial control, and there are disputes over some of the facts in the thriller.

237

Perot's first political appointment came in 1979, as head of the Texas War Against Drugs, initiated by Clements. This promptly brought out the authoritarian in Perot, according to Texas liberals. John Duncan, then the head of the state's civil liberties union, has claimed that Perot did an excellent job in 'laying a foundation for a fascist state'. He recommended measures which increased the penalties for trafficking and weakened constitutional safeguards requiring police to have warrants for drug searches and, with the governor's support, pushed them through the state legislature. He eased rules governing the evidence police needed to convict drug dealers, and new laws imposed penalties on landlords who failed to 'unobtrusively co-operate' with police searching for phones to tap. Another provision limited the liability of officers who might abuse their trust during break-ins and wire-tappings. Civil rights campaigners, such as Duncan and Diana Ragdale, a former Dallas city councillor, criticize Perot for his 'demagogic' methods in getting the measures through the legislature. They claim he preyed on widespread public fears about drugs. But Perot supporters argue that the Dallas drugs problem was so grave that exceptional measures were needed to combat the traffickers.

The liberals might have been appalled, but Perot gained widespread support from ordinary Texans fed up with the scale of the drugs problem. Even some who opposed him, such as Democrat city councillor Al Lipscomb, the first black candidate to stand for election as mayor of Dallas, now concede that Perot was right. Lipscomb's passionate support for Perot comes as a surprise. For years, he has been a left-wing firebrand councillor in Dallas, and he is a most unPerot-like figure. Yet, he says: 'Perot *is* Superman.'

Perot encouraged the development of anti-drugs education programmes for schoolchildren. A Michigan University survey has suggested that drug abuse among children in Texas has decreased, and the education programmes have become models for other states.

Perot's hatred of drugs has, however, driven him to make

what some consider extreme statements. In 1988, in meetings with police officers, he was heard by reporters to advocate the cordoning off of inner-city areas, such as south Dallas, and sending in police squads to conduct house-to-house searches for drugs. The reaction was predictable. Racial minority groups, which are concentrated in the inner-city areas, accused Perot of racism. He responded in a huff: 'It bothers me a lot to have spent twenty years of my life and tens of millions of dollars trying to help the minorities and get the kind of reaction I'm getting.' Now he is denying he ever espoused the idea: 'I did not say it, and it was just one of those unfortunate things that got into print,' he told the *Dallas Morning News* last April.

Assessments of his chairmanship of a state education reform committee in the mid-1980s also widely differ. 'He is a benevolent dictator,' says Bryan Eppstein, a Texan political consultant and pollster. 'When he sets his sights on something he doesn't give up until he gets it. He has a track record of taking away people's right to vote,' he says, referring to Perot's recommendation, in 1986, that the state board of education be changed from an elective body to one appointed by the governor.

Perot believed that the board was under the thumb of various special interests in education. But his proposal, which was agreed to by the legislature until the electorate reversed that decision in a referendum two years later, left the impression that Perot believed there are limits to democracy. The people do not always know best, seemed to be the implication.

Perot's style of chairing the reform committee worried many observers at the time. His us-and-them attitude was all very well when it concerned drug dealers, but his brusque handling of teachers was politically inept. Texan education *was* in a mess. The state, one of the richest, was ranked forty-fourth in America for educational achievement. The high school drop-out rate was among the highest in the

United States. Perot got to work with his usual enthusiasm and struck at a hallowed institution in Texas: American football. He mounted a ferocious assault on the state's 12,000 football coaches and on the Texan obsession with the game.

'It was the bravest thing I have seen an individual who cared about the outcome do,' said Ed Small, an Austin lawyer and member of the reform committee. Small is a fan of the football side he used to play for, but he backed Perot's argument that too much time was spent at school playing football. He supported Perot's 'no pass, no play' rule, which required athletes to pass all their exams in regular tests if they wanted to pursue their sport. However, Small questions the rigidity of the rule. 'Kids involved in school sports are less likely to drop out,' he says.

The no pass, no play rule received most of the media coverage of the Perot-led committee's recommendations. Other proposals included reducing the size of the average class from 31 to 22, which was well-received, pre-kindergarten services for children from disadvantaged families, an increase in teachers' pay and the introduction of competency tests for teachers. The latter proposal resulted in the walk-out of one of the major teaching associations, and guaranteed a fight for the reform all the way to the state legislature.

'Whenever he says he wants to bring people together to sort out the problems of the country, we just laugh,' says Annette Cootes, of the Texas Teachers' Association. 'He did not want to negotiate. We bore the brunt of his witticisms, and he can be a funny guy, and all he did was dismiss us as flat-earth people.'

Small rejects the teachers' picture of Perot's chairmanship. 'Yes, if he became president and we had another Bay of Pigs, I would not worry about him backing down,' he says. 'He does stay in a fight longer than most people, but he does listen.'

To drive his measures through the legislature, Perot used

240

his financial clout, hiring lobbyists, including those who worked for the teachers and other opponents of the reforms. Carl Parker, the Republican state senator, believes Perot was masterful in his handling of the state legislature. 'He came in and found out how the system worked,' he says.

However, in terms of academic achievement, Texas has moved only to 43rd place. Less than 1 per cent of teachers failed the competency tests, a result that suggests Perot was misguided in believing that poor teacher quality was responsible for the failings of Texas education. Perot argues that improvement will take time to come through, and possibly will not be seen until early next century.

In November, when Perot asks Americans to decide if he is a fit man to occupy the White House, his personality and private and business life will be nearly all that voters can judge him on. Should they choose the philanthropist who has given more than $120 million to charitable causes? Or should they reject him for spending his money in an apparent attempt to gain the favour of influential politicians?

How should Americans reconcile the three different versions of why Perot wanted to give up his commission in the Navy and leave the service early? When he applied for a discharge, the young Perot wrote to the Navy Secretary, complaining about the immorality he encountered on board. 'I have found the navy to be a fairly Godless organization', he wrote, and he said he would no longer enjoy the prospect of hearing the 'drunken tales of moral emptiness and seeing promiscuity on the part of married men'. Years later, he told a newspaper that he had wanted to leave because he was dissatisfied with the Navy's promotion system and its hidebound bureaucracy. Recently, he has claimed he wanted a discharge because the captain of his destroyer asked him to hand over money from the crew's recreation fund to pay for the redecoration of his cabin – an allegation disputed by the captain.

Perot served as a junior naval officer for four years, before joining IBM as a salesman in Dallas. After meeting his 1962 sales quota in January of that year, and becoming frustrated with IBM's inflexible bureaucracy, he left and set up the software processing firm Electronic Data Systems (EDS). His firm expanded rapidly after he secured major state contracts across America to design software to process public health insurance claims.

Perot's competitive zeal earned him widespread respect, but also criticism. His business methods were twice investigated by congressional committees unhappy with the high level of profits he was securing from state health agencies, as much as 200 per cent in one case, and disturbed by the high-pressure lobbying and massive political contributions that seemed to accompany bids for contracts. By 1974 he had become the largest individual financial contributor to political campaigns in America.

When he sold EDS to General Motors for $2.5 billion and joined the car-maker's board, Perot was already a household name in America because of his attempt to fly two plane-loads of food and supplies into Hanoi for American prisoners of war in North Vietnam. A fight with the GM board added to his fame as a straight-talking populist. He attacked GM's old-fashioned management style and its inability to see off Japanese competition. GM gave him $700 million to go away.

As he attacked GM and US industry in general for betraying the American people, so he continued to breathe fire towards the White House for another treachery, as he saw it, of the boys who fought in Vietnam. For years Perot has believed that there are still American servicemen captive in North Vietnam, and that Washington is involved in a cover-up.

Perot likes people to know he calls the shots. In 1988, two Dallas police officers found themselves being summoned by a furious Perot for accusing his daughter-in-law, Sarah, of being a rich kid who could get away with anything. The officers made their comments after they joined a motorcycle policeman who had stopped Sarah for speeding and discovered a handgun concealed in the glove compartment of her car, an offence in Texas which can earn a $2,000 fine or a year in jail. The motorcycle officer let Sarah off, which sparked the comments from the other policemen.

Instead of thanking the officers for not pressing charges, he 'chewed us out', according to traffic officer Billy Powell. Perot was criticized in the local press, which pointed out that he had been campaigning for a weakening of the powers of the Dallas Police Citizens Review Board, a police complaints body, which would make it harder for ordinary citizens to seek redress for police misconduct. One rule for the rich and one for the poor, they sneered.

The incident is explained away by friends as an example of Perot's protective instincts towards his five sons and daughters and his wife, Margot. His determination to shield them is every bit as strong as the thick wall that surrounds his 22-acre estate, 15 minutes' drive from downtown Dallas.

Fearing a bruising presidential campaign, he has told his new campaign managers, Ed Rollins, one of the architects of Ronald Reagan's landslide election victory in 1984, and Hamilton Jordan, who helped to win the presidency for Jimmy Carter, that they cannot use his family for electioneering purposes.

The Perots are a 'very family family', according to one of Margot Perot's oldest friends. They spend a great deal of time socializing among themselves and with a close-knit circle of friends. Despite being one of America's wealthiest citizens, Perot does not pursue the glitzy lifestyle enjoyed by some Texan tycoons. He runs an old Gulfstream jet, rather than a more up-to-date aircraft, he drives a 1984 Oldsmobile saloon and does not use a chauffeur. The Perots' choice of Dallas charitable balls is telling: they prefer the refined black-tie Crystal Ball to the unrestrained, at times outrageous, Cattle Baron's Ball. In the 1970s, when Dallas was in the midst of an extraordinary boom, the Perots, who joined the ranks of the very wealthy at that time, kept well away from Dallas new money.

The disdain Perot clearly felt for what has been described as the 'better nouveau than never' set provides an insight into his character. In some ways, Perot has much in common with the old East Coast tradition of clean-living captains of industry committed to the family, the work ethic and business success.

Perot has passed on sober ideals to his family, Ross Jr, thirty-three, Nancy, thirty-one, Suzanne, twenty-seven, Carolyn, twenty-four, and Katherine, twenty-one. According to Anne Dittmar, a family friend: 'They are responsible, not flashy.' Ross Jr and Nancy work for their father. Katherine lives at the family home during holidays from the University of North Carolina, and Suzanne lives in New York, where she works for Christie's, the auction house. Three of his children are married, and he has five grandchildren.

Ross Jr, who is in charge of Perot's vast real-estate holdings and the development of an industrial airport at Fort Worth, which could make the family more than $1 billion, is described by friends as self-motivated and as competitive as his father. If his father makes it to the White House, he would be put in charge of all of the family's business affairs.

Perot the patriot, Perot the prejudiced, Perot the publicist . . . America knows the man well. Perot the politician has, until now, been a purely local phenomenon. Without even declaring his official candidacy he has, however, eclipsed the president and his chief rival in the public's interest, and left Republican and Democrat officials worrying about whether his is a bandwagon running on the volatile fuel of protest or the real energy of new ideas. According to Tom Luce, one of his close aides: 'This campaign is about Ross Perot's way of getting things done.' Precisely.

20 June 1992

When bubbly flowed like barley water

Rex Bellamy

Chris Evert was between marriages and approaching the end of her shelf-life as a contender for major championships. Perhaps feeling her age, she left a poolside dinner party at Eastbourne as the jollities were winding down – or, for those players and camp followers with a taste for boisterous excess, winding up. She was not the first to leave. Dan Maskell and *The Times* were already in the hotel foyer, talking of this and that. Evert joined us and began to explore Maskell's memory of such former champions as Helen Wills Moody and Alice Marble.

Maskell was ever a man for detail, and any exploration of his long and retentive memory tends to be rewarding if time-consuming. Playing gooseberry, I thought at first that Evert was merely being sociable. About half an hour later – no fault of the affably garrulous Maskell – it had become evident that her curiosity was genuine and deep. This prompted the further thought that all of us become more interested in history as we consciously come closer to being a part of it.

That chance meeting jumps to the front of the mind because, after forty-three years at the microphone, eighty-four-year-old Maskell has retired. 'I'll be there, but not in the course of duty,' he says. 'I haven't missed a single day's play since 1929 and I'm not about to start now.' He has no doubts about his personal favourite players. 'Rod Laver – a truly great champion – and Martina Navratilova.'

His familiar tones will no longer be heard at just the moment when, in biblical terms, Wimbledon's allotted span has expired. It is precisely seventy years since the championships moved from Worple Road in south-west London to Wimbledon Park Road (now Church Road), and the challenge rounds were abolished.

To take the second point first, until 1922 the holders of three championships – both singles, plus the men's doubles – were asked to play only one match, against the winners of all-comers' tournaments. The women's and mixed doubles did not become official championships until 1913, and never used the challenge round system.

So 1922 was important for two reasons: the shift to new premises and the abolition of challenge rounds. These innovations were almost drowned at birth and certainly had a good dunking, because those 1922 championships were the wettest on record. It rained every day and the tournament finished on a Wednesday, having lasted fifteen days instead of the scheduled twelve.

Even the venerable Maskell was not broadcasting in those days. Indeed, it was not until a year later that, at the age of fifteen, he was taken on the Queen's Club staff as a ball-boy. But 1922 did introduce the medium at which he was to excel, because that was the year of the first sports commentary on British radio (a fight between Georges Carpentier and Ted 'Kid' Lewis at Olympia).

Born in 1877, the Wimbledon championships eventually became so popular that they outgrew the Worple Road grounds. The crux came in 1919 when the crowds overtaxed the resources of the police and the tolerance of local residents. The decision to move to a larger site was taken in 1920, but it took two years for today's premises to be selected, purchased and prepared. The cost, about £140,000, was met by the issue of £50 debenture shares (good for five years) which guaranteed tickets for every day of the championships.

What is now Church Road was formerly a cart track between a lakeside golf course and a cattle farm, destined to accommodate the prime stock of tennis. Somerset Road

246

was just a footpath, and the entire area was an old private park in the process of piecemeal dissolution.

In 1922 the new All England Club was a bleak, concrete structure unadorned by today's omnipresent Virginia creeper. In deference to the traditions of Worple Road, where the main court was the centre court in fact as well as name, the appellation was retained at the new grounds – although it had little logical claim to central status until the four new courts of 'North Wimbledon' were used for the first time in 1980. In 1922 the complex consisted of the centre court and 12 others, numbered from 3 to 13. Court 2 was opened in 1923 and Court 1 in 1924.

The first singles champions at the tournament's new home were Australian and French: Gerald Patterson and Suzanne Lenglen. Patterson was the favourite nephew of an operatic soprano, Dame Nellie Melba, whose professional name (later applied to a dessert, a sauce, and a thin variety of toast) commemorated the fact that she had been born in Melbourne. Patterson hit the ball uncommonly hard and few opponents could ride the storm well enough to exploit his comparatively dodgy backhand.

Lenglen's box office appeal was such that queues outside the grounds whiled away the waiting hours by singing a pun: 'There's a Lenglen trail a-winding.' In 1922 she won the singles and shared both the available doubles titles, without conceding a set in any event. Her enduring renown is based partly on her supreme status as a match-winner, partly on the balletic images raised by her tennis, and partly on the revolutionary, liberalizing influence of her personality and sartorial innovations – colourful bandeaux and elegant but unfashionably short dresses. Unfashionably short, that is, until she made such deviations from the norm fashionable. Her entourage included Ted Tinling, high society couturier and man-about-tennis, who wrote that 'she developed her star status to the point of transforming herself, physically and dresswise, from the ugly duckling of her beginnings to the bird of paradise she became.'

Lenglen had an engaging habit of taking an occasional nip from a flash of cognac (or absorbing lumps of cognac-soaked sugar) during changeovers. Which brings us to that unsung hero of British tennis, Randolph Lycett, who was Patterson's ultimate victim in the men's singles. Lycett was a high-stepper who did not always regard drinking champagne as incompatible with playing tennis at Wimbledon.

There is a misconception that British players were eminent in Wimbledon men's singles between the wars. In fact only three reached the final: Lycett (the 1922 runner-up), 'Bunny' Austin (runner-up in 1932 and 1938), and Fred Perry, champion in 1934, 1935 and 1936. Moreover Lycett, although he was born in Birmingham and died in Jersey, was an Anglo-Australian who honed his tennis in Australia and, in 1911, declined an invitation to play for what was then an 'Australasian' Davis Cup team.

Lycett shared the Wimbledon men's doubles title in three consecutive years, with as many different partners, and also won the mixed doubles three times, always with Elizabeth Ryan. In 1922 he contested all three finals. But for better or worse his reputation is partly founded on his extraordinary, resilient self-indulgence during a 1921 quarter-final with Zenzo Shimidzu of Japan in the all-comers' singles.

The records tell us merely that Shimidzu won 6-3, 9-11, 3-6, 6-2, 10-8. They do not tell us that the match was played on an unusually hot day – and that Lycett, having previously fortified himself with gin, went on court with a bottle of champagne in an ice bucket and imbibed with such regularity that eventually, when not reeling about the court, he took to resting languidly on the grass between shots and slurps.

Shimidzu, who observed all this with inscrutable courtesy, was no mug. He had been runner-up to Bill Tilden in the 1920 all-comers' singles. Lycett did well to finish such a match and come so close to winning it, though he may have been unaware of the result until he read the papers next morning. Today we would be thankful for small mercies if a

British player, drunk or sober, could play the kind of match Lycett played in the last championships contested at Worple Road.

Come Wimbledon 1992, we should remember all that from seventy years ago: the first championships on their present site, the first year without challenge rounds, the tournament that lasted fifteen days, Lenglen and Lycett and Dame Nellie Melba's nephew – and cognac and champagne. These days tennis players drink water, in various guises. And it shows.

20 June 1992

Index